Praise for the Sunshine Girl series

"I was on the edge of my seat from the very first page."
—R. L. Stine, author of *Goosebumps*

"The plot moves along smoothly and rapidly, and the writing is graceful and wonderfully polished . . . It's hard not to finish *The Haunting of Sunshine Girl*."
—*Time Magazine*

"McKenzie's skill telling the story of a young girl who inadvertently moves into a haunted house with her clueless mother is a thing that slips up behind and puts a cold white hand right down your spine and just won't let go."
—Wes Craven, filmmaker

"For a truly 'adorkable' heroine and a lot of mischief and Monopoly-playing ghosts, pick this up!"
—*USA Today*

"Teens who loved *Goosebumps* will be spooked and satisfied by the adventures of Sunshine."
—*New York Daily News*

"For *Harry Potter* and *Twilight* fans, get ready for *The Haunting of Sunshine Girl*."
—*Yahoo!*

"Enthralling! Shivers of anticipation creep up and terrifying, ancient revelations come thick and fast. *Sunshine Girl* is a winner for fans of teen horror!"
—Anya Allyn, author of *The Dark Carousel* series

"Suspenseful, exciting and endlessly entertaining."
—Kirkus Reviews

"*The Haunting of Sunshine Girl* by Paige McKenzie is based on the YouTube web series phenomena and will prove to be an enduringly popular addition to school and community library YA fiction collections."
—Midwest Book Review

"Sunshine's powers are unique. She doesn't just help humans transition to the afterlife; her empathy allows her to feel connections to their whole lived experience, a power that proves both dangerous and useful . . . Sunshine continues to be a likable protagonist who strives to grow into herself and her unusual role in life. A cliff-hanger ending will have fans clamoring for the third installment."
—Booklist

"Read if you dare!"
—Seventeen Magazine

"Fans ready to graduate from R. L. Stine's *Goosebumps* (Scholastic) or those looking for a mix of Carolyn Keene's *Nancy Drew* and DC Comic's *Scooby Doo* will find just what they need in this paranormal series. Verdict: Teens who enjoyed the previous volume or the author's YouTube channel will dive into this latest entry of ghost mischief."
—School Library Review

The Sacrifice of
Sunshine Girl

Also by Paige McKenzie (with Alyssa Sheinmel)

The Haunting of Sunshine Girl
The Awakening of Sunshine Girl

The Sacrifice of Sunshine Girl

BOOK THREE
The Haunting of Sunshine Girl series

PAIGE MCKENZIE

WITH NANCY OHLIN

Story by Nick Hagen & Nancy Ohlin

Based on the web series created by Nick Hagen

Illustrations by Paige McKenzie

WEINSTEIN
BOOKS

Published in the United States by Weinstein Books,
an imprint of Perseus Books,
a division of PBG Publishing, LLC, a subsidiary of Hachette Book Group, Inc.
www.weinsteinbooks.com

Library of Congress Cataloging-in-Publication Data is available for this book.
ISBN 978-1-60286-298-2 (print)
ISBN 978-1-60286-299-9 (e-book)

Published by Weinstein Books
A member of the Perseus Books Group
www.weinsteinbooks.com

Weinstein Books are available at special discounts for bulk purchases in the U.S.
by corporations, institutions, and other organizations. For more information,
please contact the Special Markets Department at the Perseus Books Group,
2300 Chestnut Street, Suite 200, Philadelphia, PA 19103, call (800) 810-4145, ext. 5000,
or e-mail special.markets@perseusbooks.com.

Editorial production by *Marra*thon Production Services.
www.marrathoneditorial.com

Book design by Jane Raese
Set in 11-point Baskerville

FIRST EDITION

1 3 5 7 9 10 8 6 4 2

For Nick,
my wizard behind the curtain

The Sacrifice of
Sunshine Girl

She Was Supposed to Die Today

She was supposed to die today.

The prophecy was unfolding as planned, on schedule, so elegantly. She had finally made the decision to sacrifice herself for the greater good.

Then, just like that, she changed her mind, thanks to her boyfriend and his confounded map. The little halfling appeared and rescued her, completing the reversal.

How very tedious.

Still, today isn't over yet. Even now, as she lies there surrounded by friends and family, my dark servants are rising out of the ground, preparing to soul terminate the humans. What grand theater it will be!

At the end—at the very end, when the five-pointed star is completed—the world will be washed in fire and reborn as the new kingdom. My kingdom.

And then I will convince my beloved to join me at my side. What a pair we will make—the ultimate combination of light, dark, and everything in between.

But first, the girl. The prophecy. The party to end all parties.

Let the carnage begin.

CHAPTER 1
My So-Called Death

Sunshine?

The voice is insistent, piercing through my foggy brain haze.

"Sunshine!"

I blink. Gray light, a blurry figure. *Figures*—plural. My temples throb, and my mouth feels like a giant, yucky cotton ball. Prickly needles press painfully into the backs of my arms and legs. The air against my skin is a cold, clammy blanket.

"Sunshine, are you all right? You hit your head and lost consciousness for a few minutes."

A face hovers over me. Several faces, actually. A tall, tall man in a fancy gray suit. A kind-looking woman in pastel nurse's scrubs and clogs.

And a cute guy in a brown leather jacket. He rakes his hand through his tousled, tawny hair and gives me a lopsided grin. "Sunshine," he exhales. The way he says my name in that dreamy deep voice sets my heart aflutter.

Wait. *Sets my heart aflutter?* What century is this? Am I having a retro dream?

"Thank goodness you're alive!" The nurse kneels down at my side and pushes back her long red curls. She touches my forehead tenderly; her vanilla lotion smell is familiar and comforting. "I can't believe . . . we thought you were . . . I don't know what I would have done if . . ." Her words unravel as she begins to tear up.

I rub my eyes. Information floods my scrambled synapses. The nurse is my mom, Kat Griffith. My human mom.

"Where's the owl?" I ask her groggily.

"What owl?" Mom asks, confused. Behind her the man in the suit squares his shoulders and gives a little cough. That's Aidan, my not-human dad.

"The owl that was here before," I say. "With that girl?"

And then it comes to me. I *know* that girl. She's Anna Wilde, who is ten and dead and invisible to most people. The owl is her favorite stuffed toy.

I tried to kill myself earlier, and Anna saved my life.

I tear up too as I remember.

"You're okay now, Sunshine," the leather jacket guy murmurs. Nolan, my brilliant and awesome boyfriend. No wonder my heart was set aflutter before.

Nolan is wrong, though. I'm *not* okay, not really. Because I am a luiseach, an elite guardian angel-superhero who fights demons and helps the dead cross over to the other side.

"Her heart rate is very elevated," Mom says, pressing her cool fingers against my wrist.

"That's normal—for her," Aidan replies.

Other memories come rushing back. Earlier I learned that my very existence was going to jeopardize the future of the human race, civilization, the world as we know it. Major stuff.

And so I split the ground open with my special luiseach knife and plunged in like a sacrificial lamb.

"Her pulse is starting to regulate," Mom says.

Aidan peers at his sleek steel watch. "That took a little more time than usual, but it's understandable, given the circumstances."

Then everything went crazy, haywire, out of control. Just as I took that plunge, I learned that my death was going to make the situation much, much worse. So naturally, I decided to bail. But I couldn't. I was falling into an abyss with no way to reverse or rewind—on top of which, a zillion demons were waiting for me down below.

Thank goodness Anna appeared out of nowhere with her stuffed owl and pulled me to safety. Once we were aboveground and free and clear of the demons, she let go . . .

My smile vanishes.

The demons. They're still down there.

"*Oh my gosh, oh my gosh, oh my gosh,*" I mutter under my breath. I hoist myself up on my elbows and try to stand up. My brain swirls with nausea and dizziness.

"What do you think you're doing, young lady?" Mom puts a firm but gentle hand on my chest. "You can't move until I'm done checking your vitals! And we have no idea what sort of trauma your head, neck, and spine may have sustained . . ."

"Mom, you need to help me up. There were demons down there, and—"

"*Demons?*" Aidan interrupts sharply.

"Aidan, can we close the ground back up? Like, immediately? I saw hundreds of them, maybe thousands. Dark spirits too. What if they try to climb out or fly out or trapeze-artist out or . . ." Fear is fueling me now, and I'm babbling at the speed of light. Aidan isn't just my dad and my mentor—he's also a super-big-deal luiseach. If anyone would know how to undo what I did, it's him.

His brow furrows as he glances over his shoulder. That's when I notice the others standing nearby: my friends Ashley and Lucio . . . and Victoria, who is Anna's mom . . . and Helena, who is my bio-mom, not that I like thinking about my genes being linked to her genes in any way whatsoever.

Aidan reaches a hand in Helena's direction. The two of them used to be a super-big-deal luiseach couple until they had a bad break-up—not your typical "we need to spend time apart and date other people" break-up, but a "one of us wants to kill our infant daughter for the greater good and the other totally doesn't" break-up.

That infant daughter was me. Helena tried to kill me again this morning, just before I tried to kill myself. Yup, it's been a busy day.

"The incantation," Aidan says quickly, and Helena nods and joins his side. They confer in low voices. Lucio starts to follow Helena with an expression of pure rage . . . no one can blame him, considering that she had his parents executed sixteen years ago . . . but Aidan gives him a warning look, and he retreats with clenched fists.

"Can someone please explain to me what's going on?" Ashley bursts out. "First, the earth splits open, like, like, in the new *Star Wars* movie. Then Sunshine, you *levitate* . . . and thrash around, drop into a ginormous hole, fly back out, and crash-land in this Goth lady's—" she gestures to Victoria "—front yard. Is this some sort of demented magic trick? Is this what people in Washington do to freak out the tourists?"

I stand up slowly and peer around. This time Mom doesn't try to stop me, although she does give me one of her extremely stern nurse-mom looks.

Whoa. Ashley is right. Victoria's yard looks postapocalyptic, like *Pride and Prejudice and Zombies* postapocalyptic. (My literary idol Jane Austen is rolling over in her grave right now.) Jagged, gaping chasms crisscross the pine-needle-littered lawn. Chasms that *I* created with my luiseach knife. The dark, brooding ever-greens don't help. Neither do the dying spring flowers that are brittle and hoar-white with frost.

I frown. There was something else here before. *Someone* else. A man in black. Where did he go? Did I imagine him?

"Are you okay?" Nolan joins me at my side. I feel a rush of warmth as I always do when I'm with him—not just because I'm madly in love with him but because he's my protector. Pro-tectors have an instant radiator effect on their luiseach. (Every luiseach has a protector and a mentor.)

"I'm okay. Well, *ish*. How about you?" I reply. That's when I notice the cut on Nolan's left temple, crusted with blood. Helena did that to him.

"Are you all right?" I ask worriedly.

"I'm fine. Your mom checked me out. Listen, Sunshine, to-day isn't the way I imagined saying 'welcome back' to you after not seeing you for three months. Well, except for the part when we, um . . ."

Kissed for the first time, I finish in my head. Said "I love you" to each other for the first time.

He smiles shyly. I smile back.

If only we were alone right now, but no. Just then Aidan and Helena sweep by us and position themselves in the center of the war-zone lawn. They look very serious and ceremonious. What are they up to? Can Helena even be trusted, after everything? They close their eyes, extend their palms upward, and begin chanting in unison—strange, ancient words.

This must be the incantation Aidan mentioned. I don't know what the words mean, yet a deep part of me recognizes them, reacts to their magic.

"Excuse me a sec," I say to Nolan. He nods, comprehending.

I step forward and take my place to the left of Aidan, away from Helena. I begin to chant, my words mumbly and improvised at first, then clearer and more sure.

Something reacts.

A sudden frigid wind blasts across the yard and pushes against us. Wobbling, I dig my Chuck Taylors into the ground to steady myself. Aidan and Helena remain still as statues and continue chanting.

The wind intensifies. Pine branches crack and tumble to the ground. An entire tree falls with an ominous *thud*. Slate tiles blow off the roof. A stone bird fountain splits in two.

What is happening? Are *we* doing that?

It occurs to me that I should get Mom and Ashley out of there. But Nolan being Nolan, he knows exactly what I need and ushers the two of them toward the street. Mom protests; Ashley doesn't protest at all and in fact is screeching hysterically about returning to Austin *immediately*.

The earth is shaking now. The walls of the chasms start to close, inch by shuddering inch. The incantation is working. We are keeping the demon army at bay.

I shutter my eyelids and go into a sort of trance. I chant faster and faster, the words tumbling over each other, my voice hoarse with urgency . . .

Someone screams.

My eyelids fly open. *Oh, freak*. Nearby, a humungous wild animal is crawling out of one of the chasms. It peers around hungrily and leaps onto its nearest prey: Victoria.

I blink. It's not a wild animal. It's a demon. A *serpent*-demon.

We are too late. They are coming for us.

CHAPTER 2

The Attack of the Serpent-Demons

The attack has begun.

The serpent-demon has a long, thick body with no arms or legs. Its green scales glow grotesquely in the wan light. Horns thrust out and curl backward from its head. Hissing and grinning, it proceeds to wrap itself around Victoria's slim, fragile body. She flails at it, but it is too swift and strong. Plus, she can't see it because she's an ex-luiseach and doesn't have luiseach powers anymore.

Lucio rushes forward like a football player on steroids.

"*No!*" Aidan commands him.

Lucio stops in his tracks. He can't see the creature either, even though he is a full-on, card-carrying luiseach. Not sure why. "But Aidan! Something's happening to Victoria! We've got to—"

Victoria screams again. The serpent-demon has coiled itself completely around her and is squeezing, squeezing. Its face is a breath away from her face.

"Victoria, close your mouth!" Aidan orders her. She stares at him wildly but obeys, whimpering in terror; he was her mentor when she was a luiseach, so she listens to him.

The creature laughs and flicks its tongue at the thin, hard line of Victoria's lips, its yellow eyes gleaming. Victoria tries to pull away, but it keeps flicking, flicking . . . and soon her mouth begins to open slowly, excruciatingly as though by force.

Oh no. That's how it will kill her. Not by squeezing her to death but by slipping into her mouth and down her throat. Once inside it will possess her and wipe out her soul. Stop the beating of her heart. After it is finished with her, the memory of her will fade in our minds, like she was never here.

And then it will turn on the rest of us.

I tip my face to the sky. *Anna, where are you? Your mom needs you!* But I can't feel her spirit anywhere.

Helena, who is no longer chanting, inspects her perfectly manicured nails. She has very small, dainty hands—for a murderer, that is. Or is it murderess?

"What's the plan, Aidan dearest?" she trills. Her tone is sarcastic but with a subtle undercurrent of anxiety. Has she never dealt with a demon onslaught before? Still, part of her probably wants to see Victoria suffer—after all, Victoria *was* a double agent for Aidan.

"Continue with the incantation, Helena!" Aidan instructs her.

"Why should I? Victoria did betray me, after all."

"We can discuss that later. We need to stop this now, not

just for Victoria's sake but for all our sakes. You know what will happen if . . ."

Aidan doesn't finish his sentence. He loosens his gunmetal gray tie and strides toward Victoria and the serpent-demon. Very James Bond of him. Sighing, Helena resumes chanting. So do I, although in Aidan's absence I automatically move away from her. Lucio, ever protective, places himself between Helena and me. It must be taking every ounce of self-control for him not to go after Helena right here and now. But he wouldn't disobey Aidan, and he knows what's at stake.

Aidan circles the creature, which is too busy demon–French-kissing Victoria to notice him. As I chant, I do a quick visual sweep of the perimeter. The chasms are closing, but not fast enough. I spot two more serpent-demons crawling out: one black, one red. There may be others. There *will* be others. Demons . . . dark spirits . . . an army of pure evil . . .

The serpent-demon on Victoria finally detects Aidan's presence. It whips its head around 180 degrees and bares its lethal fangs with a low, gurgling hiss.

Aidan grabs its neck with lightning speed. Startled, it loosens its grip on Victoria just long enough for her to wriggle away and hurl herself to the ground.

The creature and Aidan wrestle. Out of the corner of my eye I see that the red serpent-demon and the black serpent-demon have cleared the chasm. The red one speed-slithers toward Helena and Lucio and me. The black one speed-slithers off in the direction of the street.

Nolan and Mom and Ashley!

Panic grips my chest. They're human—they can't defend themselves. I have to do something, anything, *now*.

My luiseach knife. I reach into the back pocket of my jeans, but of course, it's not there. Ack!

"Sunshine! By the fountain!" I hear Nolan shout from the street, pointing me to the knife.

Nolan to the rescue again. I send him a mental "thank you" surrounded by hearts and X's and O's. I notice that Ashley is trying to open the driver's side of her little blue hybrid car but keeps dropping the keys. Clumsiness is *my* thing, but terror can have the same effect, I guess. Nolan is attempting to steer Mom around to the passenger side, but to no avail; she keeps pointing to me and arguing with him. *Listen to Nolan, Mom!*

Aidan is still wrestling with the serpent-demon. Lucio is lifting Victoria to her feet. I check out the other two serpent-demons . . . if I run fast enough, I might be able to get to the knife just before the closest one, the red one, reaches striking distance.

I break into a sprint.

"Sunshine, what are you doing?" Lucio yells.

The red serpent-demon pivots and speed-slithers in my direction. I combat-roll onto the ground and reach for the handle of the knife.

My fingers close around it just as the creature catches up to me and prepares to strike. I can feel its hot, rancid breath on my face as it flicks its tongue at me.

I jump to my feet and step back. The knife burns and twitches in my grip. Its blade bears the faint echoes of its past incarnations: a torch, a storm, the epic instrument that split the earth open . . .

Now!

I fling the knife—or rather, the knife flings itself—toward the charged gray sky. It swoops and arcs like a bird and nose-dives down, down, down.

The blade hits the earth and pierces it. It creates a swirling cloud of dirt and smoke and pine.

The cloud funnels up, up, up and explodes . . . and a gigantic eagle rises up from the chaos. It flaps its massive wings—they must span at least twelve feet—with a sound as deafening as helicopter blades.

Helena abruptly stops chanting. She glances at the monster eagle and then at me, her brown eyes wide with shock.

Yup, that's right, I did that, I want to say to her smugly. But this is not the time for teen-daughter attitude. Not that I'm her daughter in any way that matters.

The eagle fixes its laser gaze on the red serpent-demon at my side and swoops in for the kill. The creature screams and screams as the eagle sinks its razor talons into its throat. Ochre-colored blood sprays everywhere. *Gross.* The creature flops to the ground and sizzles, dissolves into nothingness.

Then the eagle directs its attention to the serpent-demon that is—was—wrestling with Aidan. The creature is now trying to speed-slither into the nearest chasm. But the chasm is almost closed up—all the chasms are almost closed up—and the eagle seizes the creature by its neck and proceeds to shake it to death. Old school but effective.

The eagle dispenses with the third serpent-demon in the same way. I feel a huge whoosh of relief. Nolan and Mom and Ashley are safe. We are all safe.

At least for now.

Victoria is shivering and crying. Lucio has stripped down to his cargo shorts and is using his T-shirt to wipe blood and dirt and tears from her face. The earth tremors shudder to a complete stop. The chasms have all disappeared, and things are back to normal again.

Well, maybe "normal" isn't the right word. Nothing has been normal since I turned sixteen and came into my luiseach powers and the invisible world became visible to me. Stuff no one should ever have to see or experience.

Aidan appears at my side. "Are you all right?"

"I'm fine, D— . . . Aidan. Ai-*dan*."

His milky green cat eyes, identical to my own, flash with surprise. Did I seriously almost call him "Dad"? Maybe I did suffer a head injury, after all.

Aidan starts to say something but then turns to Helena. "Do you finally—*finally*—understand why we have to keep her alive?" he says gruffly.

"Sentimental nonsense," Helena mutters. She busies herself with a loose strand of hair and shoves it back into her bun. She and I have the same curly brown hair, except that hers is perfect and mine is a perpetual, freaky frizzball (and thanks to a little encounter I had with a fire demon recently, it's now a short, *fried* frizzball).

"No, it's not that. Her powers . . . we were wrong about . . . Helena, you need to speak to the other luiseach and convince them!"

At Aidan's mention of the "other luiseach" Lucio visibly tenses. I reach over and squeeze his hand. I notice Nolan noticing my hand from across the lawn, and I remove it hastily. Not that he has any reason to be jealous of me comforting a cute half-naked guy—Lucio and I are just friends, 99.9 percent just friends.

Plus, Nolan doesn't know everything I've learned recently, including what Helena did to Lucio's mom and dad.

Helena gazes at Aidan and then at me. She seems to be considering something. To kill me or not to kill me? What method to use, maybe? Earlier today she tried to choke me. When I was a baby she tried to suffocate me while pretending to nurse me. I'm pretty sure a therapist would have a field day with our relationship.

Helena slants her cold, eagle gaze back at Aidan. "I need to take this up with my luiseach council," she says finally.

Aidan arches an eyebrow. "Your luiseach council? What on earth is that?"

"A lot has changed since we went our separate ways, *dearest*."

CHAPTER 3

Blood and More Blood

White walls, beeping machines, the smells of iodine and disinfectant. I wanted to go straight home after the demon smack-down at Victoria's, but Mom wouldn't hear of it. So now I'm stuck at Ridgemont Hospital, where she works as the head of the neonatal nursing unit, and I'm getting poked and prodded for no good reason.

Leads and wires cover my body. A nurse I don't recognize—her nametag says "Beverly"—hovers over me with a clipboard. She jots down notes as she glances over her shoulder at the blinking numbers on a monitor.

A second nurse walks into the room, pulling on a pair of latex gloves with a brisk *snap, snap.* She is carrying a basket full of empty collection tubes.

"Afternoon, ladies," she calls out in a friendly voice.

Beverly gives her a chin nod. "Our patient's all ready for you, Latoya."

"Great. The lab needs these samples ASAP. Kat's down

there now to make certain they put a rush on everything," says Latoya.

"If anyone can light a fire under their butts, it's our Kat," Beverly says, chuckling.

"May I please go home now?" I ask, shifting carefully so I don't unplug myself. "I'm fine. Really."

Beverly pats my shoulder. "I'm sure you are, hon. Your mom just wants to be a hundred percent that everything's A-okay. We're just gonna run a couple of tests and have Dr. Kothari give the results a look-see."

"Are you right or left-handed, sweetheart?" Latoya asks me.

"Right."

"Allrighty, then." Latoya takes a piece of rubber tubing out and ties it securely around my left bicep. "Make a fist for me?"

I obey, trying to ignore the pinchy pressure of the rubber tubing. If I know anything from living with Mom for sixteen years, it's that nurses don't take no for an answer. Latoya presses several points on my forearm, finds a bumpy blue vein, and swabs it with iodine. "Sharp sting, okay?"

"Um, okay."

I wince as she pierces my skin with the long, thin hypodermic needle. The collection tube attached to the needle quickly begins to fill with dark red blood. When the tube is full, Latoya switches it out for another.

The sight of my own blood has always made me feel queasy, so I look away and try to think happy thoughts.

Happy thoughts, happy thoughts, happy thoughts. Vanilla ice cream from Scoops 'N Smiles. Taking pictures with my Nikon F5, my sweet-sixteen present from Mom, on a slightly cloudy, perfect-light day. My dog Oscar wearing a sequiny, powder-blue tutu.

(Second-grade me used to like dressing him up.) Pizza and movie nights with Mom. The day we brought my cat, Lex Luthor, home from the SPCA. Sleepovers with Ashley back when Mom and I used to live in Austin. Antique stores and flea markets. Anything Jane Austen.

And Nolan. Always Nolan. The way his hair falls across his forehead. His goofy, crooked smile. His amazing mind. His warm lips . . .

Where is he, anyway? When we got to the hospital Mom insisted he get examined too—and also Victoria, although she had to sign in under an alias, as she did technically die here in the ICU on New Year's. (No one knows how she managed to resuscitate herself—is it because she had just enough leftover luiseach in her to undo that demon's mortal attack?)

I'm not sure where Aidan and Lucio went off to. I think Ashley is downstairs at the hospital gift shop buying me trashy magazines and jelly beans and other get-well presents.

As for Helena, I hope she went back to where she came from, wherever that is. I have a better chance of staying alive that way. The thing is, she didn't always have homicidal feelings toward me. When she was pregnant with me, she was your typical joyful, expectant mom. But on the other hand she was extremely *not* typical—ditto Aidan—because they were too busy conducting scientific experiments on the unborn me to try to create some kind of mutant super-luiseach. Then, at the exact moment of my birth, at the Llevar la Luz luiseach training compound in Mexico, a massive shockwave of energy apparently blasted out into the universe. Several pregnant luiseach women at the compound spontaneously miscarried, as did other pregnant luiseach women around the world. Some of them even died.

And so Helena came to believe—and still believes—that the luiseach race is doomed as long as I am alive.

"Hello, hello!" Mom—my real mom, my only mom—sweeps into the room wearing ladybug and sunflower scrubs. "Sunshine, how are you feeling? Beverly, how are her vitals? Latoya, the lab is standing by for those samples," she says all in one breath.

"Aye, aye, captain," Latoya says with a mock salute. She gathers the neatly labeled dark red tubes, winks at me, and takes off.

Beverly hands her clipboard to Mom. "Her vitals are all within range, Kat . . . except that her temp is running a bit high."

"That's okay. She's, uh, getting over a bad cold."

Mom knows by now that as a luiseach, my base body temperature runs high. But she can't let anyone know my true, non-human identity.

She takes the clipboard from Beverly and scans the information. She nods to herself and regards me with anxious eyes.

"No dizziness?" she asks me.

"Nope."

"How about nausea?"

"No nausea. Mom, can't we just—"

Mom's pager beeps. She pulls it out of her pocket and reads the message on the screen. "*Oh!* My goodness. Beverly, did you know about the situation in the ER?"

"You mean the arson incident in the shopping mall? The ER's backed up six ways to Sunday."

I sit up slightly. "Wait. What arson incident at the mall?"

"They've just admitted one of the victims. She's thirty-two weeks, and she went into premature labor. They're prepping her for a C-section now. Come with me," Mom says to Beverly.

"Seriously, Mom. What's happening?" I demand.

"Nothing for you to worry about, sweetie. Just stay put. Dr. Kothari will be by soon to check on you. You remember him, right? He's the funny one with the tattoo of a . . ." Mom's words drift away as she sweeps out of the room, Beverly at her heels.

Arson incident at the mall?

Ridgemont isn't exactly a sleepy little town, but it's not a violent-crime kind of place either. The worst crime I know of was when Anna's dad murdered her while he was possessed, and that was over a year ago, before Mom and I moved here from Texas.

My gaze lands on the small TV screen hanging from the ceiling. I wonder if this mall situation has made the news yet? I find the remote control and click ON.

A blond newscaster named Traci is saying something about a tragedy. I crank up the volume.

"—again, one person is dead and a dozen people were hospitalized as a result of the arson at the Ridgemont Mall. Police have a suspect in custody at this time. Her name is Mabel Ostricher . . ."

A photo of Mabel Ostricher pops up on the screen. White hair, blue eyes, rosy cheeks . . . holy crackers, I *know* her! She is the nice lady who volunteers at the Salvation Army where I shop sometimes. Last October when I was there she showed me a picture of her new grandson. Luke . . . no, Liam. She was planning to fly to San Diego to meet him and help out around the house while her daughter recovered from her labor.

"The police have told us that the eighty-year-old retired schoolteacher put perfume-soaked clothes into a number of trash containers throughout the mall and lit them with matches . . ."

Sweet old Mrs. Ostricher tried to burn down the mall? That can't be true. There has to be a mistake.

"The Ridgemont Mall has been closed until further notice. Anyone with information about this crime is urged to call the number that you see on your screen."

This isn't possible. Mrs. Ostricher and I have exchanged stories about our pets. I told her all about Oscar and Lex Luthor. She told me all about her morkie—Princess?—and her two cats—Fluffles and Snowflake? Something like that.

"And in other news . . . the International Center for Climate Research in Helsinki has issued a report. According to their findings, the global warming trend has been mysteriously shifting in the other direction over the past six months, with temperatures dropping to below-record levels across all seven continents . . ."

I click off the TV and shake my head incredulously. None of this makes any sense. Maybe Mrs. Ostricher was drugged? Or suffering from serious dementia? Or somebody forced her?

And then an awful, terrible, horrible realization dawns on me.

Could Mrs. Ostricher be possessed? Like Mr. Wilde was when he murdered his beloved ten-year-old daughter?

Oh my gosh.

The newscaster said Mrs. Ostricher was in police custody. This means that she is likely down at the station right now with a building full of people—all potential victims.

I have to get down there *immediately.*

I start to peel one of the leads off my body . . . and stop. Not smart. I've practically grown up in hospitals, doodling and doing homework at the nurses' station while Mom finished up her shift. When a lead comes off, things start beeping like crazy and nurses hurry to your room. There's no way for them or for the machines to tell the difference between a loose lead and no heartbeat.

If I try to escape, a horde of nurses will descend on me, and I can't exactly explain to them that I have to skedaddle out of here and over to the police station to exorcise a demon . : .

But there's someone else who can. *Aidan.*

I reach for my phone, which thankfully is sitting on my little bed tray table next to my Styrofoam cup of water and a stack of hospital pamphlets. I pick up the phone and type a message.

Mall arson lady is at the police station. She could be possessed?
I'm stuck at the hospital.

Aidan writes back immediately:

Helena and I are already on it.

Helena and I are already on it. I get a weird ping in my stomach because, well, *Helena.* But right now she and Aidan have to work together to exorcise the demon that is probably inside Mrs. Ostricher—because, really, what else can we do here?

Another message pops up from Aidan.

How are you feeling? What did the doctors say?

I reply:

I'm totally fine. Just waiting to be discharged.

"Sunshine Griffith?"

I glance up from my phone. Latoya is standing in the door-way holding a big syringe. Argh, *another* shot? Behind her a random man passes by with a bouquet of colorful *GET WELL* balloons.

"Hi, Sunshine. I'm Latoya, one of the nurses," she says.

"Um . . . I know. Hi again."

"I need to draw your blood for your labs, okay, sweetheart?"

I blink. "But . . . you just did that. Like five minutes ago."

"It'll be over very quickly. You won't feel a thing, I promise."

Latoya shuts the door behind her and begins walking toward me slowly. Her mouth twists into a strange grin as she holds up the syringe and pushes lightly at it. Clear droplets squirt out of the needle and cascade to the floor.

A sizzling sound. A burnt chemical smell. The liquid has left a scorch mark in the linoleum.

My heart pounds violently in my chest.

This is *not* Latoya. Or not entirely Latoya, anyway. There is a demon inside of her. Although why isn't the temperature drop-ping, like it usually does when a dark or light spirit is close by?

I lift my right hand crossing-guard style. "Stop!" I shout. With my other hand I send a frantic text to Aidan.

DEMON IN ROOM

Latoya continues walking toward me . . . slowly, slowly. Clos-ing my eyes, I visualize shooting a wave of extreme pain in her direction. I have no idea what made me think to do that; it just came to me.

My eyelids fly open as Latoya shrieks and drops the syringe. It breaks, and the liquid spills. More sizzling, more burnt chemical smells . . . and the liquid leaves a wake of black scorch marks across the floor.

I watch, practically hypnotized as the blackness seeps and spreads. That could have been me, that could have been me, that could have been me . . .

Focus! I tell myself.

I take a deep, centering breath and shoot more pain at Latoya. She shrieks again and doubles over.

Another idea comes to me.

I rip all the leads off my body.

Everything begins beeping like mad. Footsteps pound down the hall. Latoya straightens and hisses at the doorway like a wild animal.

She turns to me, her eyes glowing nuclear red. "You cannot stop him," she growls in a man's voice.

And then she flings the door open, practically ripping it off its hinges, and runs away.

CHAPTER 4

Home Again

Y*ou cannot stop him.*

Stop who?

Home from the hospital, I lie in my comfy bed with my fleecy *Star Trek* blanket scrunched up to my chin. Lex Luthor, who is all black except for the white patches on his face and his chest, is a warm, purring puddle near my feet. Oscar naps on the carpet, thumping his tail. I've been sort of napping for the last hour but sort of not.

This is the first time I've been in my room, in my house, since New Year's, when I met Aidan for the first time and he almost immediately hauled me off to Llevar la Luz. He wanted me to go there to hone my luiseach skills, but just as importantly, he wanted to hide me from Helena, who was out looking for me so she could finish what she started sixteen years ago.

I wish I could relax and just enjoy being here with Lex Luthor and Oscar and all my stuff, but I can't.

I burrow under my blanket even further. At least I don't have to worry about the Latoya demon anymore. After receiving my distress text, Aidan somehow managed to get to the hospital in time to intercept her. She was driving out of the parking lot in a stolen minivan and about to mow down a couple of orderlies in an attempt to escape. Aidan exorcised the demon. And magically erased the orderlies' memories of the event. And magically erased Latoya's memories of the event too and convinced her that she needed to take the rest of the day off to recover from her very sudden, very bad headache. Like I said, he's a super-big-deal luiseach.

And while Aidan was busy with Latoya, Helena apparently went to the police station and dealt with Mrs. Ostricher's demon.

Yay, teamwork?

Poor Mrs. Ostricher. She must have no clue why she is locked up in a holding cell. And how will she react when she learns about what she did? Have the police officers already told her? I hope the shock didn't—doesn't—give her a heart attack. I wonder if Aidan might be able to find her a good lawyer to defend her in court.

Your honor, my client pleads not guilty by reason of demonic possession . . .

Outside my window the sky is dark blue with twilight. My clothes feel warm and itchy against my skin, and it occurs to me that I'm still wearing the same jeans, T-shirt, and sweater I was wearing on Ashley's and my road trip from Llevar la Luz . . . and this morning at Victoria's . . . and this afternoon at the hospital. I seriously need to take a shower and change (and get a haircut to fix my fireballed frizzball . . . and, if Ashley had her druthers, put on some makeup or maybe even totally overhaul my look—less Salvation Army and retro, more H&M and current).

But I am beyond exhausted. Like emotionally and physically wrung-out-like-a-wet-rag exhausted. Like I-could-close-my-eyes-and-sleep-for-the-next-decade exhausted.

What is happening in Ridgemont? When I left here in January, things were bad—but not *this* bad.

I peek over the edge of my blanket and peer around my room. At least nothing has changed in here. Everything is pink. Pepto-Bismol pink, to be exact. Pink shag carpet, pink rose wallpaper, even a pink light switch. (This was our landlord's design concept, not mine.) Dr. Hoo, my beloved white taxidermied owl that matches Anna's stuffed toy, perches on a shelf above my desk as though standing guard over my antique typewriter and glass unicorn figurines. I found him in an antique store just outside of Austin; he was so *me* that I couldn't *not* buy him. As for the figurines, Mom has given me one every year for Christmas starting at age five, after my kindergarten teacher read *The Last Unicorn* to our class. On the floor my vintage clothes and prized Jane Austen collection spill out of my duffel bag, which still bares traces of the reddish dust that seemed to cover everything at Llevar la Luz. My stuffed animals Theodore Bear, Bear Brontë, Beary Grant, Giraffey, and Pupperoni are perched against the wall, neat as soldiers.

Between my bedroom and Mom's bedroom is the bathroom where Anna's ghost first came to me. Her dad, possessed by a water demon, had killed her by drowning her.

What is it that they say about silver linings? There really isn't one here, except that Anna has become my friend—and my savior on more than one occasion.

Suddenly all of this . . . this . . . *insanity* comes crashing down on me. I start to cry—quietly at first, then loudly with my whole body shaking uncontrollably. My life feels so . . . awful. Overwhelming. Only hours ago I met my biological mother for the first time since I was born, only to almost die at her hands—again. I tried to kill myself. I decided *not* to kill myself. I faced down a serpent-demon—*three* serpent-demons. I then faced down another demon at the hospital.

Plus, a lovely old lady tried to burn down the mall.

Plus, Helena and her "luiseach council," whoever they are, may vote to execute me.

Plus, there is that man in black I keep seeing.

I didn't sign up for any of this. Not for the first time, I wonder how I can un-luiseach myself, like Victoria did.

Eventually my pity party sob session runs out of steam. I won't be able to fix my sorry life or the sorry state of the world by holing up in my room and crying. I take a few deep yoga breaths and reach for a box of tissues—there isn't one, so I swipe my yucky, drippy nose against the back of my sweater sleeve—and glance at the mint-green 1950s clock radio on my nightstand. It's almost dinnertime, and I realize I'm starving—I don't remember the last time I ate. A bag of potato chips at that rest stop in Idaho? I didn't have anything at the hospital. It would be beyond awesome if Mom ordered in an extra-cheese and pepperoni pizza and we had a movie night, like we do every week. *Did,* rather, before I took off for Mexico with Aidan to become a super-luiseach who could save humanity. *Ha.*

Where is everybody, anyway? Except for Oscar's snoring and Lex Luthor's purring, the house seems eerily still. After Aidan dispensed with the Latoya demon, he insisted on driving me home—once Dr. Kothari had discharged me, that is, with strict orders to rest for twenty-four hours. Nolan texted and said that he and Victoria had been discharged too and that he was going to head home to check in with his parents while Lucio drove Victoria to her house. I thought I heard Mom and Ashley downstairs earlier? (At the hospital Ashley showered me with presents from the gift shop: a pile of celebrity gossip magazines, candy, and a book called *Endless Longing* with a cover of a hunky, shirtless nineteenth-century guy who is just about to kiss a sweet, blushing nineteenth-century girl. "Because you like historical stuff," was Ashley's explanation.)

I rise out of bed—Lex Luthor meows in annoyance at me for disturbing his cozy napping spot—and look around for my phone. I wonder if Nolan has texted.

He has. Seven times.

Are you all right?

Is it okay if I come over?

I miss you.

Are you all right?

I miss you.

Can I come over?

Okay, I'm coming over.

A smile tugs at my lips. The thought of seeing Nolan and spending time with him—we *did* just officially become boyfriend-girlfriend today—lifts my mood. Is he already here? I glance out the window; beyond the tops of the pine trees I can see his big, beat-up navy blue Chrysler parked on the curb behind an old-fashioned black sedan, and my heart does a silly little happy dance. Maybe he's downstairs with Mom and Ashley— and Aidan too, if he stuck around after dropping me off.

I put on my fuzzy bunny slippers and poke my head out the door. I hear faint voices drifting up from downstairs. I proceed quietly down the steps. Oscar and Lex Luthor follow, thinking it's their dinnertime too.

As I near the first-floor landing I can hear the voices more clearly. They are coming from the living room—hushed, angry whispers. Who is arguing?

I stop, press myself against the wall next to the framed poster of the Austin skyline, and listen.

"Let me address your council. They need to understand that Sunshine is not the enemy. The darkness is—or more importantly, whoever has been organizing the darkness." That's Aidan.

"She is making us weak. Her very existence has enabled the darkness to grow because she put an end to the birth of new luiseach, upset the balance. *They* are taking over. Just today in Ridgemont alone there was the old woman and the nurse at the hospital. And we have been receiving reports about similar incidents from all around the world. In addition, there is the climate issue." That's Helena.

Wait . . . Helena is in my *house? But how and why and when and* . . . My hand moves to my back jeans pocket. Good, my knife is there, just in case she decides to pull any moves.

Also, what climate issue? And then I remember hearing that news item at the hospital, about temperatures decreasing all over the world.

"Our birth rates were declining decades, centuries before Sunshine was born. Besides, you see how powerful she is. You and I, we created something incredible. A miracle. She is going to save our kind, not destroy it." Aidan again.

"*Excuse me!*" That's Mom. "I know I'm not one of you, and I don't understand half of what you're talking about. But lady, if you try to harm my daughter again, I will see to it that you . . . you . . . well, all I can say is, you'll regret it! Honestly, what kind of *mother* are you? What kind of *luiseach* are you? I thought you people were supposed to be on the side of good. You should be in jail, not sitting in my living room sipping Earl Grey tea."

"Yeah, I'm with Mrs. Griffith on that." That's Lucio, who sounds like he's speaking through gritted teeth, ready to drag Helena to jail himself . . . or worse. He's here too?

"Lucio, right?" That's Mom again. "You can call me Kat. And by the way, thank you for looking after my daughter in Mexico."

"You were with Sunshine in Mexico?" That's Nolan.

"Um . . . yeah. Why do you want to know?" asks Lucio.

"We haven't officially met. I'm Nolan Foster. Sunshine's boy-friend."

"*Oh.*"

I never told Nolan that Lucio was at Llevar la Luz the whole time I was there. Or that Aidan is Lucio's mentor too. Or that Lucio and I sort-of kissed while I was there, although I couldn't go through with it because I loved *him*, not Lucio.

I never told Lucio that I had a boyfriend either. My boy-friend-protector.

But one difficult, awkward conversation at a time.

I unpeel myself from the wall next to the Austin poster and trot down the last few steps. I suppose I need to be part of this "family" meeting, even though the subject at hand appears to be whether or not to eliminate me. *Great.* It *seems* like Aidan is winning the debate, but maybe that's just wishful thinking.

When I reach the first-floor landing a cool draft hits my face. The front door is open a crack, letting in the cold. Springtime in Ridgemont.

I see a shadowy movement through the square glass pane.

Who's missing from this party? Victoria? Ashley?

I tiptoe over to the door, trying to keep my footsteps quiet on the hardwood floor, and peer through the crack.

There is no one there.

No, someone *is* there. Or *was.*

Goosebumps prickle my arms as I open the door further. An engine roars, tires squeal . . . and that vintage black sedan, the one that was parked in front of Nolan's Chrysler, speeds away. It disappears around the corner, but before it does I catch a glimpse of the driver.

He is wearing a black hat. One of those hats like you see in 1940s gangster movies.

It's *him.*

CHAPTER 5

The Man in Black

I saw him again!" I shout as I run into the living room. Oscar follows at my heels, yipping and barking. Lex Luthor is at the front door, sniffing and hissing, his back arched like an upside-down U and his tail puffed up like a rabid raccoon's.

Everyone stops talking and stares at me. Helena sits stiffly on a plastic folding chair and sips tea from a chipped Texas Rangers mug (which is surreal in a time-warp way considering that neither the Rangers nor plastic folding chairs existed in the eighteenth century or nineteenth century or whenever she was born—luiseach do age but very, very slowly). Aidan towers next to her with his hand resting elegantly on the top of the mantel.

Lucio is on the couch next to Mom. Nolan, who is wearing his gold wire-rimmed glasses, sits cross-legged on the floor with a notebook, pen, and map. *The* map. The map with the pentagram, the map that saved my life earlier today.

Nolan and Lucio both leap to their feet when I enter the room. Mom also leaps to her feet. She is already reaching into

the pockets of her ladybug and sunflower scrubs for a thermometer or stethoscope or whatever. "Why aren't you in bed? Dr.
Kothari was very clear. Twenty-four hours of—"

"Saw who, Sunshine?" Aidan interrupts.

"The man in black!" I blurt out.

"*What* man in black? Clarify, please."

"He's a . . . I've seen him a few times now, mostly from a distance. I've been meaning to tell you guys about him, but every
time I tried, something came up and . . . anyway, this time he
was at our front door. *Our front door.* Just now, right this second.
I saw him through the little glass thingy. But when I opened the
door he was driving away."

Aidan strides to the window and peers cautiously through
the Venetian blinds. His jaw is clenched, and his shoulders are
rigid with tension. "When and where did you see him previ-
ously, Sunshine?"

"Well, the first time was in January at the Seattle Airport,
when you and I traveled to Mexico. The second time was . . . in
that village, the one near Llevar la Luz. When that demon was
setting fire to everything."

"Wait. What demon? What fire?" Mom demands.

"I'll explain later, Mom. I saw him again this morning, Aidan.
Just before I . . . when I fell into the . . ." I hesitate.

Helena stands up abruptly. Tea sloshes out of her mug and
onto her dress, but she doesn't seem to notice.

"What did he look like, exactly?" she asks me calmly. Not
for the first time, I notice we are the same height and have the
same mouth.

I describe his long black coat and old-fashioned black hat. It's
weird speaking with Helena, acting like we're on the same side;

the last time we exchanged words she was just about to choke the life out of me, and even now she is trying to convince Aidan that I need to be put down like some dangerous animal.

"But it's not his outfit that made me notice him," I continue. "He has this . . . I don't know how to describe it . . . this aura of darkness about him. Like that creepy shadow around the moon . . ."

"Penumbra," Nolan speaks up.

I point to Nolan and nod *yes yes yes*. "That! Penumbra! It's really, really strong around this guy."

Nolan frowns, considering this. Then he gets down on all fours and begins scanning the map from right to left, his lips moving as though ticking off numbers. I stole this map from Aidan's laboratory before leaving Llevar la Luz. Aidan had circled four locations and written a date next to each; the dates correspond with four mysterious luiseach deaths that took place four years apart starting in the year of my birth. But that was as far as Aidan got.

I figured if anyone could detect a pattern, it was Nolan. And I was right. Somewhere in his brilliant Einstein mind he figured out that he had to rip the map in half and flip the right and left halves. Then he drew a pentagram on the map with his own blood (I'm sure he would have used a pen if he'd had one at the time), connecting the four locations and adding a fifth—Ridgemont.

I was number five. I was supposed to die today.

Helena takes a deep, shuddering breath.

"Helena?" Aidan says.

She says something, but her voice is so low that I don't hear at first.

"Who is it? Do you know him?" I ask.

She won't look at me. "It's Dubu," she says quietly to Aidan.

"*Dubu?*" Aidan barks. "But we thought he was—"

"He's *not*," Helena cuts in.

"How do you know?"

"I just do."

Aidan clasps his hands behind his back and begins to pace around the living room. Helena watches him nervously.

"Um, does anyone want to clue me in? Who is this Dubu person?" I ask.

Aidan stops his pacing and fixes his milky green cat eyes on Helena. He looks furious . . . afraid . . . *something*. I can't quite put my finger on it.

"You're certain Dubu is still alive?" Aidan says to her.

Helena barely nods. Her cheeks are bright red.

"So *he* is the one who's responsible for all this? The one who has been organizing the darkness?"

Helena nods again. "It's the most plausible explanation."

"May I ask why you chose not to bring this up earlier?"

"Who. Is. Dubu?!" I persist.

Aidan walks over to the window again and gazes out at the empty street beyond the tall bushes and pine trees.

"Dubu is a Markon," he says finally.

"A mark on what?" I ask.

"*Markon.* M-A-R-K-O-N. A super-demon."

I gulp. *A super-demon?* Because regular old demons aren't bad enough?

"What is a . . . how can they . . . I mean, why didn't you tell me about these Markons in Mexico, Aidan? You know, during my 'How to Become a Luiseach in Ten Easy Steps' seminars?"

"I didn't know about them either," Lucio informs me.

"We thought they were all dead. There were only three of them to begin with," Aidan explains.

"Why has Dubu been following *her?*" Helena tips her head in my direction. "What is he after?"

"The fifth point on the pentagram," Nolan says suddenly.

All eyes turn to him. Nolan rises to his feet and holds up the map.

"See this pentagram?" He traces his finger over the bloody lines as though playing a macabre game of connect the dots. "Hokkaido, Japan. Rapa Nui, also known as Easter Island. The Chukchi Peninsula in Russia. The Cape York Peninsula in Queensland, Australia."

His finger lands on Ridgemont, Washington, which has no date next to it. *Yet.*

"Ridgemont is the fifth point on the pentagram," he says. "These other four points are where the previous mysterious luiseach deaths occurred."

"*What mysterious luiseach deaths?*" Mom cries out.

"This Dubu person, super-demon, whatever . . . I think this is all part of his plan. Or part of *a* plan that he's helping to implement," Nolan plunges on. "He expected a luiseach death here in Ridgemont today. It was planned, it was organized. Sunshine, if you . . . if things had gone differently this morning, the fifth point of the pentagram would have been complete. So it's good that you're alive. For all sorts of reasons," he adds, his face coloring.

"But what's Dubu's end game?" Lucio asks.

"When I was, um"—*falling into the demon pit and about to die a horrible death*—"I had this vision that completing the pentagram would have unleashed something major. Like a spell. Like a really bad, powerful spell that stretched across the whole planet. It felt very . . . doomsdayish."

Aidan's brow furrows. "You saw this?"

"Yup."

"Oh, honey." Mom comes over to me and wraps her arms around me tightly. I can feel her trembling.

Helena studies us curiously. *This is how a real mom acts,* I want to say to her.

"But you didn't complete the pentagram. So you're safe now? The world is safe?" Mom adds in a half-hopeful, half-desperate tone.

"I wish that were the case, Katherine . . . *Kat,*" Aidan says. "But given the information we have before us, I'm inclined to think that Dubu will not rest until Sunshine is . . . until the pentagram is complete."

Until the pentagram is complete.

"Then we have to get Sunshine out of Ridgemont, *now!*" Mom practically shouts at him. "You have to take her back to Mexico! It's the only way!"

"Running may not be an option," Aidan replies evenly. "We have no idea what a Markon—what Dubu—is capable of. It's been a very long time since our kind has engaged with him, with any Markon."

He narrows his eyes at Helena before addressing Mom again.

"He may have the ability to track Sunshine down no matter where she is and bring her back to Ridgemont. We just don't know," he finishes.

"But—" Mom protests.

Aidan holds up a hand, silencing her, and turns to the rest

of us. "It seems to me that we have two priorities here. One, protect Sunshine. Two, figure out what this pentagram spell is and how we can stop or reverse it. And to accomplish all this, we must put our differences aside and work together. I trust we are in agreement on this, Helena?"

"If your interpretation of events is accurate, then . . . *perhaps*. I will relay all this to the council," Helena says coolly.

"Please do. And of course there is a third priority. I must track down Dubu and destroy him," Aidan adds.

"You? What about all the working together stuff? Shouldn't we *all* be searching for Dubu?" I say.

"No. I am the only one who can handle Dubu."

I gesture to Helena. "Not even her?"

"*No.*"

Something inscrutable passes between Aidan and Helena—some sizzly, darkly charged, estranged-married-couple vibe. What is going on between them? And what does Dubu have to do with it?

"You know very well that it is extremely difficult to destroy a Markon. It is practically impossible. No luiseach has ever done so single-handedly," Helena points out to Aidan.

"Nevertheless," he says tersely.

Just then the front door creaks open. Oscar barks. Lex Luthor hisses and puffs out his rabid raccoon tail.

Aidan and I exchange a glance. We are both thinking the same thing.

He's back.

Aidan is at the door in three quick strides. Lucio and I follow, and so does Helena. We take our positions, ready to defend.

A figure in black appears in the doorway.

But it's not Dubu; it's Victoria.

Ashley is right behind her, carrying four big, flat boxes from Ridgemont Pizza. Her confused glance bounces from Aidan to Helena to Lucio to me.

"Hey, it's just me and Vicky. We got two pepperoni and two vegetarian. What's up with the *Fantastic Four* act?"

CHAPTER 6

All Roads Lead to Rome

It's late, and almost everyone has left. Mom and Ashley are upstairs in my room, setting up the queen-sized air mattress for Ashley (and Lex Luthor–proofing it with blankets so he doesn't puncture it with his claws). Aidan and I sit on the front porch—or rather, I sit on the rickety old swing while he paces across the creaky floorboards.

He seems to be doing a lot of pacing tonight.

The sky is black and clear with a sprinkling of stars, and the moon is a perfect gibbous. I am a phases-of-the-moon expert, thanks to Mom, who taught me a bunch of memorization tricks for my fifth-grade science quiz. "Gibbous" because it looks like a gibbon monkey sitting sideways, "crescent" because it looks like the letter C . . .

A cool breeze swishes gently through the pine trees, and I can almost pretend that Aidan and I are just hanging out and enjoying the evening, having some father-daughter chill time.

Except we're not.

"We need a detailed plan in place to ensure you are protected," Aidan says as he paces. "We cannot underestimate Dubu's abilities—or his intentions."

"I can protect myself. You trained me well in Mexico," I assure him.

"Not well enough. In fact, we must resume your training immediately. Monday morning. And until further notice I want either myself, Helena, or Lucio near you at all times. I have discussed it with them both, and they have agreed. Nolan, Kat, and Victoria can provide extra eyes and ears. Everyone will have a military-grade GPS-enabled cell phone that can reach me directly and immediately in case something happens."

"Um, isn't that overkill? Also, excuse me . . . *Helena?* Dubu isn't the only one who wants me dead. Isn't being alone with her the same as being alone with him?"

"No. Helena and I spoke again before she left, and we . . . she has given me assurances regarding your . . ." Aidan stops pacing and clears his throat. "The bottom line is, she has promised not to harm you or to let harm befall you. Her council is on their way to Ridgemont from Peru now, and—"

"Her council is on their way here?" I interrupt, alarmed. "Why?"

"Helena has to confer with them about you—about everything. Also, it's crucial that we mend the rift and bring the luiseach community together. Sixteen years is long enough. Dark times lie ahead, and we cannot afford to be divided."

I bite my lip and scrunch up my nose, which is my go-to expression when I have complicated stuff to mull over. When I was born and released that luiseach-killing energy wave, Helena's immediate response was to try to destroy me like a lab specimen gone wrong. She thought it was the only way to save our race. Aidan insisted on keeping me alive. Most of the luiseach community was on Helena's side. Aidan's only allies were Victoria, who was still a luiseach then, and Lucio's parents, Argi and Jairo.

Outnumbered and out of options, Aidan lied to Helena, saying he'd had a change of heart; he said he would take me into the jungle and kill me himself. But instead, he and Victoria transported me far, far away and left me at a random hospital in Austin, where a neonatal nurse named Katherine Marie Griffith promptly fell in love with me and took me home with her.

It didn't take Helena long to figure out that Aidan had fabricated my death. She left Llevar la Luz and took her followers with her—after she had Lucio's parents executed for not revealing my location. These days Team Aidan consists of Aidan, Lucio, Victoria, and me. And because Victoria isn't really a luiseach anymore, that puts our number at three and a half. On the other side of the rift is Team Helena, which is Helena plus all the other luiseach on the planet, including this council.

I guess Aidan is right about the need to mend the rift? The thing is, I'm the one who caused the rift to begin with. Will the council accept Aidan's theory that it's in everyone's best interests to keep me alive? Or will they go all Salem-Witch-Trials on me?

"Who's on this council?" I ask Aidan. "Do you know them? What's their purpose? Did any of them live at Llevar la Luz when you and Helena were . . . um, you know . . . when you guys were married? I mean, together-married versus not-together-married?" Seriously, could I sound more awkward?

Aidan shakes his head. "She has not given me names or other details, so no. I can only guess as to the members' identities."

"And?"

"We can discuss that later. We have more pressing matters before us. Like what happens from here on out. As I said, Helena and Lucio and I will take turns guarding you around the clock, in eight-hour shifts. We will not . . . violate your privacy. We'll just be nearby, out of sight, so we can take action at the first sign of trouble. Tomorrow I will pass out the new cell phones to everyone and provide detailed and explicit instructions. And you and I can resume our training on Monday morning at five."

"*Five a.m.?*"

"Yes. You will be returning to school, and we need to fit in at least two hours each day—more on the weekends."

School on Monday. Ugh, I had almost forgotten about that. Although Nolan will be there in at least a few of my classes, so that's an uplifting, glass-half-full thought.

"Aidan?"

"Yes?"

I scoot over on the porch swing and indicate that he should join me. He frowns at the broken, peeling-paint seat but sits down anyway, folds his hands in his lap, and waits for me to speak.

"Aidan, I need to know more about this Dubu."

"I have told you everything you need to know."

"No, you haven't. All you've told me is that he's a super-demon who may want me killed as part of his evil pentagram-themed master plan. Have you ever met him? Has Helena? Actually she seems to know way more about him than you do. Why is that?"

Is it my imagination, or did Aidan stop breathing there for a moment?

"That is not relevant," he says finally. His voice is steady, even, without emotion.

"Yes, it is, Aidan! The guy, demon, whatever, appears to be

after me. And you said that he's behind the organized darkness too. What exactly is that, 'the organized darkness'?"

"I can explain," someone says quietly. I detect her lavender and spice perfume before I see her.

Aidan and I glance up.

Helena emerges from the shadows and fog and steps onto the porch.

Aidan stands up abruptly. "I thought you had gone."

"I had an important errand to run. Aidan, the girl needs to be brought up to speed."

"I am taking care of that."

"Not really, no. You haven't changed, have you? You've always been so . . . *selective* in your sharing of information." Helena turns to me and regards me coldly. "Listen carefully, please. In the past few years there has been increased demonic activity all over the world. And in the past few weeks and months the demonic activity has been escalating at a dramatic rate. The most likely conclusion is that Dubu is orchestrating this—*has* been all along. As a Markon, he commands all demons and dark spirits. He is their king, if you will."

Increased demonic activity all over the world? That doesn't sound good at all.

"Um, okay . . . but why now?" I ask.

"We saw similar spikes in demonic activity leading up to the other four luiseach deaths," she replies. "Except this time the activity is much more intense, much more frequent than what we saw before those other deaths. Everything seems to be coming to a head."

"*The pentagram spell,*" I say with a shudder. "What is that phrase? 'All roads lead to Rome.' Except here it's 'all roads lead to the pentagram.'"

"Yes, something like that. Although Ancient Rome was far preferable to this era. Remember when Marcus Aurelius was in power, dearest? The people and the culture were so—"

"Helena," Aidan says warningly.

When Marcus Aurelius was in power? My history of ancient civilizations trivia is a little rusty, but wasn't that almost two thousand years ago?

Exactly how old *are* my birth parents? Aidan has always been vague on that point. He looks to be forty, fifty tops—and Helena looks even younger.

It occurs to me too that this is the first time I've been alone with my birth parents. I don't even know how to process the experience. This is what it would have been like if Helena had made a very different choice sixteen years ago, but it's too weird and too painful for me to go there right now.

Aidan turns to leave. "We must go, Helena. Sunshine needs her sleep. We can continue this conversation with her at another time."

"Sunshine. It's such a . . . *quaint* name, isn't it? So 1975," Helena says sarcastically.

"We must go, Helena," Aidan repeats more insistently. "Sunshine, I am taking the first shift. I will be in the vicinity if you need me."

With that, he takes off and strides briskly through the front yard.

Helena starts to follow, then turns back. "I almost forgot. I have something for you."

I stare at her suspiciously. "You do?"

She glances over her shoulder as if to make sure Aidan is out of earshot, then she reaches into the pocket of her dress and pulls out a shiny object.

It gleams ominously in the moonlight. For a second it occurs to me that it might be a weapon. I stumble back on the porch, bracing myself for the worst, and quietly reach into my back pocket for my luiseach knife . . .

But it's not a weapon. It's a necklace.

Helena cocks her head and studies me with a knowing smile. Can she read the fear on my face?

"Problem?" she purrs.

"Nope, no problem. I'm good."

She steps forward until we're eye to eye. She's no taller than I am, and yet she's so . . . flipping *terrifying*. How does she do that?

She presses the necklace into my palm and closes my fingers over it. "Wear it at all times. As long as it is on your person, you will have enhanced protection against all demons—including Dubu."

Startled, I open my hand to inspect the necklace. A star-shaped charm hangs from a delicate gold chain. The charm has a symbol on it—a hieroglyph?

"W-what is it?" I stammer. "W-where did you get it?"

"He gave it to me as a gift. During the October Revolution."

"The October . . . what? *Who* gave it to you as a gift?"

"But it has to be our secret, so please don't speak of it to anyone, not even your father—*especially* your father. Make sure you conceal it under your clothing, and please don't misinterpret this gesture. I have no interest in saving your life. I only care about saving the future of the luiseach race. It appears these two things coincide, at least for the moment."

And then Helena disappears back into the shadows.

CHAPTER 7

The Nacho Cheese Sisterhood

Under my PJs Helena's gold necklace is cool and almost imperceptible against my skin. And yet it feels heavy, oppressive, like the proverbial albatross around the ancient mariner's neck from that poem we studied in freshman English.

What *is* this necklace, really? She made it sound like the demon-repellent version of a silver cross or garlic garland for vampires. Is that true, or is this a trick? Is it actually going to weaken me or sicken me instead of making me stronger? And why is it such a big, huge secret?

If the necklace is for real, then how much "enhanced protection" will it give me against demons? Against Dubu himself?

Why can't Aidan especially know?

Sighing, I roll over in my bed. My mint-green clock radio tells me it's almost 1 A.M. Aidan mentioned he was taking the first shift. Where is he right now? Sitting in his car, hiding in the garage, pacing up and down the sidewalk?

"Hey, Sun?" Ashley whispers from across the room.

"Hey, Ash?" I whisper back.

"Are you asleep?"

"Nope. Are you asleep?"

"Nope."

We giggle quietly. We used to say this to each other during our sleepovers back in Austin, starting from when we were ten. During those epic overnights Ashley would paint my toenails shiny pink and style my unruly frizzball with sparkly barrettes and headbands, all over my objections. We argued over what movies to watch on Netflix; I wanted film noir and screwball comedies from the 1940s and 1950s, and she wanted only the most recent releases, preferably with lots of romance and hot guys. She regaled me with endless stories about her various crushes, and I had no such stories to reciprocate with. She and I never had a lot in common even then except for our shared obsession with nacho cheese–flavored popcorn and instant hot chocolate with tiny marshmallows. But *something*—an invisible bond, a fierce, tenacious loyalty—always kept us together. I know without question that she would do anything for me and absolutely ditto me for her.

We called ourselves the Nacho Cheese Sisterhood.

Ashley clicks on a light, then props herself up on the air mattress and swats aside the random collection of sheets and blankets. Lex Luthor sleeps at her side—he and Ashley are super-tight, among other reasons because she always snuck him food under the table when she was over for a meal in Austin. He seems to have made a little cat-cave for himself under one of the blankets.

"Why can't you sleep? I mean, you haven't slept in, like, a week, right?" Ashley asks.

"Dunno. You should be super-tired too after everything."

"Yeah, well." She pulls back her long blond hair and secures it with a scrunchie. "Soooo, Sunny-G, are you going to tell me what's going on? You need to tell me, like, *everything*. When I picked you up in Mexico you told me that you *had to had to had to* get back here to keep your boyfriend from dumping you for another girl. Which was a lie. You also said your long-lost dad— that Aidan guy—wasn't who you thought he'd be. And then that freak show in Vicky's front yard happened . . . seriously, what *was* that? Like, are you guys some kind of cult?"

"Um, not exactly."

I sit up and click on the antique gooseneck lamp on my nightstand, buying myself time to come up with answers to her questions. What version of the truth should I tell her? What combination of facts and little white lies? Not even Mom knows all the details—just the broad brushstrokes, including the fact that her daughter, whom she believed for sixteen long years to be human, is not.

Ashley *does* deserve an explanation. Last week in Mexico I found out—actually, I had this telepathic vision, which seems to be one of my new luiseach super powers—that Helena had taken Nolan prisoner in Victoria's house in order to bait me. Victoria was pretending to be on Team Helena for spying purposes. I *had* to rescue Nolan, so I tricked Ashley into picking me up at Llevar la Luz—the story about Nolan worked, at least temporarily—and driving me all the way to Ridgemont. Aidan and Lucio followed us, not like caravan followed but movie-car-chase-scene followed.

When we got to Victoria's I convinced Helena to set Nolan loose in exchange for me. Of course, my lovely bio-mom then tried to strangle me to death, although she changed her mind in the end. Could she not go through with it, after all? Does she have a couple of maternal neurons in her brain amongst the hundred billion crazy ones? But something tells me she may try again. I guess it all depends on this "council" of hers, whatever that is. Who are they? *Where* are they? Are they really on their way here, like Aidan said? How did Helena convince them to make the journey to Ridgemont from . . . where was it . . . Peru? Did she call them, videochat with them, or engage in telepathic messaging?

Found daughter. Should I eliminate her or not eliminate her? Please advise.

The point is, I owe Ashley a lot. Including the truth. Or part of the truth anyway.

After a moment I decide on a carefully edited version of what I told Mom.

By the time I'm done Ashley's jaw is practically to the floor.

"Soooo . . . you're like a *magical fairy?*" she says finally.

"Sort of. Not exactly. More like a guardian angel with, uh, superpowers."

"How did this happen? Did you accidentally swallow a potion? Were you in a laboratory accident? Did you get bitten by a spider from outer space?"

"I was born this way. Aidan and Helena are also luiseach."

"That's insane. So how many of you are there?"

"I'm not sure. Lots, I *think.* Aidan says there may be tens of thousands of us spread around the world. The problem is, there are also lots of demons and dark spirits out there who are doing evil. Even now they may be hatching some evil doomsday plan to unleash Armageddon and overthrow civilization. You aren't able to see these creatures—I can, and Aidan and Helena can, and I'm not sure who else can. I was fighting against three of them on Victoria's front yard."

"Get out of town!"

"No, really. It's my job. It's what luiseach are supposed to do."

"*Wow.*"

Ashley unties her hair and ties it back up again. She crosses her legs in a lotus position and then uncrosses them. "Okay. This evil doomsday plan. Is it happening soon?"

"Maybe. Probably. We're not sure."

"And you're going to try to stop it?"

"Oh, yeah, definitely."

Ashley nods to herself. "In that case I'm staying in Ridgemont with you. You can't be going through all this scary demon drama without your bestie around."

I'm startled. I wasn't expecting this. At the same time I feel relieved, touched, grateful. And also happy—Ashley and I haven't spent any quality time together since Mom and I moved here last August. Unless you count the past few crazy days as quality time, which I most certainly don't.

Although going through more scary demon drama together isn't exactly quality time either.

"That's really sweet of you. But it could be dangerous . . ."

"If you're right, it'll be dangerous everywhere, Austin included. I'd rather be here with you and the rest of your guardian angel squad."

"What about school? Spring break is almost over."

"I'll talk to my parents, tell them there's an emergency here or something. They never say no to me—well, except maybe that time I asked if I could trade in my hybrid for a BMW convertible. Okay, yeah, the hybrid *was* my sweet-sixteen birthday present. Oh, and when I asked if I could date that super-hot guy from UT Austin. I'll get my teachers to email me my homework and stuff. They all love me, so it's totally cool."

"Really?"

"Really."

Ashley truly is my Nacho Cheese Sister.

CHAPTER 8

Back to School

Monday morning. Ashley and I walk to school together, our backpacks slapping against our backs. The neighborhood is quiet—no kids waiting for the bus, no grown-ups leaving for work. I can practically imagine the tumbleweeds blowing down the street, it's that desolate. The only sign of life besides us is a crow pecking at a patch of dirt.

The day is typical Ridgemont—somber gray sky, cool temperature, major fog, the threat of drizzle hovering perpetually in the air. Being accustomed to the hot, dry Austin climate and having packed only a small overnight bag before picking me up in Mexico, Ashley was completely unprepared wardrobe-wise. Right now she's wearing my vintage pearl-white cardigan over her pink sundress and also my beige-y wool tights, which she's not thrilled about—"because I look like someone's grandma" were her exact words. But of course she's exaggerating, because she can basically wear anything and exude supermodel gorgeousness.

I yawn. And yawn again. My day started at 4:45 A.M., when

I made myself roll out of bed, throw on some clothes, and meet with Aidan to train in the park. The training was very difficult and seriously martial arts—he actually put a blindfold on me, gave me a stick, and challenged me to locate and knock down a bag of salt potatoes hanging from a tree. In under ten seconds. I jokingly called the exercise "luiseach party piñata," but Aidan wasn't amused.

"So what's your school like?" Ashley inquires as we turn onto Evergreen Street, which is kind of a misnomer because the pine trees here are more brown than green. "Are there lots of cute guys?"

I laugh. Ashley is notoriously boy crazy. She was on-off with Cory Cooper forever back at our old high school in Austin. I've never known her to be single for more than a week or two.

"I haven't noticed. But I'm sure there are," I reply.

"Does *he* go here? The one with the fancy ink on his right hand?"

"You mean Lucio? No."

"Even his *name* is dreamy," Ashley swoons. "What's his relationship status? Spill!"

I glance surreptitiously over my shoulder. I know Lucio is back there somewhere, following me—his shift started right after Aidan's. I spot him about half a block behind us. He gives me a little nod; I nod back.

"What. Is. His. Relationship. Status?" Ashley repeats impatiently. "Does he have a girlfriend? Concentrate, Sunny-G. This is important."

"Um . . . no. I don't think so. But I think he might"—*have a big, huge crush on me,* I want to say—"be getting over a previous relationship?"

Ashley grins and shrugs. "No worries. I can help him forget her."

"Um . . . okay."

"Do you have any deets? A name? Maybe I can check her out on Facebook."

"Sorry, I don't."

Although maybe I should confide in her about what happened—*almost* happened—with Lucio? But Ashley's not always 100 percent reliable about keeping secrets, and what if she accidentally blurts it to Nolan?

When Lucio almost kissed me in Mexico and I pulled back, he misunderstood, thinking I needed more time, and he said he would wait for me. I didn't tell him about Nolan then or that more time wasn't the issue. Of course now he knows about Nolan, so maybe he's over me and ready to move on? Lucio's the first guy I ever kissed, or almost kissed.

I like to think the kiss I shared with Nolan on Saturday was my *real* first time.

"Hey, new topic. Your dad's not as bad as you said. *And* he has awesome taste in clothes!" Ashley declares. "It was nice of him to arrange the school stuff for me. And the ballet lessons too."

"Yeah, that's Aidan for you."

After finding out about the Ashley-wanting-to-stay-in-Ridgemont plan, Aidan somehow arranged for her to transfer to Ridgemont High for the rest of the spring semester. He managed to sell her parents on this plan too—among other things, because Ashley plans to be a professional dancer someday, he fixed it so that she'd be able to take private dance classes with some famous ballerina who happens to live near here. Aidan

is weirdly powerful, even with boring, nonparanormal matters
like navigating school bureaucracies and organizing lessons. He
did a similar thing for me too, arranging for me to take a spontaneous leave of absence from school while he and I were in
Mexico.

"Oh, and your dad gave me this awesome new cell that's like
a Bat phone or something. He said I need to carry it with me at
all times. He also said I'm not supposed to leave your side. Well,
I'm *not* not supposed to leave your side ever," Ashley amends
with a hair flip.

"That sentence is confusing."

"Whatever, Ms. Grammatically Correct English Nerd. Anyway it's all good because everyone's bodyguarding you. Me,
Vicky, your dad, your mom, your psycho-freak other mom,
your boyfriend . . . and my dreamy future boyfriend, Lucio. I
wouldn't mind being bodyguarded by him, if you know what I
mean." She giggles and jabs me hard with her elbow.

"*Ow!*"

My backpack slides down my shoulder, and I push it back
up absent-mindedly. That's another thing . . . I don't know how
I feel about this "bodyguarding" business. Aidan may think I
need round-the-clock luiseach protection (him, Lucio, Helena),
plus extra sets of human eyes and ears (Nolan, Mom, Victoria, and now Ashley). But honestly, I can take care of myself.
Besides, what if we're all wrong and Dubu isn't targeting me
personally? What if his plan, *the* plan, is more complicated than
"have Sunshine killed and unleash the doomsday or whatever
spell"? Right now all we have are theories.

I touch the gold necklace hanging around my neck, hidden
under layers of plaid. If Helena is telling the truth, I may not

even *need* bodyguarding from Dubu or other demons. Not as much, anyway. But how will I know if she's lying? What is her game? Maybe I can ask Nolan to research the necklace for me without actually mentioning the necklace. Like, were there any talismans throughout history that provided protection against the dark side?

I peek at my watch: twenty minutes until homeroom. In Mexico it would be time for Lucio's and my daily ten-mile run through the jungle. I feel a strange disconnect, like I'm here and not here, like this is all a dream. Part of me is still back at Llevar la Luz, training with Lucio and Aidan from dawn till dusk and collapsing at the end of the day exhausted but exhilarated.

At Llevar la Luz I came into my own. Of course, it wasn't all Wonder Woman empowerment—far from it. I watched a man die. I became aware of a bunch of painful truths about myself, about Helena, about Aidan, and about the history of the luiseach.

On the plus side, though, I learned how to help multiple spirits move on at the same time. I even taught spirits how to move on by themselves, which is part of Aidan's Plan B in case the luiseach extinction thing really goes down and human spirits are left to fend for themselves. Apparently I'm the only luiseach who can actually do this.

We turn onto Old Schoolhouse Road, and there it is: good old Ridgemont High. It's still the same gray, depressing concrete monolith. Cars jockey for spots in the parking lot. Students swarm as one through the front entrance. My palms are sweaty, and I realize I'm nervous. I've been gone for three whole months. I wonder if anything's changed? Will I be able to catch up in all my classes?

Ashley jabs me with her elbow again. "Oooh, who's that hottie?"

"Who?"

"The one in the red polo shirt," she says, pointing.

"He's on the varsity football team. Jamal something. I guess you're already over Lucio?" I joke.

Ashley grins. "Ha ha."

Suddenly the temperature dips.

I reach up and wrap my blue owl-print scarf around my neck. It's then that I sense the spirit nearby: a young woman who died just hours ago. Her name was Kirsten, and she woke in the middle of the night because her baby was crying. Bleary-eyed, she headed down to the kitchen to warm up a bottle, but she stumbled on the stairs and fell twenty steps. She hit her head hard on the marble foyer. Kirsten was dead before her girlfriend, Ruth, woke up and called 9-1-1.

She's the first light spirit who has come to me since Saturday morning, when way too *many* light spirits came to me and nearly caused me to freeze to death. It must be the fact that Aidan, Helena, and Lucio are here too. Translation: I'm not the only luiseach in the area.

I stop in the middle of the sidewalk and hold out my right hand to Kirsten.

Ashley stops too. "Um, Sunshine? What are you doing? Cuz if you're trying to get that Jamal guy's attention, there may be a less awkward way—"

"*Shhhh.*"

I close my eyes and concentrate. I try to pull Kirsten to me— slowly, gently. She's afraid and resists at first.

It's okay. Let me help you. I want you to be at peace, I say silently.

Her resistance eases a little. She billows toward me, her long strawberry-blond hair matted with blood, her face contorted with sadness and shock. She and Ruth were going to get married this summer at a B&B in the mountains. Their daughter, Eden, just turned six months old.

"Sunshine?"

"Ash, be quiet!"

Kirsten is close to me now, so close that my fingertips are freezing cold, on the verge of frostbite.

You're almost there. I can feel the love in your heart. I can feel your strength. I know how much you miss Ruth and Eden, but they'll be all right. You'll be able to watch over them soon, forever.

In response Kirsten's spirit flickers and begins to bloom into a ball of light.

Yes. Just let it happen. Just become one with the light.

Suddenly her sad face morphs into . . . jeepers creepers, what *is* that? Hatred. Malice. Evil. Her blue eyes glow red, and her mouth twists into a malevolent smile.

Startled, I stumble back. But Kirsten manages to grab my outstretched hand. Her fingers dig into my wrist.

"*Deditio,*" she mutters in a deep, guttural voice.

"W-what?" I stammer. I try to wrench my arm away, but Kirsten's grip is like iron.

"Sunshine, what's wrong?" I hear Ashley cry out.

Then I feel Helena's gold necklace grow hot against my skin. *What's happening?* At the same moment Kirsten—or what used to be Kirsten—shrieks and lets go. She vanishes into a nearby tree—or rather, she flies right at it, into it, and disappears.

For a second the whole tree turns blood-red. Then it's back to tree-colored.

I rub my wrist, dazed. I know light spirits can turn dark if they're left on Earth too long. But a few hours isn't "too long"—not even close. How did Kirsten manage to speed up her light-to-dark journey so dramatically? Was she an anomaly, a mutant?

Or did she have assistance?

I peer around. No Dubu, no black sedan. Still, maybe he can control and convert spirits from far away?

I can feel Helena's gold necklace returning to cool. *Huh*. Did it actually work just now to repel Kirsten?

Lucio jogs up to Ashley and me. "Sunshine, what happened?" he demands breathlessly. "I saw that light spirit, that woman, but then she disappeared, and it looked like you were struggling . . ." Lucio can see light spirits but not dark spirits or demons—not yet anyway—whereas I've been able to see both for a while now.

Ashley tucks a strand of hair behind her ear and flashes him a radiant smile. "Oh, hey. Lucio, right? We had pizza together at Sunshine's house the other night. She was just performing one of her Loose Peach magic tricks. You're a Loose Peach too, right?"

"Luiseach," I correct her. "I was helping that spirit cross over, Lucio. Except all of sudden she turned dark, and . . ."

But Lucio isn't listening to me. He is staring at my right wrist.

I follow his gaze—and stifle a scream.

Kirsten left a mark when she grabbed me. Thin black lines in an intricate spider-web pattern.

I touch them and try to rub them away.

The spider-web twitches. Then doubles in size.

CHAPTER 9

Spellbound

Before homeroom Lucio and Nolan stand at my locker and inspect my wrist. The mark is still there, although it's faded somewhat to a dull pearly gray and returned to its original size.

I'm trying not to freak out about it—any more than I already have, anyway.

It's seriously gross and creepy, and I want my boring old wrist back.

Nolan leans forward, studying the mark closely.

"I remember now . . . there's a phenomenon called stigmata in the Christian tradition," he says thoughtfully. "Stigmata are believed to be miraculous marks and such that are found on the human body, perhaps echoing the crucifixion marks of Jesus Christ. I'm not sure if there is an equivalent phenomenon in demonology. I'll have to do the research."

Nolan is an Internet genius. He is also a genius with dusty old books, the kind that are hidden away in obscure corners of university libraries and contain ancient, esoteric information about demons and the like. He's basically a genius, *period*, which is one of the reasons I love him.

"Does it hurt, Sunshine?" Lucio asks with a concerned expression.

"No. But I really, really, *really* want it to go away."

"Of course, it could be something less symbolic. For instance, it could be the paranormal equivalent of a bruise or allergic reaction," Nolan continues.

A bruise or an allergic reaction? I consider these possibilities, which sound so everyday and no-big-deal, like I tripped and fell (which I do on a regular basis) or accidentally ate a scallop (which I'm mildly allergic to).

If only.

Just then Ashley breezes by with crabby old Vice Principal D'Angelo and flutters her fingers hello at us. Her gaze lingers on Lucio, who seems oblivious to the special attention. I offered to take her to the front office earlier and get her settled in, but she said she'd be fine. Which obviously she is. Mr. D'Angelo is cracking up at something she just said. I swear that girl could charm a pool full of hungry piranhas.

I haven't shown her the spider-web mark yet—I didn't want to frighten her.

"I'll look into all this. I'll also look into the business of light spirits morphing into dark spirits so soon after death," Nolan is saying. "Oh, and what was it that the Kirsten spirit said to you?"

"Ded-something," I reply.

Nolan pulls out his notebook and flips it open. "As in D-E-A-D?"

"I'm not sure. It sounded more like a foreign word. Maybe Italian? Or Spanish? *Ded . . . ded-ee . . .*" I pause and shake my head. "I'm sorry, I can't remember. Things were happening pretty fast and furious."

"No worries. I just learned about a search engine that searches for multisyllabic words with just one of its syllables. I'll get on it."

Nolan looks adorable today in a moss-green flannel shirt and his buttery-soft brown leather jacket, given to him by his namesake grandfather. Lucio actually looks adorable too in his faded jeans and a black T-shirt with a picture of his motorcycle, Clementine.

Waves of students pass by, talking and laughing. Lucio peers around curiously, shyly—which is weird, because I've never known Lucio to be shy. But I realize that he's never been inside a real high school—or a real school of any kind. He spent his whole life at Llevar la Luz. The compound was his school, and Aidan has been his only teacher.

"Do you want me—I mean, *us*—to show you around?" I say to Lucio. I glance at my wrist quickly; the spider-web mark is fainter and smaller now. *Go away*, I will it silently.

"Thanks, but I'd better take off," Lucio replies. "By the way, I'm meeting with your dad later this morning. I'll fill him in on what happened with your Kirsten spirit. He might have some ideas? In the meantime I'll be nearby. Just call or text if you need me, and I'll get to you fast as lightning."

"That would be over three hundred million feet per second," Nolan points out.

"Yeah, I might be a tiny bit slower than that," Lucio laughs. "Hey, so I'll see you tonight at the library, dude. It's on Bernadino Avenue, right?"

"Right. At the corner of Second Street. I'll be there at seven sharp."

"What's this about the library?" I ask Nolan after Lucio leaves.

"Your dad asked us to do some research."

"On what?"

"Well, pentagrams, for one. Aidan wants us to figure out the significance of the pentagram and also how to stop or reverse the spell. I already uncovered some interesting information at the library yesterday afternoon. Lucio and I are going to pick up where I left off."

I'm not sure what I think about my boyfriend and the guy with a crush on me working together. They'll get along just fine and never talk about me, right? *Right?* Although maybe I'm being a delusional, egocentric princess about this, acting like boys are fighting over me when really there are bigger, more important things happening.

Like trying to stop a possible apocalypse.

"Your friend Lucio is a pretty smart guy," Nolan remarks.

He says "your friend Lucio" with a funny catch in his voice. I know he's asking me the question by not asking me the question.

"We really are just friends," I tell him softly. "He grew up at Llevar la Luz after Helena . . . after she had his parents killed."

Nolan stares at me. "*Seriously?* That's horrible."

"Aidan is Lucio's mentor, just like he's my mentor and was Victoria's mentor when she was a luiseach. But Aidan is also the only parent Lucio has ever really known. Which makes Lucio and me kind of like a brother and sister. You know, like, um . . . Princess Leia and Luke Skywalker?"

Nolan frowns. Is he remembering that Princess Leia and Luke Skywalker kissed before they figured out they were related? And not a peck on the cheek kiss either, but a borderline make-out kiss?

Fortunately the first-period warning bell sounds. Saved by the bell!

"Algebra. Gotta go." I lean over to hug him—then stop, overwhelmed by a wave of nausea. I step back and take some deep breaths.

"Sunshine?" Nolan asks, worried.

"I'm fine. It's just, um . . ."

When I was born Aidan cast some weird luiseach spell on me that keeps me from being able to have close physical contact with anyone I'm in love with. He explained all this to me in Mexico, why I felt woozy and sick every time I touched Nolan or Nolan touched me. Apparently, Aidan wanted me to focus on my luiseach duties and not get distracted—I seem to recall that he also used the words "weakened" and "compromised"—by a boyfriend. I think he also had a nice luiseach husband in mind some day so I could contribute a bunch of nice luiseach babies to our waning population. (A luiseach and a human can't produce a luiseach child.)

I'm not sure how Nolan and I managed to share that amazing, epic, Jane-Eyre-and-Mr.-Rochester's-first-kiss kiss on Saturday when we thought it was the end of the world. Maybe fear, adrenalin, and our intense feelings for each other trumped Aidan's draconian antilove magic?

I've almost forgiven Aidan for this control-freak-father move. Almost.

"I'm going to tell Aidan to lift the spell," I announce, suddenly inspired. "Yes, that's it! He has to! You and I can't keep . . . that is . . . we should be able to . . . um, whenever we want, and . . ." I stop, flustered, heat creeping into my cheeks.

"Actually, I think Aidan's right," Nolan declares.

"I'm sorry, what?"

"I mean, not for forever. Just until Dubu is apprehended and you're safe again."

"But—"

"Your life is at stake, and I don't want me . . . *us* . . . to get in the way. I don't want our relationship to distract or weaken or compromise you, like Aidan said. If anything happened to you . . ." He clears his throat and shoves his hands into his jacket pockets, not looking at me.

"Oh, Nolan . . ." I reach out to touch his arm, but he moves away. My heart sinks.

"So you're telling me you *agree* with Aidan?"

"No. Yes. Well, just for now. I *am* your protector, after all. I have to protect you no matter what."

This day isn't turning out as I expected. Light spirits are acting different, and so is my boyfriend.

CHAPTER 10

Sense and Sensibility and Spirits

By the time fourth period English rolls around, I'm in a better mood. Nolan texted and asked me out on a coffee date after school. The spider-web mark on my wrist has faded and shrunk some more and is almost completely gone. *Big* relief.

Also, English is my favorite subject, and according to the online syllabus we're doing *Sense and Sensibility* this week. Of course, I've already read it fifteen times and memorized my favorite passages, but still . . . you can never read enough Jane Austen.

As the late bell rings, I hurry into Room 124 and scoot into an empty seat behind Tiffany Ramirez and in front of Linus Wing. I peer around. I know Nolan isn't in this section—I think he might have Mr. McAllister for English?—and neither, apparently, is Ashley. *Oh well.*

Someone else is missing too.

I tap Tiffany on the shoulder. "What happened to Ms. Chen?"

She turns around. Her perfume smells like honeysuckle and butterscotch, and her lip-gloss is neon orange. "What? She just had her baby, like, last night. Babies, plural. Twins. We have a sub."

I remember Ms. Chen's big, exciting baby announcement from last fall. "But she wasn't due till next month, right? I heard her telling Ms. Ferguson she was going to become a mom on Mother's Day."

Tiffany shrugs. "I guess the twins came early. Where have you been anyway?"

Before I'm forced to improvise a cover—family emergency, lingering mystery illness, anything but "in the middle of a Mexican jungle training to fight demons and help ghosts pass into the afterlife"—she rushes on. "Oh, hey, do you want to join the spring dance committee? We're totally looking for volunteers." She reaches into her backpack, pulls out a yellow flier, and thrusts it at me with a smile that reveals two rows of sparkly purple braces.

"Um, I'm kind of—"

"Just think about it, okay, Griffith? It's a super-fun time, *and* you get community service credit."

"How is the spring dance committee community service?"

"Ms. Sayed's in charge, and she arranged it with Principal Henderson. The proceeds from the dance are going to a local charity. Come on, Griffith, it's time you gave something back, don't you think? There are a lot of needy people out there. Life isn't all about makeup and boys and fancy vacations, you know?"

"Um, *excuse* me?"

At that moment the sub—or the person I'm assuming is the sub, anyway—enters the room, teetering precariously on platform shoes. She doesn't look like a teacher at all but more of an eighties rocker: dyed platinum blond hair, black lace tutu over leopard-print leggings, and puffy hot-pink top. Chunky glasses dominate her pale, pretty face.

I squint. There's something familiar about her. Where have I seen her before?

"Hello, class. I'm Ms. Warkomski," she announces in a squeaky voice. Turning around, she writes on the board: W-A-R-K-O-M-S-K-Y. Flustered, she quickly erases the Y with the palm of her hand and replaces it with an I.

An English teacher who doesn't know how to spell her own name? This isn't good.

Ms. Warkomski peers over the top of her glasses, spots the teacher's desk, and sits down carefully, fluffing and smoothing her black lace tutu. She riffles through some papers, picks up a pen, sets it down, and picks up another.

"So!" She adjusts her glasses and smiles at us. "Let's discuss books, shall we?"

Let's discuss books?

"Has anyone read anything good lately?" she goes on.

Several people giggle.

A guy in the front row—Isaac, I think—raises his hand. "Ms. W? We're doing *Sense and Sensibility* this week."

Ms. Warkomski nods quickly and pushes her glasses up her nose. "Oh, right. Of course! I love Charles Dickens, don't you? Who can tell me his main themes in this novel?"

Charles Dickens?

And then it slowly dawns on me.

Ms. Warkomski isn't Ms. Warkomski—she's Victoria in disguise.

Aidan must have planted her here to help keep an eye on me. Just like he planted her in my art class last fall. That was the class where I met Nolan, where we bonded over our mutual dorkiness and speculations about the strange new art teacher who dressed like a member of a witch's coven.

Victoria didn't know how to fake being an art teacher either. I remember her opening line during the first class: *Let's make some art, shall we?*

"H-hello?"

Another latecomer. This time it's a student: skinny, shoulders hunched, dark blond bowl cut. He's dressed in a navy blazer that's two sizes too big for him, a white button-down shirt, and wrinkled khakis. Also tortoiseshell glasses that are crooked on his thin, pock-marked face. He's standing awkwardly in the doorway with a slip of paper in his hand while his other hand rests on a brand-new-looking rolling backpack.

"Oh! Come right on in! The more the merrier!" Victoria calls out.

The student walks into the room and immediately trips. A fellow tripper! His cheeks flame crimson as he rights himself and offers Victoria the slip of paper, his eyes averted.

Victoria reads over the slip of paper. "I see! It seems we have a new student. Welcome, new student! Please take a seat. It says here your name is . . . how do you say that?"

"B-Bastian," he stammers. "Bastian Jansen." He glances around, slinks into an empty seat across from Tiffany, and parks his backpack next to him.

"Hello, Bastian Jansen! Class, please welcome your new classmate!" Victoria trills.

Tiffany leans across the aisle and hands Bastian a yellow

flier. "Welcome to Ridgemont High! You should totally join our spring dance committee!"

Bastian takes the flier from her and stares at it.

"It's upside down," I whisper.

He rights it immediately and stares at it some more.

Victoria beams. "Now, where were we? Oh, yes. Let's talk about Charles Dickens, shall we?"

I sigh and lean back in my seat. Should I correct her or let someone else do it? Victoria's babbling on about the name Charles and did his family call him Charles or Charlie or Chuck, and eventually I start to tune her out. I pull my English binder out of my backpack and find a clean page. My last notes from December are on Shakespeare's play *Hamlet*.

To be or not to be, I write next to the old notes. *If I assume my father's noble person.* I doodle Hamlet's sword, a cup of poison, a skull. Then I cross all that out and doodle a picture of Lex Luthor. Then Oscar. Then a pentagram.

Below that, I write:

Why are luiseach dying in a pentagram pattern?

Why every four years?

How did they die? Were they killed, and if so, by whom? Humans? Other luiseach? (It can't have been demons because demons can't permanently destroy luiseach.)

What will happen if/when the fifth and final death occurs?

If we stop Dubu, will that stop the pentagram spell?

Out of the corner of my eye I notice Bastian is doodling too—is that a castle? Or a cathedral? He's a good artist. I wonder where he transferred from. Obviously someplace where they wear navy blazers and khakis to school.

I decorate my pentagram drawing with stripes and pol-ka-dots and smiley faces. Someone taps me on the shoulder. I turn around, and Linus Wing whispers, "Is there a test in his-tory?"

I flip to a blank page in my binder and write: *No idea.* I hold it up for Linus to see. Just then I notice that the spider-web mark on my right wrist has reappeared. Except the shape has changed—the thin black lines are in a slightly different formation.

I bite my lip to keep from crying out. What's going on?

A cold wind sweeps through the room.

Startled, I drop my binder to the floor. Papers flutter every-where. Linus picks up a few, as do Bastian and Tiffany.

I take the papers from them and stuff them back into my binder. I glance around nervously—is it Kirsten again? Or Dubu?

No, it's a teenaged boy. A light spirit, not dark. Not yet any-way. He perches on the windowsill next to the bust of Shake-speare and kicks his feet against the flimsy radiator grate steadily, rhythmically. His name is Wesley, and he suffered from severe depression. Finally it became too much for him and he jumped off the High Falls Bridge.

Victoria is copying words onto the blackboard from Ms. Chen's computer: *Elinor Dashwood, Colonel Brandon, love, marriage, socioeconomic class.* She's finally figured out to Google "Jane Aus-ten." I twist slightly in my chair and reach my hand toward the windowsill, toward Wesley. He's frowning at his shoes as he kicks at the radiator grate with a sound only I can hear. *Clang, clang, clang.*

Wesley, it's okay. I'm here for you. You've suffered a lifetime of dark-ness. Now it's time for you to feel peace, serenity, closure.

I need him to come closer so I can touch him and help him move on. Part of me is afraid, though—what if he pulls a Kirsten and turns into a dark spirit? But I can't let fear rule me. It's my duty to help light spirits, and at the moment Wesley is a light spirit.

Surrender, Wesley. Surrender to the light. It will be so wonderful there, I promise.

Wesley stops kicking and raises his gaze. He looks at me with a curious expression.

Actually, he looks *past* me. At someone else.

I turn around.

He's looking at . . . Bastian. And Bastian seems to be looking right at him too.

"Bastian?" I say in a low, surprised voice.

Bastian shakes his head and covers his ears with his hands like he's trying to tune something out. He bends over his notebook and resumes his doodling. His pen scratches furiously across the white page.

Can Bastian *see* Wesley? But that's not possible.

Then, just like that, Wesley's spirit blossoms into light and vanishes—quietly, peacefully.

But *I* didn't do that. I didn't even touch him.

The skin on my right wrist prickles.

My spider-web mark has vanished too.

Cat and Mouse

It would probably be more efficient if I just ended her life right now. I have the means and the ability . . . and multiple opportunities, given how freely she goes about her business. I thought he would hide her away somewhere, perhaps in Llevar la Luz or one of the other luiseach compounds, as it is difficult for me to penetrate their protective magic.

But no.

Perhaps he believes he can use her to draw me out of the shadows? He is arrogant, as always. Arrogant and foolish. Just like that time in Constantinople.

Although he does seem to be keeping tabs on her. I have noticed him shadowing her. Also his pupil, that boy who believes himself to be an orphan.

And also my beloved.

Does she know? That I am here?

Strangely it turns out that I do not mind the wait with regards to the girl. Efficiency is not the priority. I am starting to relish the prospect of a cat-and-mouse game—the slow, delicious tango of stalk, retreat, repeat. The prophecy will be fulfilled, so why not savor the ride?

My beloved once called me a sadist. If by that she meant I enjoy causing the suffering of those who deserve to suffer, then yes, I am a sadist. I myself prefer the term "justice minded." After all, I am merely restoring the balance that his ancestors and their followers destroyed so long ago, so unjustly, during the First War.

In any case, I had the feeling she liked my sadism, understood it. She too is quite the sadist, even though she would never admit to it. We are two of a kind, both willing to do what must be done for the greater good. Which necessarily involves the suffering of others, of the wrongdoers—and also some innocents.

Indeed, she may suffer when I finally soul terminate the girl. But her suffering will not last, as she too wants the girl dead.

As for his suffering . . . that is another matter altogether.

For that I plan to have a front-row seat.

CHAPTER 11

The Color of Sunshine

unshine!" the barista guy calls out. "Your drinks are ready!"

Nolan and I walk over to the counter to pick up our cappuccinos. We're at the Dream Bean Coffee Shop, which opened up in downtown Ridgemont while I was in Mexico. It used to be a sad little Chinese takeout place sandwiched between the hardware store and the dry cleaner's. Now it's a trendy-looking café, or what passes for trendy in Ridgemont—paintings by local artists cover the pumpkin-colored walls, and a huge crystal chandelier hangs over a motley assortment of antique tables and chairs.

"Is that a made-up name?" the barista guy asks as he hands me my mug.

"No, it's my real name."

"You're like that actress, Moon Beam something."

I don't explain to him that Mom named me Sunshine because I made her feel like she was in a perpetual state of sunshine. Which makes me wonder—what did Aidan and Helena originally call me? Did they make a list of cute baby names while

I was growing in her belly, or were they too busy conducting scientific experiments in order to turn me into a mutant freak? I can't imagine not being called Sunshine. Of course, I also can't imagine not being Kat Griffith's daughter, not growing up in our sunny little house in Austin. Especially as the alternative was probably a gravesite in the jungle surrounding Llevar la Luz.

My phone beeps with a text.

Are you okay? When are you coming home?

This is, like, the twentieth text Mom has sent me today.

Nolan and I just got to the coffee place.
I'll be home in about an hour.

     Be safe, Sunshine. Love you!

Love you too, Mom!

Nolan and I return to our table with our drinks and a banana-nut muffin to share. Sitting down, I reach for the muffin to split it in half, and Nolan does the same thing at the same time. His fingertips accidentally brush against mine.

No queasiness. I smile and twine my fingers through his. He smiles back, then startles like a frightened rabbit and pulls away.

"Sorry! I can't. We can't."

"But we're just holding hands!" I point out.

"Still."

Nolan is taking this new dating protocol thing way too seriously. It's like we're a couple in a Victorian novel—deeply in love but unable to show physical affection because of society's rules, which would be kind of romantic except that it's not. It's frustrating. I waited a long time for us to act like a real boy-friend-girlfriend, and now I have to wait even longer. *Ugh.*

I take a sip of my cappuccino. The espresso is strong, and the milky foam tickles my lips. "So, um . . . something weird happened in English today. *Two* weird things. No, make that three."

"Tell me. By the way, you have foam all over your chin."

"Oh!" I swipe at my chin with the back of my sleeve. "Okay, so first of all, Victoria is my new English teacher."

"Seriously?"

I explain about "Ms. Warkomski" and her rocker get-up. "Ms. Chen just happened to have her babies yesterday, like a month early, and Victoria just happened to be the new sub."

"Wow."

"You don't think Aidan actually . . . I mean, is he *that* powerful? Can he cast a spell to make babies be born early? That's crazy, right?"

"Knowing him, it's entirely possible."

"True. Anyway, I think he wanted another bodyguard or whatever to keep an eye on me."

"Did you talk to Victoria after class?"

"No. I tried, but she just winked and waved me away. I think she's trying to stay . . . what's that word?"

"Incognito."

"Yup, that's it. It sounds like a coffee drink—'I'll have an in-cognito, please! With an extra espresso shot!'"

Nolan grins. He is one of the few people on this planet who appreciates my super-dork sense of humor. "'Incognito' comes from the Latin word 'incognitus,' meaning 'unknown.' What's the second thing?" he asks.

"Huh?"

"The second weird thing that happened in English."

"Oh right."

I take a bite of the banana-nut muffin and gather my thoughts. "There's a new student in the class. Besides me, that is, although I'm not *new* so much as *reinstated*. His name is Bastian something."

"Yeah, I think he's in a couple of my classes too." Nolan nods. "Bastian Jansen."

"Yes, him! So we're all listening to Victoria going on about Charles Dickens. The best of times, the worst of times, the French Revolution, blah, blah, blah. When we're actually *supposed* to be discussing Jane Austen, which she eventually gets around to . . . anyway, all of a sudden this spirit shows up. A light spirit. Like, our age, which was so sad, especially because he committed suicide. I start to help him move on, but then I notice that . . . well, this is going to sound insane . . . but I notice that Bastian is reacting to the spirit too."

"Reacting how?"

"Bastian was looking right at the spirit, and he seemed kind of . . . well, uncomfortable. Agitated."

Nolan considers this. "Is it possible that he just *sensed* the spirit? Humans do sometimes feel the presence of a spirit without actually being able to see it."

"Maybe, but . . . *argh,* I don't know."

"It's possible too that he knew the guy who died? Maybe they had some sort of connection? The spirit could have been reaching out to Bastian."

"I guess so. Maybe. But then the spirit moved on without me touching him."

"You're becoming more powerful. You're enabling spirits

to move on without your help, which is what Aidan wanted, right?" Nolan cocks his head. "So what's the third weird thing?"

I hold out my right wrist, which is smooth and unmarred. "The spider-web thingy . . . during Victoria's class it reappeared. In a slightly different pattern. Then when Wesley's spirit moved on, it disappeared."

Nolan inspects the spot where the mark used to be. "That's odd. Do you remember what the pattern looked like?"

"Sort of?"

"Can you draw it for me?"

He slides his notebook and pen across the table as I make a quick sketch. He puts on his gold wire-rimmed glasses to study the sketch, then moves his lips soundlessly as he counts the lines.

"It's the same number of lines as before, except rearranged," he says after a moment. "I don't understand."

"I don't understand either."

"I'll look into it. Lucio and I are meeting at the library in"—he glances at his watch—"exactly forty-eight minutes. We have a lot of work to do on the subject of pentagrams, of course, but we'll check out these other things too."

"Thank you!" I break off another piece of the muffin. "You mentioned before that you uncovered some stuff on pentagrams at the library yesterday? When you were there by yourself?"

"Yes."

"So what did you find?"

"Well, so pentagrams have a long and fascinating tradition in many cultures. Of course, first and foremost it's a mathematical shape, a five-pointed star. The word comes from the Greek: 'pente,' five, and 'gramme,' line. It is a simple star polygon—the simplest star polygon."

I nod, remembering my sophomore-year geometry. "Right."

"A pentagram consists of fifteen line segments and ten points."

"You mean *five* points."

"Five on the outer tips of the star and five on the pentagon that forms in the middle of the star. See?"

"Nope, not really."

Nolan flips to a clean page in his notebook and begins sketching. "One, two, three, four, five, six, seven, eight, nine, ten," he counts.

"Okay, *now* I get it."

"Anyway, that's the mathematical piece of it. The history of its symbolism is more interesting."

"Interesting how?"

"Well, the normal pentagram has various meanings. The five senses, the five wounds of Jesus Christ, etcetera, etcetera. Some believe that the top point of the pentagram represents good because it's the superiority of spirit over matter. Like the top point is the heavens and the lower four points are earth, air, fire, and water." Nolan adds, "There are other meanings attached to the pentagram too. One creation myth relates it to Chronus, a serpentine god with three heads."

I think about the three nasty serpent-demons we encountered on Saturday. "Are his three heads all snake heads?"

"Actually no. He has a lion head, a bull head, and a human head. He supposedly placed seeds in five spots on Earth so he could create the cosmos—the universe."

"Huh." I do a mental double-take. "Back up. Did you say *normal* pentagram? Is there such a thing as an *abnormal* pentagram?"

"That's where things get *really* interesting." Nolan rotates his notebook a few degrees so the pentagram is tipped on its side. "See how there's no more single top point that goes straight up but instead two top points that go sort of northeast and north-west? Occultists and others believe this type of reversed penta-gram symbolizes evil—the triumph of matter over the heavens. Some even think the northeast and northwest points are the horns of a goat."

"Like a demonic goat, not a nice, cute farmy goat."

"Exactly."

We lapse into silence and sip our cappuccinos. An old jazz tune plays softly over the speakers—Billie Holiday is singing "Let's Fall in Love." At the next table a girl giggles and leans into the curve of her boyfriend's neck; he holds her close and kisses the top of her head.

Longing tugs at my heart, and for a moment I forget all about pentagrams. All I can think about is Nolan. I imagine leaning into the curve of his neck and Nolan holding me close and kiss-ing the top of my head.

Nolan is watching them too. "Soon," he says quietly.

"How soon?"

"When I know you're safe."

After we finish our coffees Nolan insists on driving me home on his way to the library. We don't talk about dark spirits or demons or anything creepy-scary in the car, just silly stuff like the biology teacher's new toupee and the ugly cat-puke color they painted the cafeteria walls over spring break. I also tell him about Tiffany Ramirez's spring dance committee.

"Yes," Nolan says emphatically, turning onto my street.

"Yes . . . what?"

"Yes, I'll go to the spring dance with you."

I blush, and my heart does a goofy, giddy somersault. "I didn't realize I'd asked you."

"Fine, I'm asking *you*. We can go as friends . . ."

". . . unless you and Lucio have solved the pentagram puzzle and Aidan has caught Dubu and put him in demon jail or whatever. The dance is, like, a couple of weeks away. Then we can go as not-just-friends."

"Yes, okay. I'd like that."

When we reach my house he parks his car to walk me to the porch.

"I'll call you later?" he says.

"Yes, please!"

I stand on my tiptoes and kiss him lightly on the lips—quickly, before he can react.

"That's not very just-friends," he chides me.

"Yeah, I know."

He gives me a little wave and walks back to his car.

My heart is still doing goofy, giddy somersaults.

Humming the Billie Holiday song, I turn and start to open the front door, but it's locked. I thought Mom and Ashley were home—maybe they went grocery shopping for dinner stuff?

I reach into my pocket for my key. There's a movement behind me.

"Nolan, did you forget something?" I say as I turn around.

But Nolan isn't there. No one is there. I glance around, suddenly panicked—could it be Dubu? But he's not there either.

Somewhere in the pine trees I see a movement. Is it Helena, who is supposed to be watching me between four and midnight?

I hear a faint fluttering sound, like the sound of feathers. Then . . . silence.

My gaze drops to the porch floor, where there's a dead bird at my feet.

It's bright yellow.

The color of sunshine.

CHAPTER 12
Bye, Bye Birdie

I drop to my knees and look at the bird closely to make sure it's really dead. It really is. Its eyes are black and dull. Its chest is eerily still.

Was it the work of a neighborhood cat? But there are no neighborhood cats that I know of, and Lex Luthor is strictly indoors. The bird has no bite marks or scratches. There is no blood.

I also don't recognize this particular kind of bird. I'm not an expert, but it looks exotic, out of place. Mostly it's just sparrows and blue jays and crows around here. This one is small and bright yellow with white-ringed eyes. Could it be someone's missing pet? Did it escape from its cage and fly out the window?

"What happened to you?" I ask the bird.

One of its wings flutters. *Good golly, it's still alive!*

The porch swing creaks. Pine needles scuttle against my ankles. My blue owl scarf flaps against my face.

The bird isn't alive—it's just the wind blowing and stirring its feathers.

Biting back my disappointment, I unravel my scarf and gently, carefully wrap its tiny body. I unlock the front door and bring the bundle inside.

Mom and Ashley are cooking in the kitchen. A delicious, buttery, oniony smell fills the air.

"Hey there, Sunshine State! I'm so glad you're home!" Mom calls out. She wipes her hands on her faded brown Longhorns T-shirt and rushes up to hug me. She smells like butter and onions too. Ashley stands at the stove, frying little dumplings in a skillet, her long hair knotted back with a pink scrunchie.

"Ashley's teaching me how to make her grandmother's pierogi recipe. How was your first day back? Did Aidan and Lucio keep you safe—and that woman too?" Mom refuses to say Helena's name.

"My first day was fine. *Ish.*" I don't want to tell them about the Kirsten spirit or the Wesley spirit just yet. "I found a dead bird."

Mom frowns. "You mean at your school?"

"No, on our front porch. Just now."

"What?"

I hold out the scarf-covered bundle. Ashley turns off the stove and joins us. Lex Luthor trots into the kitchen, tail high, and sniffs curiously.

"Aww." Ashley makes a sad face when she sees the bird. "We should bury it in the backyard and give it a little funeral. Maybe plant some pretty flowers."

"That would be nice," I agree. "I thought we might make posters and post them around the neighborhood. You know, in case this is someone's pet."

"Totally! I can help with the posters." Ashley reaches into her back pocket, pulls out her phone, and takes a picture.

"I've never seen a bird like this before. I wonder what kind it is?" says Mom.

"I don't know, but maybe Nolan can find out. He's good at stuff like that," I reply.

"Here, Sunny-G, text him our poster photo," Ashley suggests.

She sends me the photo, and I quickly forward it to Nolan with a brief message about what happened. He texts back immediately and says he'll check it out while he's at the library with Lucio.

After dinner Mom, Ashley, and I go to the backyard to bury the bird. It's chilly out, like winter-coat chilly, and the sky swirls with twilight colors: lavender, pink, and gold.

Mom puts the bird in an empty shoebox lined with an old shawl. I dig a hole under a Douglas fir tree, put the box in it, and cover it with dirt. Ashley finds a snowdrop plant near the chain-link fence that surrounds our property and transplants it next to the grave. The tiny white flowers droop forlornly. Then I stick a splintery piece of two-by-four in the ground on which I've scribbled the words "R.I.P. BIRD" in magic marker. Maybe I can make a nicer marker later.

"Bye bye, birdie. We hope you have a nice life in birdie heaven," Ashley says, blowing kisses at the grave.

Mom says a little prayer. I close my eyes and try to sense the bird's spirit. Can I help it cross over? I've never done that with a nonhuman spirit. But I don't feel or see anything. Either I don't have that ability or the bird is already gone.

That night I lie in bed tossing and turning. Ashley is asleep on her air mattress. She's definitely out because she's snoring lightly and also muttering in her sleep—something about what to wear for the spring dance. (While we were getting into our PJs she saw Tiffany's yellow flier sitting on my desk and immediately insisted we both join the spring dance committee plus go dress shopping together.) Lex Luthor is curled up at her feet. Oscar isn't in the room; I think he got used to sleeping with Mom while I was away in Mexico.

I glance at my mint-green clock radio: 2:12 A.M. Not a good time to be wide awake and staring up at the ceiling. I try counting sheep, then elephants, then brontosauruses, but none of that works. I run through my favorite passages from my favorite Victorian novels, but that doesn't work either. My brain is buzzing and whirling with a million thoughts. The dead yellow bird. Dubu. The pentagram spell. The four mysterious luiseach deaths. Latoya. Mrs. Ostricher. Wesley. Kirsten. Helena and her council. My spider-web mark, which thankfully hasn't returned, although I keep touching my right wrist and checking it for new creepy, bumpy lines.

Nolan called earlier. He said that he and Lucio hadn't gotten very far at the library but that they were going to try again tomorrow night.

So many mysteries and so few answers.

I have no idea what time it is when I finally pass out, exhausted from all my restless churning and cogitating. My REM-sleep-deprived brain immediately plunges into dream mode.

In the dream it's night, and I'm sitting alone on the bank of a big, still lake. The moon is high and silvery bright. Trees swish in the cool breeze. It's magical and mysterious and quiet except for the steady hum of crickets and the occasional plaintive cry of a loon, a lone loon.

The loon is way across the lake. After a while it begins to swim toward me in a straight line that perfectly bisects the round body of water. As it gets closer, I can make out its black head and tiny, piercing red eyes. Its wings are mottled black and white.

The loon gets closer and closer . . . and then suddenly it begins to morph into some other creature. The dead yellow bird! Except that the bird isn't dead—it's alive. It tries to tell me something, but its beak is taped shut with black tape.

Blood gushes out of the bird's eyes . . .

I wake up screaming and realize in horror that across the room Ashley's mouth is taped shut with black tape too. I try to get up to help her, but my hands and feet are bound to the bed with heavy iron chains.

At the same time I notice the spider-web marks have returned—not just on my wrist but all over. They pulse and multiply, pulse and multiply, pulse and multiply. I scream as they take over my entire body . . .

But I'm not awake. I'm still in my dream. I can't get out of my dream. My limbs feel heavy as lead, and my mind is thick and soupy and confused.

Then the dream shifts, and the darkness is gone. The chains and marks are gone. Bright light floods my vision.

Aidan and Helena are in a room. Where are they? Aidan is wearing a navy suit and matching tie that I don't recognize, and Helena is wearing a long, lacey white dress and a silver ring with an unusual C-shaped design—some kind of symbol? Or a rune?

"Does she know? What Markons are capable of?" Helena is asking.

"No. And I'd like to keep it that way," replies Aidan.

"But he's going to kill her. I thought you wanted to prevent that."

"I intend to kill him first."

"That means—"

"Yes, I'm fully aware. There is no other option."

"But you can't do it alone."

"I must."

Darkness. The bright light is gone. Aidan and Helena are gone.

Then the darkness twists slowly like a surreal kaleidoscope. Browns and blacks and reds bleed into each other and form a muddled image of Dubu's face.

The muddled image sharpens into focus. Dubu is laughing.

"*Deditio,*" he whispers in my ear.

"*No!*" I hear Aidan shout from far away.

"*No!*" I scream as Dubu wraps his six-fingered hands around my neck.

Six fingers?

I wake up in a tangle of sheets and cold sweat—this time for real. I reach under my pillow for my knife and hold it up to Dubu's throat.

But he isn't there.

It's just my room, same as it was before. Ashley's stretched out on the air mattress and murmuring about peep-toe pumps. The mint-green clock flashes 4:35 A.M. Almost time to wake up and get ready to train with Aidan.

I reach up and touch Helena's necklace. It's still there—warm against my skin, then cooler, then cool.

Did something activate it?

Lex Luthor jumps off of the air mattress, slinks across the pink shag carpet, and leaps onto my bed. He blinks up at Dr. Hoo and hisses.

I glance up.

Dr. Hoo's beak is taped shut with black tape.

CHAPTER 13
The Telltale Suit

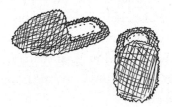

It's still dark outside when I rush downstairs in my PJs and peer out the square glass pane. The ghost of the full moon hovers on the horizon. Fog blankets the dense grove of pine trees.

I spot the familiar figure standing on the front porch reading a newspaper—a French-language newspaper.

Tall. Unsmiling. A navy suit with a matching tie. Short, immaculately styled, almost-black hair.

Just the person I needed.

I open the door and wave Aidan in.

"You need to see this!" I whisper frantically.

"See what? Sunshine, you're"—Aidan glances at his steel watch—"twenty minutes early for your training session."

"Forget about that. Come upstairs—quietly, so you don't wake Mom and Ashley. I think Dubu was here again."

"*What?*"

"I think he did something to Dr. Hoo!"

I close and lock the door behind Aidan and gesture for him to follow me up the stairs. But first he insists on searching the first floor of the house.

"There is no one down here," he says when he's finished.

"I know that. He's gone. Come on, you need to see Dr. Hoo!"

"Who or what is a Dr. Hoo?" Aidan whispers as we enter my very messy room, which is practically wall-to-wall with Ashley's and my clothes. I wish I had at least made the bed, but "battle-field conditions," as Mom would say, meaning you do what you can in the midst of chaos.

Ashley's still snoring and sleep-talking on the air mattress. Aidan glances around curiously, and I realize this is the first time he's ever been in my *real* room, with my *real* stuff, as my temporary room at Llevar la Luz was pretty Spartan and aus-tere and not me at all.

"Dr. Hoo is my owl. My stuffed taxidermy owl. Dubu or some other dark superpower-overlord covered its beak with black tape. *See?*"

"No, I don't see."

I do a double-take. On the shelf above my desk Dr. Hoo's beak is back to normal. There's no sign of the black tape.

Puzzled, I stand up on my desk chair and touch his beak. It's perfectly smooth, not sticky-tacky as though it was all taped up a few minutes ago. Everything else appears to be undisturbed too: my glass unicorn figurines, my antique typewriter, my books, my Nikon F5.

"But . . . but . . . it was just . . . Aidan, you have to believe me! I swear, the tape was there when I woke up!"

"Explain, please."

Ashley stirs and yawns. I step off the chair, trying not to fall on my face in the process, and gesture for Aidan to follow me back downstairs.

Once we're on the porch again I plunge into the details. "I had this dream last night. Actually it was more like super-early this morning—like, just now. And it wasn't just a dream, it was a nightmare. When I woke up, Lex Luthor—that's my cat—was looking up at Dr. Hoo and acting all weird. Hissing. That's when I saw the black tape on Dr. Hoo's beak."

Aidan mulls this over. "Is it possible that this Dr. Hoo incident was part of your nightmare?"

"No! I mean, I don't think so. Although I'm not a hundred percent sure."

Aidan mulls some more. "I suggest that you get dressed. We can continue discussing this matter during our training exercises."

I look down. Good golly, I'm still in my Care Bear PJs and fuzzy slippers. How embarrassing is that? And then I remember Helena's necklace. I forgot about it in all the chaos. I quickly reach up to make sure it's hidden under my pajama top, out of Aidan's sight. It is.

"Be right back," I mumble.

"Of course. And please bring Dr. Hoot with you."

"You mean Dr. *Hoo?*"

"Yes, Dr. Hoo."

Upstairs I grab some clothes and my Chuck Taylors from my closet and tiptoe to the bathroom, being careful not to disturb Ashley and Mom. I brush my teeth and wash my face simultaneously to save time, studying my reflection in the mirror—frizzball frizzier than usual, pale skin paler, black circles under my milky green cat eyes. (Even in the dim bathroom light my pupils don't get big—they never get big.) Ashley told me yesterday we need a girls' day at a spa, which sounded silly—mud wraps and papaya facials and getting massaged with hot rocks?—but maybe she's right. Although honestly I'd settle for a good night's sleep and a mini-vacation from luiseach duty.

A few minutes later I'm back on the porch with Dr. Hoo tucked under one arm and a couple of granola bars for my pre-training breakfast.

"May I see your owl specimen, please? I wish to inspect him."

I pat Dr. Hoo's head and hand him over to Aidan. He takes him from me and runs a hand over his dusty white feathers.

"Interesting," he murmurs.

"*What's* interesting?"

Aidan doesn't answer but instead reaches into his pocket and pulls out a small silver device. It looks like something Mom might use at the hospital to examine patients.

Aidan touches the device to Dr. Hoo's black-speckled head and wings . . . then his legs . . . then all over.

"Um . . . what are you doing?" I ask curiously.

"I am trying to detect an energy signature."

"A what?"

"As you know, the presence of a dark spirit or a demon can lower the temperature of the air, often quite dramatically. Although not always, as Helena and I have been discovering more and more. In any case, Markons have always been different. They have the ability to keep the temperature around them the same, if they wish. It is one of the many ways they have of masking their presence. However, one thing they are apparently unable to mask is the almost undetectable energy signature they leave behind. Helena's cousin Dulcetta, who is a luiseach, of course, created a prototype of this instrument during the Renaissance. It is not unlike a Geiger counter."

"During the . . . Renaissance? Wasn't that, like, five hundred years ago?"

"Yes, something like that."

So Helena has some cousin who was alive during the Renaissance period. And the other day Helena and Aidan were talking about Ancient Rome as though they'd actually been there. Are luiseach really capable of living for hundreds, even thousands of years? Will *I* live that long too?

That is, if I manage to avoid being the fifth point on the pentagram . . .

Aidan shakes the silver device and waves it around Dr. Hoo again. The device emits a low, strange whirring sound, and I almost expect Dr. Hoo to hoot back.

"What does that noise mean?"

"The instrument is picking up a very faint energy signature."

A chill runs down my spine. I feel at once terrified and vindicated. "So *now* do you believe me that Dubu was here? Or maybe one of his Markon cohorts? How many Markons did you say there were?"

Aidan tucks the device into his jacket pocket and checks his sleek steel watch. "Come with me. We are going to train down by the river today. You will learn how to control large bodies of water and also fight water demons more effectively. We will go in my car, and I will drop you off at your school afterward."

"But what about Dr. Hoo? And aren't you going to answer my question? My questions?"

"Bring the owl specimen with you. I would like to examine it further."

He turns and heads toward the street.

I sigh. Are all fathers this secretive? And bossy? And all-around annoying?

I grab my backpack from inside the house and close the door behind me. The morning sky is gray—what else is new?—and the air is damp and heavy with the smell of pine needles and moss. Munching on a granola bar, I hurry my steps to keep up with Aidan. My feet crunch on gravel as I half walk, half run down the long driveway.

Aidan's car is parked across the street. As usual, the other houses on our cul-de-sac show no signs of life—no kids waiting for the bus, no adults driving off to work. People *do* live in them, but Mom and I have yet to meet a single neighbor. Everyone seems to keep to themselves.

As Aidan approaches the driver's side door of his car he reaches into his pocket and extracts a key. Behind him, I stare at his broad back, at his navy suit.

A troubling thought flits through my mind.

He was wearing that exact same suit in my dream. A suit I've never seen before.

Which means . . .

"Aidan?"

"Yes?"

"Earlier this morning . . . were you with Helena? And did you guys have a conversation? About me, about Dubu?"

Aidan turns around slowly and stares at me. "What did you say?"

"I'm right, aren't I? Because you and she were in my dream. Except that part of the dream wasn't a dream. I just figured it out. You were wearing that suit. She was wearing a white dress and this artsy-looking silver ring with a design that looked like the letter C."

Aidan raises an eyebrow. "You *saw* all this?"

"I saw *and* heard. Helena said . . . let's see . . . she asked you if I knew what Markons were capable of. You said no and that you preferred to keep it that way. What did you mean by that?"

"It is not important."

"And then she said something about—"

But my words are drowned out by the loud screeching of tires. Aidan and I whirl around—just in time to see a red SUV speeding toward us.

CHAPTER 14
A Lie by Any Other Name

Sunshine, look out!" Aidan shouts.

As the red SUV bears down on us, tires screeching, Aidan dives toward me and pushes me out of the way. I tumble into the middle of the street, out of the car's path, my right shoulder hitting the pavement, hard.

The SUV changes course quickly, tweaking left by 45 degrees, and guns toward me. Not Aidan . . . *me*. Adrenalin pumping through my veins, my instincts on hyper-alert, I roll away just in the nick of time. A shockwave of heat and noise and burning rubber hits me as the SUV passes within inches of my head.

The car makes a hasty U-turn and comes after me again.

Out of the corner of my eye I see Aidan sprinting toward me. I leap to my feet, but I lose my balance on a dangling shoelace—*stupid sneakers!*—and stumble backward. The SUV is almost upon me now.

Just then I feel Helena's necklace grow hot against my skin.

At the same instant—*literally* the same instant—the SUV careens out of control.

The runaway car passes about six inches from where I'm lying on the ground. It hits the curb, spins out of control, and—*crash!*—slams into a massive pine tree.

Broken glass, crunching metal. I'm still lying on the pavement, trying to stop my shaking and trembling and general freaking out. I reach for Dr. Hoo, who landed next to me, a little dirty but unharmed.

"Dear God! Sunshine, are you all right?" Aidan is at my side.

"I'm fine. Just a little rattled. And mad, gosh darn it! Let's nab the driver!"

Aidan grabs my hand, helps me to my feet, and we hurry over to the SUV. The front of the car is accordioned against the tree and smoke plumes from the engine. There are glass shards everywhere.

We step carefully over the debris and peer inside the driver's side window.

There's no one in the car.

"Wait a sec. Did the person get away?" I ask, confused.

Aidan shakes his head. "Impossible. I had my eyes on the car the entire time."

"Then how . . . who . . ."

"*What have you done to my vehicle?*"

A woman marches up to us, dressed in a housecoat and slippers. Her grayish-blond hair is done up in large pink curlers.

"I'm calling the police! You thieves stole my car and destroyed it!" she yells, shaking a fist at us.

Aidan steps forward and smiles. Aidan never smiles.

"No, madam. That is not what happened at all. Someone *did*

steal your car. But in making his escape, he drove off so quickly that he almost ran us over. He crashed into the tree and got away on foot."

Aidan's voice is calm and soothing and hypnotic. The woman blinks at him, dazed.

"Yes, that's what must've happened. Sorry, I didn't mean to jump to conclusions. I live over there in that raised ranch. My name's Patty Hillman." She points to a sad-looking white house with faded brown shutters at the end of the cul-de-sac. A neighbor, finally.

"Hi Patty. I'm Sunshine Griffith. My mom, Kat, and I live over there." I wave Dr. Hoo in the direction of our house, which probably used to be white but is now a dingy gray. "And this is Aidan . . . um . . ." Wait, I don't know his last name. Does he *have* a last name? "He's my dad. He lives . . . um . . . out of state."

"You should go back to your home now. Your coffee is getting cold, and your cat, Petunia, is waiting for her breakfast," Aidan tells Patty in the same calm, soothing, hypnotic voice. "I will call the police for you and file a report. A hired sedan will be here at nine to take you to your dentist's appointment and then bring you home. Your own car will be returned to you by the end of the day, fully repaired."

"Why, thank you. That's mighty kind of you," Patty says, still sounding dazed. She turns around and walks mechanically back to her house.

I gape at Aidan. "How did you do that? What did you do to her?"

"I did what needed to be done."

"How did you know about her cat and her coffee and her dentist's appointment and all that?"

"Sunshine, that information was available to you as well. You simply chose not to receive it."

"What does that even mean?"

But Aidan ignores my question. *Again.* Instead, he pulls the silver device out of his pocket and waves it at the passenger's side window of the SUV.

It makes the strange whirring sound—louder this time.

"Dubu *was* here. Or at the very least, he touched this car recently. I believe that Markons have the ability to manipulate objects from a distance."

"But why would he try to run me over? So he can hurt me? Scare me? Send me a warning? He's a demon, so it's not like he can kill me," I point out.

A shadow crosses Aidan's face.

What is he not telling me?

Then I remember his and Helena's conversation, the one in my vision.

Does she know? What Markons are capable of?

No. And I'd like to keep it that way.

But he's going to kill her. I thought you wanted to prevent that.

I intend to kill him first.

That means—

Yes, I'm fully aware. There is no other option.

"Markons can kill luiseach, can't they?" I say slowly.

Aidan doesn't answer. He doesn't have to. I *know.*

"Why did you lie to me?"

"I did not lie. I simply obscured the truth. I had to protect you. If you knew, you might become frightened and lose your focus. These are dangerous times, and I need you at your best, at your sharpest."

I squeeze my fists. I want to yell, scream, demand to know why he always keeps things from me, manipulates me, tries to control me . . . all in the name of "protecting" me.

But at the moment my brain is stuck on the other thing.

Markons can kill luiseach.

The Book of Prophecy

Honestly, he started it.

Or rather, his ancestors did: the Original Ones, the high-and-mighty King Adis and Queen Uiri.

That war changed everything. Until then the three of us—my brothers and I—ruled the world. The luiseach were . . . nothing. Mere annoyances, like mosquitoes on a glorious summer night. Under our guidance our dark servants were free to possess as they pleased, gathering energy and more energy every time they performed a soul termination.

Of course we let the luiseach have a crumb here and there . . . the occasional moving-on of a light spirit. We wanted them to feel useful, important. Duped into thinking that the balance was actually equitable, that they were fulfilling their stupid, saintly mission.

Then the balance began to shift in the other direction. The luiseach grew stronger; their number grew. More and more light spirits moved on successfully. Eventually the luiseach started interfering with our soul terminations and even managed to terminate many of our own.

When Adis and Uiri declared war on us—actually declared war as though the luiseach were some sort of sovereign nation—we were surprised: Were they that arrogant to think they could shift the balance entirely? But we were not unprepared. My brothers and I terminated most of the first wave of luiseach soldiers, and our dark servants managed to capture the rest.

The luiseach would not surrender, though. Such persistent, pesky mosquitoes. The battle raged on for years, unbeknownst to most of the humans on the planet—among other things, because there happened to be other wars going on at the same time. The tribal conflicts in Europe and China and Africa and so forth. We fought, dark against light, across several continents . . .

. . . and also in the invisible realm.

That's where things got messy.

How did Adis and Uiri know to do that? Sacrifice themselves to fight against Markons in the spiritual plane? That is a highly protected secret from the Book of Prophecy that is known only to the top echelon of our kind.

In the end I barely escaped.

My dear brothers perished, as did Adis and Uiri, who remained in the spiritual plane too long.

After news reached our dark servants that two of their three leaders had been terminated, many of them fled, vanished into the void. The luiseach declared victory, and Adis and Uiri's eldest daughter, Laoise, immediately took the reins.

I ordered my remaining servants to retreat. For almost two millennia. It was not an admission of defeat—far from it. Instead, I used the time to mobilize.

Now the time of mobilizing is over. The prophecy is unfolding. I am ready to engage again, and I have brought some very fine reinforcements.

One in particular.

Our victory will be swift, and the aftermath will be glorious. Brutal. Bloody.

Perhaps I shall get a new hat for the occasion?

CHAPTER 15
More Questions

t noon I head outside to meet up with Lucio and Nolan in the school parking lot. Only seniors are allowed to leave the building at lunchtime, but I managed to sneak out a back entrance. I think Nolan convinced one of the secretaries in the front office that he had a doctor's appointment. He can be very convincing, not like Aidan-mind-control-convincing, but convincing in that he's a nerdy, straight-A student with zero detentions on his record so no one would ever suspect him of breaking the rules.

Outside it seems like the temperature has fallen since this morning—it feels more like November than April—so I button my vintage poodle sweater all the way up to my neck. My fingers stumble on Helena's gold chain, which I tuck carefully under the collar of my Beatles T-shirt.

Did the mystery necklace save me from the SUV this morning? Was Helena telling the truth about the necklace's powers, after all? It has activated at least twice so far—with the SUV and with the Kirsten spirit.

Why does *Helena* seem more interested than Aidan in keeping me safe from Dubu?

Because, news flash, Aidan whatever-your-last-name-is, not cluing me in to the fact that Markons can kill luiseach is not keeping me safe. It's the opposite, in fact.

The two guys are waiting for me next to Nolan's Chrysler.

Nolan smiles happily when he sees me. Then his smile vanishes.

"What's wrong, Sunshine?"

"Nothing. I'm fine," I reassure him.

"No, you're not. What happened?"

"Sunshine?" Lucio pipes up, sounding concerned.

I can't seem to keep anything from Nolan. Or Lucio, for that matter. Taking a deep breath, I tell them everything that's transpired in the last twelve hours, starting with my dream/vision mash-up and ending with the SUV incident.

"Whoah, *what?*" Lucio bursts out when I'm finished. "Dubu tried to run you over with a car? Are you all right? Was Aidan with you?"

"Maybe, sort of, and yes. We don't know for sure it was Dubu. But Aidan used this ancient silver thingy and found out that a Markon *had* touched the car at some point. He detected a—what did he call it?—an energy signature."

"I don't know anything about that," Lucio says.

Nolan opens his mouth to say something but clamps it shut and hugs me fiercely instead. The hug is brief, and I barely register the usual queasiness. In fact, I feel warm in a wonderful, swoony way. I've missed being held by him; it's only been a few days but it seems like an eternity.

Over Nolan's shoulder I can see Lucio watching us. I experience a twinge of guilt, but maybe that's dumb? Lucio and I are just friends, and I've never let him think it can be any more than that.

Except for that almost-kiss thing in Mexico.

Nolan's lips graze my hair as he pulls away. He clears his throat and extracts his notebook from his pocket and begins busily flipping through pages.

"I need to write all this down. You said Aidan used some kind of ancient silver object to detect a Markon energy signature?"

"Yes. He referred to it as a 'device.' He said it's from the Renaissance period. Is that possible? Did they *make* things like that during the Renaissance? It seemed very . . . *Star Trek,* futuristic."

"I never saw anything like that at Llevar la Luz," Lucio says. "But I do know that the luiseach have always been crazy advanced in terms of science and technology. Sunshine, are you *sure* you're okay? Do you need to see a doctor?"

"Thanks, but I'm fine. Really. Although . . ." I sigh. "I need to tell you guys one more thing. Apparently Markons—" I stop, flustered. I'm not sure how they'll react to this, especially Lucio.

"Sunshine?" Lucio prompts me.

Nolan reaches over and squeezes my arm gently, encouragingly.

"Okay, here goes. Markons can kill luiseach," I blurt out. "Did you guys know that? Did you, Lucio?"

Lucio's jaw drops. Fear flickers in his big brown eyes. "What? No! I didn't even know Markons existed until, like, three days ago!"

"Wait a second here. I thought demons and dark spirits were incapable of doing permanent damage to luiseach," Nolan points out.

"Apparently, regular old demons and dark spirits are. But Markons have extra-special powers or whatever. According to Aidan, anyway."

"How does Aidan happen to have this information?" asks Nolan.

"He didn't give me any details. Besides, I was too busy being super-mad at him for once again trying to keep stuff from me and treating me like I'm a child. Because, you know, I apparently can't handle the truth. Does he not realize that—"

Voices.

I stop midsentence as a couple of senior girls approach the Chrysler. They glance at us curiously. I smile hello at them and pretend to check my phone. Nolan and Lucio pretend to check their phones too.

The two girls pass by us, talking animatedly.

"So I heard Melissa tried to poison her boyfriend Omar with rat poison or something. He's in the hospital now in intensive care," one of them says.

"Oh my gosh, that's horrible. Is everyone going insane around here?" says the other.

"Yeah, well, did you hear about the—"

Their voices fade as they get into a silver Mini Cooper. A moment later they drive away.

I whirl around and gape at Nolan and Lucio. "Did you guys know about that?"

"I read about it in the *Ridgemont Herald* this morning. Melissa DeYoung and Omar Hassam, who were seniors here last year, I believe," Nolan replies.

"What's happening? Ridgemont used to be so peaceful. Well, *pretty* peaceful anyway," I amend.

Nolan pushes his glasses up his nose. "I'm not sure. But didn't

Aidan or Helena say something to you about increased demonic activity? This incident sounds consistent with that."

"Also the arson at the mall and that nurse at the hospital," Lucio adds. "I'm going to text Aidan and make sure he knows about the poisoning thing. If not, we need to track this Melissa girl. She might be possessed? Which means we need to unpossess her ASAP."

"Good idea," I agree.

While Lucio texts Aidan, Nolan pulls me aside.

He points to his notes. "Listen. The stuff you just told us— something doesn't add up. Not to bring up a grim subject, but . . . if Markons can kill luiseach, and a fifth luiseach death would activate the pentagram spell, then why hasn't Dubu killed you yet? I mean, yes, I know he may have been behind the SUV incident this morning. But what about before? You said you've been seeing him for a while now, right?"

"Um . . ."

I bite my lip and scrunch up my nose. Why *hasn't* Dubu killed me yet? Not that I enjoy thinking about that prospect. Far from it. But Nolan is right—it doesn't add up.

"Also, why you? Why not kill Lucio or Aidan or Helena? They're here in Ridgemont too. Wouldn't their deaths activate the pentagram spell too?" Nolan goes on.

"Um . . ."

Nolan is right about that too.

What are we missing?

Is there some reason Dubu has picked me to be the fifth luiseach victim? Is it because I'm the luiseach to end all luiseach, as Aidan claims?

Or does Dubu plan to cast a wider net and go after other luiseach too?

CHAPTER 16
Demon Drama Detox

N o, Griffith. *This* is how you make a rose! Watch and learn."

Tiffany Ramirez rolls her eyes like I'm very, very hopeless. She picks up a green pipe cleaner and slowly, deliberately twists it around a blob of pink crepe paper.

I watch. And learn. And wonder for the millionth time why I let Ashley talk me into joining the spring dance committee. It's pretty much the polar opposite of everything I'm interested in, not to mention the fact that I'm kind of busy these days with my luiseach duties plus trying to stay alive plus a million other demon-related things.

But Ashley can be very persuasive. She said I needed some "demon drama detox."

Oh, well. I guess it can't hurt to do normal once in a while.

Tiffany and I are in one of the large second-floor class-rooms—a history classroom, judging by the brightly colored maps and timelines on the walls—with a dozen other commit-tee members. I recognize a few faces but don't really know any of them by name. Tiffany and I are on decoration duty. Some other people are listening to music demo reels and debating live bands versus DJs, indie versus pop. Everyone else is working on posters or social media. At my old high school in Austin I never went to any dances, so this is all new to me. I don't even listen to music from this decade—another thing on Ashley's "to do" list for me.

Sigh.

Ashley *is* right. I do need something to distract me from all the dark stuff in my life these days. I'm trying to save humanity from getting overtaken by demons. I'm also still reeling from Aidan's very awful and very scary Markon revelation. I knew luiseach weren't immortal—even though we can live long, long lives, we can also die. We are not invulnerable. Lucio's parents died, thanks to Helena. *I* almost died twice, thanks to Helena, and on a few other occasions too, including the demon pit incident in Victoria's front yard.

And of course, those four luiseach died—the ones in Japan, Easter Island, Russia, and Australia. I wonder *how* they died? Did Dubu kill them? I'm sure many other luiseach have died too throughout our long history.

So yes, I am fully aware that luiseach are totally and completely mortal. Still, the fact that Markons can kill us—that Dubu could kill *me,* if he wanted—adds a whole other layer of terror to the big picture. It also raises more questions. Am I definitely the top candidate for the fifth luiseach death, the one that's supposed to take place in Ridgemont? Or are Lucio, Helena, and Aidan candidates too? Does Dubu plan to eliminate one of us personally?

If it's me, can Helena's necklace really save me and, by extension, save the world, as my death would set off the pentagram spell?

And is all the scary stuff that's been happening in Ridgemont this past week the equivalent of the "increased demonic activity" that those four other places experienced before the luiseach deaths?

Enough. I need to start thinking about crepe-paper roses. Even if it's just for the next hour. Demon drama detox.

And then I'll be all refreshed and ready to defend humanity from the darkness . . .

"Where's your friend? Isn't she supposed to be here too?" Tiffany asks me as she squeezes pink glitter glue onto a piece of crepe paper.

"Ashley had to stop by the bio lab. She should be here soon."

"Awesome. We need lots of volunteers. So do you have a date for the dance yet?"

"I do!"

"Wow, really? Who?"

"My boyfriend!" I love saying those words: *my boyfriend.* I think I'm still allowed to call him that, even though he's pretending we're just friends until the doomsday crisis is over. "His name is Nolan." I twirl the pipe cleaner in my hand and smile secretly—when Nolan and I first met, in Victoria's art class, he and I were making pipe-cleaner sculptures.

"You mean Nolan Foster?" Tiffany shrugs. "Yeah, I guess I can see the appeal. If you like that type. What are you going to wear?"

If I like that type? "I'm not sure. Ashley wants to take me shopping."

"I think that's a good idea, don't you?" Tiffany raises one

eyebrow and looks me up and down, taking in my Beatles T-shirt, bell-bottom jeans, and pilly, pet-hair-covered vintage poodle cardigan. "No offense, Griffith, but you could use some fashion advice."

I blink. I think she just insulted me. Yup, she definitely insulted me. Twice. I try to think of a clever comeback, but I'm so not good at those. If and when I ever think of a snappy retort, it usually happens a week later and in the middle of the night.

I seethe silently instead. Besides, why am I surprised? Tiffany has never been all that nice to me. Or to anyone, as far as I can tell. Only when she wants something, like my free labor for her spring dance committee.

"Why are you twisting your rose into a pretzel?" Tiffany asks.

"What? Oh!"

"Excuse me, hello."

Tiffany and I turn around. It's Bastian Jansen from English class. He's dressed in his usual outfit of khakis, white button-down, and baggy navy blazer, and he's dragging his rolling backpack behind him.

He frowns at a flier in his hand—not Tiffany's flier but a blue one with a picture of a chessboard on it. He clears his throat. "Is this . . . no, it's obviously not. The chess club, I mean. Don't they meet in this room?"

"On Tuesdays and Thursdays," Tiffany explains. "The spring dance committee has the room Mondays, Wednesdays, and Fridays. Why don't you stay since you're here anyway? Bennett, right?" She thrusts a handful of green pipe cleaners and pink crepe paper at him.

"B-but—" he stammers.

"Welcome to our little group! 'Scuse me, I need to check on the website design. Sunshine here can show you how to do this. You've got this, right, Griffith? Try not to mess it up!"

She flashes one of her sparkly purple smiles at Bastian and me before making her way over to a computer station.

I seethe some more.

"I'm very sorry," Bastian apologizes. He starts to return the pipe cleaners and crepe paper to the table, but he misses, and they tumble to the floor. He bends down to pick them up. "I should go. I am not meant to be here."

"I don't want to be here either," I joke. "Peer pressure."

Bastian nods and gives me an awkward wave and takes off, pulling his rolling backpack behind him. What an odd guy. I can't tell if he's super-shy or what. But I also know what it's like to be different, so I shouldn't be judgey.

In English earlier today and also yesterday I watched him, wondering why he reacted to the Wesley spirit on Monday. But he didn't do or say anything peculiar—just kept his head down and doodled a lot. Maybe Nolan is right: maybe Bastian is simply extra-sensitive to the spiritual world, as some humans can be.

I step on something. There's a faded brown leather wallet on the floor. I reach down to retrieve it.

I open the wallet. It's Bastian's; it must have fallen out of his pocket. There's a learner's permit inside with his full name—Sebastian Andras Jansen—and address and birthdate and other personal information. His last address was in Washington, DC. He turned sixteen in January. Next to the learner's permit is a school ID from somewhere called the Wheedon Academy.

I tuck the wallet into my pocket and head toward the door. Bastian can't have gotten very far.

"Griffith, where are you going? I have more stuff for you to do!" Tiffany calls out.

"I'll be back in a sec!"

I spot Bastian up ahead, turning the corner.

"Bastian!" I shout.

He keeps walking, oblivious, muttering to himself. He trips on some invisible obstacle, steadies himself, and continues. I hurry my steps. The corridor is deserted, although I can hear the distant sounds of a sports team practicing in the gym: voices shouting, whistles blowing, balls bouncing with hollow *thunk, thunk* sounds. There are inspirational posters plastered above the rows of lockers: BELIEVE IN YOURSELF! NO PAIN, NO GAIN! IT'S OKAY TO FAIL AS LONG AS YOU TRY!

I start to shout Bastian's name again when a blast of cold hits me like a tidal wave and almost knocks me over. *Where* did that come from?

And then I see. A group of light spirits—fifteen, twenty, more?—are drifting down the hall toward me. I know Lucio is somewhere nearby, probably sitting in his car in the parking lot—this is the end of his shift. Aidan and Helena can't be too far away either. But I guess the spirits decided to come to me instead?

They drift closer, closer. Suddenly the horrifying image of their deaths flashes in my head. A carbon monoxide leak killed all the residents of an apartment building just outside of Ridgemont.

My chest tightens and I choke back a sob; two of them were little kids, ages two and four—practically babies.

But there's no time for sorrow. I can feel my pulse accelerating, my body temperature plummeting, my teeth starting to chatter. I have to move the spirits on, now, quickly. Right after New Year's a horde of light spirits almost killed me by sending me into hypothermia (a fancy way of saying I almost froze) and cardiac arrhythmia (a fancy way of saying my heart rate shot through the roof), and Mom had to revive me with CPR. Later, in Mexico, Aidan nearly destroyed me trying to teach me how to handle groups of light spirits like this. I eventually managed to learn, and I began to get the hang of it, kind of. But I'm still far from an expert. In fact, on Saturday Helena sent a huge posse of light spirits my way, and I barely managed.

I also need to move these spirits on quickly so they don't turn dark, like Kirsten did.

I shut my eyes and concentrate, trying to draw the spirits even closer.

I'm here for you. Let me guide you to the other side.

"Help me!" someone cries out.

Startled, I open my eyes. Just up ahead, near a row of lockers, a figure lies crumpled on the floor, shaking and spasming.

Oh my gosh.

It's Bastian.

CHAPTER 17
Kindred Spirits

Bastian writhes on the floor, his knees curled up to his chest. The spirits move toward him and swirl around him, pleading for release.

"*Stop!*" he begs.

I run up to him and kneel down on the floor by his side. His teeth are chattering. His lips are blue.

What's happening? How can the spirits affect Bastian in this way? He's *human.*

But I can't dwell on this bizarre turn of events because he looks like he'll freeze to death if this keeps up. I'll freeze too, for that matter. Maybe I should text Lucio for backup . . . but there's no time. I jump to my feet and gather the swirling spirits to me, *will* them to me. I focus all my energy on them as I touch them one by one, trying to keep my own violent shivering at bay.

I'm so sorry your lives were cut short. Let me help you move on and find peace on the other side.

The spirits bloom into balls of bright light and disappear. None of them pulls a Kirsten and suddenly turns dark. Thank goodness. The two children go last. I bite back tears as I touch their chubby gossamer cheeks. The little boy and girl rub their eyes and give me sad, sleepy smiles as they vanish through my fingertips.

In Mexico Aidan told me I had to turn off my empathy when dealing with spirits so I can be more effective. But how can I *not* feel this? Feel the terrible, gut-wrenching grief, especially when children are involved?

But he's right that I can't let empathy make me lose my concentration, whittle away my strength. I have a job to do.

A job that I really, really hate sometimes.

The temperature in the corridor stops freefalling; the air is gradually starting to get warm again. I peel off my vintage poodle cardigan and throw it on top of Bastian.

"I'm calling 9-1-1," I tell him, reaching for my phone.

"I-I'm fine," Bastian insists.

"Yeah, no, you're not." I begin punching numbers.

"Really, I am." He struggles up to a seating position, coughs, and rubs his arms briskly with his hands. I startle. He actually *does* seem to be fine, or he's on his way there anyway. Color is returning to his face. His lips are no longer blue.

"Nine-one-one. What is the nature of your emergency?" a voice on the other end of the phone asks me.

"I'm so sorry. I dialed by mistake," I reply hastily.

I end the call and instinctively put three fingers on Bastian's wrist, the way Mom always does when she takes my pulse. His heart rate is accelerated, but over the next minute or so I can feel it slowing down, settling back to normal.

I shake my head. None of this makes any sense. Bastian's body reacted to those spirits the same way my body did . . . *does*. And he recovered the same way too—quickly. Can humans do this? Act like luiseach? Maybe Aidan knows the answer, or maybe Nolan can research it.

Bastian stands up, still rubbing his arms with his hands. He regards me uneasily.

"How did you do that?" he whispers. Behind his crooked tortoiseshell glasses, his eyes are wide and frightened.

"Do what?"

"You know . . . make the ghosts disappear."

I stare at him, shocked. "You *saw* all that?"

"Yes. I can see ghosts. I can feel them too. Their fear, their coldness."

I tuck my phone back in my pocket slowly, buying myself time to think. Bastian can see and feel ghosts. That explains his reaction to Wesley in English class. And he almost froze to death just now in response to multiple spirits.

My mind is racing, churning. What does this mean? Is he just one of those people who experience the spiritual world more vividly than others?

Or . . .

"How long have you been able to see and feel ghosts?" I ask him cautiously.

"Yes, um . . . the first time was this past winter. At Wheedon, at my old school. In Washington, DC."

This past winter.

"When this winter exactly?"

"It was . . . let's see . . . in January."

January.

Bastian can see and feel ghosts. When he does, his heart rate spikes and his body temperature plummets.

This all started in January. Which is when he turned sixteen, according to his learner's permit.

Sixteen.

Does this mean . . . ?

No, it can't possibly mean that.

Can it?

"Hey, Bastian?" I say, trying to keep my voice light and casual and no-big-deal. "Your birthday is January third, right? Or fourth? Sorry, you dropped your wallet back there, and I had to look inside to find out who it belonged to. Here."

I hand over his wallet and he takes it from me. "My birthday is January third, yes."

"And your first ghost episode happened around then?"

His brow furrows. "It was shortly after my birthday. The middle of January sometime. I remember because of the long weekend for Martin Luther King Jr. Day. Listen, please don't tell anyone about today. I beg you. If my mother and father find out, they will send me back to that . . . that *place*."

"What place?"

"The clinic, the psychiatric hospital. They sent me there after that first time."

Footsteps. I look up to see Coach Martinez coming down the corridor, a soccer ball tucked under one arm.

"Everything okay here?" Coach Martinez says, his gaze moving between Bastian and me.

"Yes!" Bastian and I say at the same time.

"We're on our way to the spring dance committee meeting!" I add, fake smiling. "We thought it was in the gym, but it turns out it's in Room 236."

"Very well. Carry on."

Coach Martinez smiles at us, and for a second his eyes glow red. But it's gone in a flash and maybe I imagined it. Or maybe it was a reflection of the sunlight streaming through the windows.

Or maybe . . .

Coach Martinez smiles again, no glowy red eyes this time, and continues down the hall.

Bastian and I wait in silence until he disappears around the corner.

First things first.

"Are you sure you didn't have any of these . . . these ghost episodes before January?" I ask Bastian in a low, furtive voice. I don't want anyone to overhear us, especially coaches who may or may not be under demonic influence.

"No. That was the first one."

"Did you have any more episodes between then and today?"

"No. Well, perhaps. I have these dreams sometimes, and ghosts appear in them. Except the dreams don't always feel like dreams. They feel real."

I nod slowly.

"Why are you asking me these questions? And you never answered *my* question: How did you make those ghosts disappear?" Bastian asks in a trembling voice.

I cross my arms over my chest. There is no way. *No way.* I was the last luiseach to be born. Bastian was born almost five months after me. He *has* to be human.

And yet . . .

An idea occurs to me. I glance around and spot a darkened classroom.

It's not locked.

"Come with me," I say, tugging on Bastian's arm.

"Why?"

"Please, just trust me."

"I suppose, yes, all right."

Bastian follows me into the classroom, not very enthusiastically. I pull down all the blinds. Then I lean against the glass pane in the door so no light can enter from the hall.

I gesture for him to stand next to me. He does, looking increasingly uncomfortable, because why is some girl cornering him in a dark room?

I check out his pupils.

They're tiny. Just like mine. And they *stay* tiny, even after a full minute.

Holy moly.

"Bastian, have you ever heard the term 'luiseach'?" I ask finally.

CHAPTER 18

A New Mentor

It's Thursday after school, and Nolan, Lucio, and I are hanging out on the front porch of my house. Well, not "hanging out," exactly: I called a meeting so we could catch up and strategize. Lucio sits on the creaky old swing and rocks back and forth on his heels. Nolan and I sit on the ugly peeling-paint steps, a bowl of nacho cheese–flavored popcorn untouched between us. (Unlike Ashley, he's not a big fan of the nacho cheese, and I have zero appetite.) The rusty bird thermometer that hangs from the railing says it's 52 degrees out, which is chilly even for Ridgemont. Mom is still at work, although she texted before and said she'd be bringing home Thai takeout for dinner.

Nolan pulls his notebook out of his backpack. "So where do you want to start? Lucio and I can fill you in on the research we've been doing at the library?"

"Actually, I want to start with something that happened yesterday at the spring dance committee meeting, and then we can talk about that other stuff," I announce.

"Spring dance committee meeting? What even is that?" Lucio asks, confused.

"Long story. I'll tell you later. Anyway, first of all, you guys have to pinkie-swear you won't tell anyone. That includes Aidan. *Especially* Aidan."

Wow, I sounded like Helena there! I touch the gold chain at my throat. I'm now keeping two big secrets from Aidan: Bastian *and* the necklace.

The two guys exchange a glance. Lucio shrugs.

"Yes, okay. We promise we won't tell anyone," Nolan says. "What's going on?"

I turn to Lucio. "Do you know of any luiseach who were born after me?"

"Of course not. But you knew that already. You were the last one," Lucio says, looking puzzled.

"But how do we know for sure? How does Aidan know? I mean, is he omniscient? Does he have a luiseach crystal ball? Superman vision?" I persist.

"Well, I know your m— . . . that *Helena*"—Lucio's expression darkens as he says her name—"oversees her part of the luiseach community. Which is almost all the luiseach left on the planet. And she would have told Aidan if new luiseach kids were being born, right? Because that would change everything."

I nod slowly. "Yeah, but hypothetically speaking, could there be one or more luiseach couples out there who maybe split off from Helena's community and she's lost touch with them? And they had a baby or babies sometime after I was born?"

"Hmm, good point. We should ask Aidan," Lucio suggests.

I shake my head. "No, that's just it. I told you, we *can't* ask Aidan. He would get suspicious."

"Suspicious about what?" Nolan pipes up.

"Suspicious about . . . okay, guys, here it is. This is top secret. Like, double-triple-*quadruple* top secret."

Lucio and Nolan exchange another glance. "Go on," Nolan says.

"*Argh,* okay."

I take a deep breath and plunge into the story about Bastian, starting with his arrival in Victoria's, a.k.a. Ms. Warkomski's English class on Monday, for Lucio's benefit, and ending with what happened yesterday after school with the group of light spirits. And, of course, his tiny pupils that are just like mine.

"So . . . I kind of told Bastian I thought he might be a luiseach," I finish.

"Wait. You did *what?*" Lucio erupts.

"I *had* to," I say defensively. "I mean, if someone had told *me* I was a luiseach when Mom and I first moved into this creepy old haunted house—no offense, house!—I wouldn't have been so confused and scared. Seriously, I thought I was going insane the first time I heard Anna's ghost. And the fact that I was the *only* one who could hear *or* see her made me feel extra-insane."

Nolan rakes a hand through his tawny hair. Usually that means he's thinking complicated thoughts. "Okay, so how did Bastian react?" he asks.

"He was confused and scared, like I was at first. Also skeptical. He's sort of like Mom—you know, scientific and rational and all 'there's no such things as ghosts.' Even though he can see them," I reply.

"You said the light spirits were drawn to him?" Nolan continues.

"Yup."

"And he started to go into a state of hypothermia?"

"Uh huh. And his heart rate went all wacky-crazy."

Nolan nods and writes something in his notebook. "Got it. So what do you know about his background?"

"Well, we talked afterward, and he told me a little bit about himself. He's adopted, for one thing, and he doesn't know anything about his biological parents. Like me for most of my life. His adoptive dad is a professor at Georgetown Law School. The dad is on sabbatical, which is like a vacation from teaching. They're living at their family's mountain retreat in Ridgemont for half a year or something while his dad writes a book on . . . international law? Treaties? War crimes? I can't remember. Next year Bastian will go back to the Wheedon Academy, which is his regular school. His adoptive mom is a psychotherapist . . . no, a psychiatrist. That means she's a doctor."

"So what's your assessment of Bastian? One to ten, ten being definitely luiseach, and one being definitely *not* luiseach?" Lucio asks.

"Hmm. I'd say eight and a half," I reply.

"Really." Lucio stands up suddenly and grabs the chain to still the creaky swing. "Eight and a half is serious. We *have* to tell Aidan immediately."

I stand up too. "*No!* I already said. That's the *opposite* of what we need to do. First of all, Bastian swore me to secrecy. Okay, yes, I know I told you guys, but that's because I need your help, and in any case, it can't go any further. We are the inner circle. Second of all, if Bastian is a luiseach, and I'm pretty sure he is— eight and a half sure—then that's a big deal. A *huge* big deal. It means my birth wasn't the end of luiseach births. If Aidan finds this out, he would tell Helena because, well, he'd *have* to. Then what? They might want to capture Bastian and perform sicko science fiction experiments on him to find out if he's special . . . to find out *why* he's special. Or they might want to capture and/or harm Bastian's biological parents, whoever they are, because they left the fold or whatever."

A muscle works in Lucio's jaw. *Ugh.* Stupid me, reminding him of what happened to his mom and dad.

"Yeah, fine," Lucio agrees gruffly. "I guess we should keep this between the three of us. For *now.* But Sunshine, you know what this means?"

"What?"

"The dude needs a mentor. And it sounds like you're it."

Me . . . a mentor?

"I can't be a mentor. I'm just learning how to do all this stuff myself!" I protest.

"Seems like you don't have a choice, though," Lucio declares.

Lucio is right.

CHAPTER 19
Bizarre Love Quadrangle

An hour later Nolan and Lucio and I are still on the porch, immersed in our conversation about Bastian and the guys' library research too. The sun is beginning to set, and I can see the first streaks of purple and gold through the pine branches.

Ashley's little blue hybrid pulls up in front of the house. She gets out and skips up to the porch, swinging her dance bag over her shoulders. She's wearing a gray Austin High hoodie over a black leotard, plus pink capri tights, leg warmers, and flip flops, despite the cold temperature. Each of her toenails is painted a different color. Her blond hair is swept back in a sleek ponytail.

She smiles at us, and her smile lingers on Lucio.

"Hey! Is this a party? Oooh, nacho cheese–flavored popcorn!"

"Hi, Ash! We're strategizing about stuff. How was your first ballet class with the Russian lady?" I ask.

"Awesome. We worked on *entrechat* and *pas de poisson* jumps. Madame Gergiev says I have 'great potential.' Her exact words, I swear. Soooo, a strategy sesh, huh? What can I do to help?"

She sidles up to Lucio and playfully slips her hand through his arm.

Lucio stares at her in surprise, then he gracefully extracts himself by bending down and retying his shoelaces. "Nolan and I were just catching Sunshine up on our research," he replies, all business.

Ashley bristles ever so slightly and gives me a subtle what's-up-with-him? look. I don't think she's used to guys saying no to her.

"Here." Nolan splays out his notebook for Ashley to see. He points to his notes, which are in small, meticulous cursive. "Sunshine, can we include Ashley in the—"

"—yes," I reply hastily. "But that's it, okay? We're now an inner circle of four. And Ashley, this stuff is top secret. I *mean* it."

"You can trust me," Ashley promises.

She sets down her dance bag and begins to read Nolan's notes. I peer over her shoulder and read along.

Aidan asked Lucio and me to research the five locations on the geographical pentagram: Hokkaido, Japan; Rapa Nui (Easter Island); the Chukchi Peninsula in Russia; the Cape York Peninsula in Queensland, Australia; and Ridgemont, Washington. We've been looking for common features (like demographics, climate, ecosystems, linguistic origins, forms of government, etc.). So far we have not found anything significant, except that these locations lie on a hypothetical pentagram and that an unexplained luiseach death took place in each of the first four locations, four years apart starting in the year of Sunshine's birth. Also, the violent crime rates in all four locations spiked in the weeks and months leading up to these luiseach deaths.

Strangely, we came across no news stories regarding the luiseach deaths. Who were the victims, and how did they die? We asked Aidan, and he said he didn't know.

*He also asked us to research demonic spells (especially those related to pentagrams) and possible ways to stop or reverse them. No findings to report yet.

* Side note: While researching demonic spells and pentagrams, we came across an oblique reference to an ancient book containing prophecies, instructions, etc. for demons and dark spirits. Not sure if this book actually existed/exists or if it is apocryphal/legendary in nature.

*Regarding the light spirit Kirsten who turned dark only hours after her death: How did this happen? Are there other spirits like her?

*Also, the Kirsten spirit grabbed Sunshine's wrist and left a spider-web-like mark on the skin. The mark has grown in size, shrunk in size, changed shape, gotten darker, gotten lighter, and disappeared altogether. It seems to be gone now? The mark was made up of ten short lines. We are searching for information on such a phenomenon.

*Sunshine found a dead bird on her front porch. (See printout of photo on following page.) The bird may or may not be connected to the current situation. We are trying to identify the bird's class, order, family, genus, and species. Definitely not native to Washington State.

Ashley gazes at Nolan in admiration. "Wow, it's like we're in college! I didn't understand half the words you wrote here! Actually, J-K, I understood most of it. This stuff is super-scary. You guys have been through a *lot!*"

"Sunshine's the one who's been through a lot," Lucio says, nodding in my direction.

"Absolutely." Nolan drapes his arm around my shoulder.

Ashley leans her head toward mine. "It's not fair that you have two hot guys fawning over you and I have zero," she whispers in my ear.

"*Shhhh!*" I shush Ashley, hoping Nolan and Lucio didn't overhear.

Although I do have to admit it's a little weird being here with the three of them. Nolan likes me . . . Ashley likes Lucio . . . Lucio likes me . . . I like Nolan. We're like some sort of bizarre love quadrangle.

Someone's phone beeps with an incoming text. Lucio pulls his cell out of his jeans pocket and peers at the screen. "It's Aidan. He wants me to head back to Llevar la Luz right away and pick up some important files for him and also take care of some other stuff. We, uh, left in kind of a hurry," he adds with a sideways glance at me.

I smile apologetically. "Sorry. I had to get home ASAP. I knew Aidan would try to stop me because, well, he has this delusional notion that he knows what's best for me."

"He *does* know what's best for you, Sunshine," Lucio says quietly. "Anyway, you don't need to worry about security because he and Helena are going to watch you in twelve-hour shifts while I'm gone. So you'll be covered."

Helena. I haven't seen her since Saturday night when she gave me the necklace, although I can feel her presence nearby during her shifts. I wonder what she's been up to? And when is her council arriving in Ridgemont? Has she spoken to them about me yet and convinced them not to execute me?

Ashley's face lights up. "Hey, I just had a major brainstorm! Maybe the *four* of us should do a road trip to Llevar la Luz. That way, Sunshine, you can escape from the demon dude and his minions. Besides, I didn't get a chance to enjoy Mexico during the two seconds I was there to rescue you. I'm talking sandy beaches, fish tacos, mango smoothies, dancing under the stars . . ."

"Hey, that's actually a great idea," Lucio agrees. "You should come with me, Sunshine. No one can step foot inside the compound unless they're invited by one of us. You'd be totally safe there—or safer than here anyway."

Nolan raises one eyebrow.

"*You should come with me, Sunshine . . . AND ASHLEY AND NOLAN,*" Ashley mutters under her breath.

I squeeze her hand really hard to shut her up. She lets out a tiny yelp.

"Thanks, you guys, but I need to stay here," I say. "Aidan may think he's going to nab Dubu singlehandedly, but I want to do my share too. Besides, I have Bastian now, remember? I can't just leave him here to fend for himself. He has no luiseach skills, and he needs training. Otherwise he's going to be as helpless and messed up as I used to be." *And still am sometimes,* I add silently.

Lucio nods. "Understood."

"Come on, Ash, let's introduce these guys to the wonderful world of nacho cheese–flavored popcorn," I suggest with a grin.

Ashley grins back. "Totes!"

As she passes the bowl around I think about the idea of escaping to Llevar la Luz. There is something so tempting about it, which is ironic because just last week I couldn't wait to get the heck out of there.

But running away isn't an option. If I really *am* Dubu's target, and if he really wants to find me, then he'll find me for darned sure.

No matter where I try to hide.

Besides, it's not just about him and me. If the pentagram spell really *is* a doomsday spell, then it's about the end of the world. And I may be the luiseach to stop that because I am *the* luiseach, the one who is destined to save humanity.

As long as I don't let myself become the fifth point on the pentagram and trigger the spell to begin with, that is.

Temptation

One of my dark servants has informed me they are on their way to this geographical location. This was not part of the prophecy, which augers neither well nor badly . . . it is merely an interesting development.

Did my beloved call them here? If so, for what purpose? Is it about the girl? Or have they become aware of the prophecy and are beginning to organize against us?

I have watched her watch the girl every day. I cannot glean if she is protecting the girl or pretending to protect the girl or observing her for some entirely different reason.

Of course, I have found myself longing to come out of hiding and approach my beloved, make myself known to her.

But I must bide my time. I cannot—I must not—do anything to jeopardize the unfolding of the glorious prophecy. No matter the temptation.

Soon, though.

Very soon.

CHAPTER 20
Hope

Bastian invites me to his house. Or rather, I invite myself and he reluctantly agrees.

I wanted somewhere very private to speak to him, which meant *my* house was not a great option. He said his parents would be out for a few hours late Saturday afternoon, so we settled on five P.M., which was fine with me, as I had my training with Aidan earlier. This time from around now through around sunrise tomorrow is technically Helena's shift—Lucio said that she and Aidan were switching off every twelve hours while he was in Mexico. But I didn't see her or even sense her presence before I left my house. If I had, I would have canceled my trip to Bastian's—I can't lead Helena (or Aidan or anyone else) to him and reveal his secret.

Although this means I'm technically without a luiseach bodyguard on this little excursion. I'll have to be extra careful.

Bastian said his house was in the middle of nowhere. Following his directions, I drive up the road that winds around

Ridge Mountain. I've actually never been up here. Along the way I spot a few modest cottages and cabins tucked away in the woods. Otherwise, it's very secluded and peaceful and nature-y. It really *is* in the middle of nowhere.

The address he gave me is at the end of the road, near the summit.

An ornate antique mailbox, a long, tree-lined driveway . . . and here's the Jansen house.

Whoa. It's not like the other houses on this road. It's a *mansion.*

When Bastian said "mountain retreat," I thought he meant like a rustic log shack with a couple of rocking chairs out front. But no. This is an elegant Italianate mini-palace with white stucco walls and stained-glass windows. A large, perfectly manicured rose garden occupies much of the front lawn, with an elaborate gold fountain at the center.

I didn't even know places like this existed in Ridgemont.

I park in the semicircular driveway and step out of the car. The front door opens before I'm halfway there, and I half-expect to see an elderly butler dressed in a tuxedo.

But instead Bastian steps out.

"Sunshine, hello," he calls out. He's dressed casually today, in jeans and a light blue cashmere pullover and black leather loafers. He actually looks nice.

"Hi! Your house is really . . . *wow*. It's gorgeous."

"It was built by my father's grandfather, Aldo Jansen. Please do come in. Minette, be quiet!" Bastian commands a small white poodle that's yipping at his heels.

He holds the door open for me, and I enter the front hallway. A crystal chandelier hangs overhead. Beautiful old oil paintings cover the walls—a combination of portraits and landscapes. The soles of my Chuck Taylors squeak against the pearly-white marble floor.

"So when are your parents coming home?" I ask him, glancing around.

"Not for a few hours at least. They're having dinner in town. Why don't we sit in the parlor?"

"You have a parlor? That's so Victorian and awesome!"

"Um, thank you."

Bastian leads me to the parlor, which truly *is* Victorian and awesome. We sit down on a red velvet settee. On top of the antique coffee table is a sterling silver tea set. Framed black-and-white photographs line the top of a baby grand piano. Classical music drifts from invisible speakers.

"J. S. Bach. His six suites for solo cello," Bastian says, gesturing to the air.

"It's really beautiful. Do you play an instrument?" I ask.

"Yes. My parents had me take piano, violin, and cello lessons from the time I was four and a half. My brother . . ." He hesitates.

"Oh, you have a brother?"

"*Had*. I . . . it is a long story. Sunshine, why did you want to speak to me?"

"Oh yeah. That."

Minette the poodle trots into the parlor, nails clicking against the polished wood floor, and jumps onto my lap. She circles around three, four, five times, then finds her spot and settles down with a contented sigh.

Like Minette, I've been going around and around this in my head—that is, how to talk to Bastian about him probably, definitely being a luiseach and about me probably, definitely becoming his luiseach mentor. In some ways there's an argument to be made that I should break all this to him slowly and gradually so he doesn't get spooked and run away, which is exactly what I wanted to do, what I almost would have given my right arm to do, when Aidan made his dramatic entrance into my life and announced matter-of-factly that he was *my* mentor and asked if I was ready to save humanity.

Bastian could still tell me to go away. That's what I did with Aidan at first and a bunch of other times too. Not that it's worked so far.

But hopefully I can convince Bastian. We *need* more luiseach to help us help humans. If Bastian truly is a luiseach—and at this point I'm almost ten-out-of-ten convinced he is—then he'll be an invaluable asset. Not to mention proof that my birth wasn't the doomsday event Helena pronounced it to be.

I pet Minette on the head and then begin.

"The thing we talked about the other day. Have you had a chance to think about it?"

"You mean the loose . . . Louise . . . I'm sorry, I've forgotten how to pronounce it. I do remember how to spell it, though. L-U-I-S-E-A-C-H."

"Luiseach," I articulate slowly. "As in, *loo* and *seech*."

"Yes, luiseach. We have a book about mythical creatures here in our library. I skimmed through it for a reference to these luiseach, but there was none. I found a mythical South American death spirit called a luison, and a mythical Chinese beast that could detect the truth called a luduan, but no luiseach."

"Yeah, well, the luiseach aren't mythical. We're quite real."

"By 'we,' you mean you and the other luiseach? How many of you are there?"

"I'm not sure exactly. Thousands maybe? Or tens of thousands? In any case, I was referring specifically to you and me just now."

Bastian drops his gaze and wrings his hands in his lap. His right leg begins to shake, and he grabs his knee to stop it. Color floods his cheeks.

"Sunshine, I don't believe I'm one of these . . . one of *you*," he says, sounding agitated. "There's nothing supernatural or paranormal about me. Perhaps my parents and the doctors were right: perhaps I *do* suffer from paranoid delusions. I'm supposed to be taking medications for these delusions, did I tell you? Except I only pretend to swallow them. I flush them down the lavatory instead."

I gasp. "I'm sorry! That sounds awful."

"Perhaps I should start taking the medicines again. Perhaps that will make the ghosts go away. I don't know . . . I don't know . . ."

He groans and buries his head in his hands.

"Oh, Bastian! I'm sorry," I repeat, although "sorry" sounds so lame. I try to imagine what it would have been like if Mom had checked me into the psychiatric ward at the hospital instead of believing me when I told her I was a guardian angel (sort of) with superpowers (sort of).

The thing is, Mom would never have done that. She's the best mom ever. She's her own special kind of guardian angel with her own special kind of superpowers.

Bastian's parents, however . . .

Although I suppose most parents, even the most kind, loving, open-minded parents might have reacted the same way?

Still, my heart aches for poor Bastian. He's obviously in a lot of emotional distress. I have to do *something*.

A brilliant light-bulb inspiration comes to me.

"Listen, I have an idea," I announce.

Bastian takes off his glasses and rubs the bridge of his nose. "What sort of idea?" he asks wearily.

"You'll see. Give me a sec. Just trust me."

I lift Minette from my lap and put her down on the settee. Then I stand up and close my eyes.

I need a light spirit to come to me—to *us,* to Bastian and me.

Reaching out my hand to an imaginary horizon, I try to visualize the invisible plane. There's a mysterious space out there between the realms of the living and the dead. Somewhere in the middle, where the recently deceased hover. A spiritual limbo. If they stay there too long, they'll become dark spirits forever. But if they manage to cross over, either on their own or with the help of a luiseach, they'll become one with the eternal light. A place of peace.

There he is. I detect a distant presence, a young man who passed away just this morning. His name was Tomas, and he lived in Vancouver, Canada. He drowned in a sailing accident.

"Sunshine? Why are you . . . please, what's happening?" Bastian asks, alarmed.

I shake my head quickly and put my finger to my lips.

I focus intently and attempt to connect with Tomas's spirit.

It's okay. Come closer. You can trust us. We'll help you move to the other side, to a better place.

A cool breeze blows through the room.

Closer, Tomas. You're almost there.

Another breeze, colder this time. I open my eyes and see Tomas's spirit standing by the piano. Seaweed and saltwater drench his longish black hair. His eyes are bloodshot, bewildered, and tormented.

Bastian rises to his feet slowly, his face drained of color. "Sunshine?" he whispers. "Do you see him?"

"Yes. Do you?"

"Yes."

"We're going to help him cross over."

"We?"

"Just reach out to him," I instruct. "Connect with him. Draw him toward you."

"I don't understand. Connect with him how? Draw him toward me how?" he asks in a panicked voice.

"Just close your eyes and listen to your instincts. You'll know what to do."

"I will?"

"You will."

"Yes, fine. I'll try."

Bastian coughs and clears his throat. He closes his eyes and lifts a trembling hand in the air. His lips move as though he's silently speaking to Tomas.

In response, Tomas passes through the baby grand piano and coffee table and billows toward us, at first in my direction then Bastian's.

Bastian's teeth begin to chatter. He steps back and shakes his head. "I-I don't think I can do this," he stammers. "I-I'm getting very cold . . . like with those g-ghosts at school. I-I can hear my pulse—it's very fast."

"That's normal. Just relax. Now reach out and touch him. Send him kind feelings, compassion. Imagine him stepping into the light," I say gently.

"B-but—"

"Just try, Bastian. *Please.*"

He takes a deep, shuddering breath and nods. Then he closes

his eyes again and lifts his hand in the air. His lips begin to move.

I watch in wonder as Tomas's translucent form brushes up against Bastian's fingertips.

Bastian stumbles backward, then stops and steadies himself.

A moment later they touch—luiseach and light spirit.

Tomas blooms into a radiant ball of light and then flickers, vanishes.

A sense of peace washes over the room.

"*Yes!* You did it! You helped a spirit cross over!" I shout with a fist pump.

Bastian's eyes open slowly. His hand is still hovering in the air.

"*I* did that?" he gasps.

"You sure did!"

He slumps down on the settee, breathing heavily.

"It was so . . . magical. So ethereal."

I grin and nod. "Right? Isn't it amazing? So *now* do you believe me? Or do you still think you're suffering from paranoid delusions?"

"I believe you."

"You've passed your luiseach initiation! I mean, not that there's a luiseach initiation, but . . . did I mention I'm going to be your mentor?"

"My mentor?"

"Yes. I'm going to train you, teach you everything you need to know about being a luiseach. We'll start today . . ." *Oh, well.* So much for slowly and gradually. I'm just too eager, excited.

Bastian stares at me, totally befuddled.

"First lesson. Telling the difference between light spirits and dark spirits. Pay attention, Bastian, because this is super important . . ."

As I plunge into my light spirits versus dark spirits lecture, which sounds alarmingly like the one Aidan gave me on the same topic, practically word for word, I feel something I haven't felt in a long time.

Hope.

Like maybe the luiseach race has a chance after all.

Because I'm not the last of my kind.

CHAPTER 21

The Detour

On my way home from Bastian's I decide to make a spontaneous detour. At the bottom of Ridge Mountain I take a left instead of a right. Right would have taken me directly downtown and then home. Left takes me home too, but through a different way, along the eastern border of the state park, then onto Route 79, and then onto Pinecone Road, which Ts at Pinecone Drive.

My visit with Bastian was . . . incredible. Game changing. Life altering. Now I'm definitely beyond just eight-and-a-half-out-of-ten sure he's a luiseach. I'm absolutely, positively ten-out-of-ten sure. I am *not* the last luiseach to be born on this planet. That mega-shock wave of energy that my birth released did not entirely doom our race!

And if Bastian exists, that means other luiseach might exist too who are younger than me.

I drive along the edge of the state park, obeying the posted thirty-miles-per-hour speed limit even though I'm the only one on the road. It's just after six, and strangely the sky is already dark, even though the sun doesn't usually set until after seven. Ominous black clouds pass across the full moon. Maybe there's a storm coming?

Now I need to make double, triple, quadruple sure I don't reveal Bastian's specialness to Helena and Aidan. Not yet. I want to tell Aidan so much because this is what he's been working toward for such a long time—the continuation of the luiseach race. The problem is Helena. Because for her, "special" might mean "science experiment fodder." And/or a death sentence for a luiseach couple, Bastian's biological parents, whoever and wherever they are. And I can't let that happen, even if Bastian's very existence on this planet is my ace in the hole, my definitive, one-hundred-percent, ten-on-a-scale-of-one-to-ten proof that my arrival on this planet sixteen years ago on August 14 didn't trigger the beginning of the end. My birth obviously triggered *something*—a number of luiseach women did miscarry that day, and several women even died while in labor, and of course it marked the beginning of the mysterious luiseach deaths in Japan and Easter Island and Australia and Russia, so there are puzzles to be solved there. *But . . .* Bastian being here among us means that August 14 wasn't the final deathblow to the long extinction of our race.

Still, I will have to tell Aidan about Bastian at some point. Just not right away. I'll have to find the right time when I'm sure Helena won't be able to do any harm to Bastian or his biological parents.

Where *is* Helena anyway? I still don't sense her presence nearby, which is fine for my own Bastian-visiting purposes but a little mysterious. I touch my gold necklace, which is tucked under the fringey purple scarf I bought at an Austin flea market last summer. Does my dear bio-mom think she doesn't have to watch me so carefully anymore because I'm wearing her mystical protective jewelry? Or does she have other, more important plans tonight? In any case, Aidan would not be happy if he found out she's blowing off her bodyguard duties, even if it's just this one time. Not that I'm going to rat her out.

A raccoon or other small animal darts across the road in front of me. I slam on the brakes, and it skitters away into the bushes. *Whew.*

Route 79 should be just a mile or so up the road. I turn on the radio, and a tear-jerky country-western song comes on. *Nope, nope, nope.* I continue turning the dial, searching for something more me. Like old, romantic jazz. Or classical . . . I loved that Bach cello piece Bastian had on at his house.

I land on a local public radio station. I'm about to bypass that too when a news item catches my attention.

". . . earlier today a man boarded a bus in downtown Ridgemont and attacked passengers with a machete . . ."

A machete?

I frown and turn up the volume.

". . . three people were rushed to the hospital with serious injuries. The assailant escaped on foot. He's believed to be armed and dangerous. Witnesses described him as a white male, early twenties, short brown hair, clean shaven, wearing a black suit, white shirt, and black tie. If anyone has any information about his whereabouts . . ."

I stop the car and shift to "park"—I'm still the only one on the road, except for the raccoons and other critters. I need to process this. Another violent crime in Ridgemont? That's . . .

how many in one week? Mrs. Ostricher last Saturday, and that girl poisoning her boyfriend, and now this.

A guy in a suit carrying a machete? It sounds surreal, like something out of a bad horror movie.

I tap my hands against the wheel, thinking, thinking.

"In other news, astronomers and astrophysicists worldwide are confounded by the appearance of a second—"

I turn off the radio and pick up my phone. Mom has texted twice:

Are you all right? When will you be home?

And:

Sunshine, please let me know if you're safe!

I get texts like these from her, like, twelve times a day. Which I don't mind because actually it's really nice having a mom who cares and worries and fusses. Especially with everything that's going on.

I'm totally fine, Mom. I'll be home soon.
I love you to the moon and back.

I look at my phone and notice my battery is running a bit low. I quickly call Nolan.

He picks up immediately. "Hey!"

His warm, familiar voice makes my heart skip a beat. "Hey. Are you busy?"

"Heading over to the library. It's just me—Lucio's not back from Llevar la Luz yet. I miss you. How did it go at Bastian's?"

"Good. Great. *Really* great. I'll fill you in later. Listen, can you add an item to your research list? I want to know if violent crimes are on the rise across the country. And around the world too while you're at it?"

"No problem."

"I know Helena mentioned all this before, but . . . well, I just want to see for myself. The numbers, kinds of crimes, and so forth. Thank you!"

"Sure, of course."

"Oh, and Nolan?"

"Hmm?"

"I miss you too."

We say our good-byes and click off. It's almost pitch-black out, and I realize I need to get a move on if I'm going to stop by Pinecone Drive before heading home for dinner.

Just then I see a movement in the headlights.

Another raccoon?

No, it's bigger. Way bigger. Maybe a dog?

No, it's not a dog either. It looks more like a coyote. Or maybe a wolf. Or maybe a mountain lion. Or a regular lion. *Yikes.*

Whatever it is, it stops in the middle of the road, sniffs the air, and pivots in my direction. It begins creeping slowly toward my car, eyes gleaming, fangs bared.

It does not look friendly.

It probably thinks I'm a predator—or worse, prey. Whatever the case, I need to get the heck out of there.

Shifting to reverse, I back up the car and start to U-turn around.

But behind me is another animal, identical to the first.

No, actually, there are *three* more of them back there. I seem to be surrounded by *four* of these not-friendly, huge, lion-like creatures.

Now what?

Whomp!

One of them jumps onto the roof of my car.

Whomp!

Now there are two of them up there. The remaining two slink up to my side windows and peer in, growling and drooling.

Must. Not. Panic.

Helena . . . Aidan . . . bodyguards! Where are you guys when I need you?

But I'm on my own here, so I need to do something. Quickly. The car horn!

I slam my hand against the middle of the steering wheel and press down—*hard*. The horn blares abruptly, loudly. The two animals at my side windows jump back, startled. At the same moment I shift into drive and gun the accelerator.

As the car jerks forward, the two animals on the roof go flying off, twist in the air, and land in a tall stand of grass by the side of the road. In my rearview mirror I can see them rise to their feet and shake themselves off.

All four animals start running after my car.

This is not good.

I press down on the accelerator and my car goes to thirty . . . forty . . . fifty . . . sixty. My palms are sweaty, and my heart is hammering in my chest. What's going on? What are these animals, and why are they coming after me? Are they possessed? I didn't sense plummeting temperatures or any of the other usual signs of demonic presence. Although didn't Aidan mention

something about that the other day? That more and more, demons and dark spirits are able to show up without the usual
chill effect? Another sign of the growing darkness, maybe?

I'm not used to Grand Prix speeding down pitch-black country roads being chased by I'm-not-sure-what. I pray I don't hit
anyone or anything or lose control.

Finally. I see the turnoff for Route 79 just ahead. I press down
on the accelerator a little more—*wah,* seventy miles per hour!—
and then spot the stop sign half-hidden by a gnarly old pine tree.

I slam on the brakes hard. The tires screech and squeal, and
my body is thrust forward as the car comes to a sudden and
ungraceful halt.

Breathless, my pulse racing, I glance in the rearview mirror.
The taillights of my car cast eerie red pools of illumination on
the dirt road.

The animals are long gone.

What *were* they?

CHAPTER 22

Missing Anna

A few minutes later I pull up in front of Three Pinecone Drive. I've managed to calm down, sort of, from the incident by the state park.

Was it an unfortunate encounter with some aggressive forest critters—or something else?

I turn off the engine, find my phone, and text Nolan.

Can you find out what wild animals are indigenous to this area? Especially the state park? And by "wild animals" I mean wolves, coyotes, mountain lions, random nondomesticated cats. Not cute little bunnies or squirrels or chipmunks.

He immediately responds:

Yes. Why? What happened? Are you okay?

I swear, Nolan is totally psychic. Not for the first time I wonder if *he's* part luiseach.

I'm fine. I'll tell you all about it later.

I'll call you, okay? Around ten?
Will you be up?

Yes, definitely! xoxo

I smile to myself. When did I start adding Xs and Os to my texting vocabulary? Is that what girlfriends do? As I put my phone away I notice the battery's nearly dead. *Argh*, I'll have to charge it when I get home. Aidan is adamant about all of us being able to maintain constant contact with his fancy high-tech phones.

I get out of the car and note that Victoria's front porch light is on and that the living room lights seem to be on too. Which means that hopefully my old art teacher—and my current English teacher—is home. As I cross the front yard I flash back to when I was here exactly a week ago along with Victoria, Nolan, Helena, Aidan, Mom, Lucio, and Ashley. You could never tell from the neatly trimmed lawn and just-budding spring bulbs that this was the site of a mini-apocalypse that day: the earth splitting open, demons crawling out, complete chaos. An anarchy of evil.

During the past week I've seen Victoria in English class every day, squirming uncomfortably in her eighties rocker outfits and Googling "Jane Austen" and whatnot every five minutes. I keep trying to get her alone so I can talk to her, just to catch up and also see how she's doing . . . but no go. It's almost like she's determined to avoid being Victoria around me. Although I guess it would be kind of a disaster if anyone at the school recognized her as Victoria Wilde, the quiet, eccentric art teacher who tragically "died" on New Year's.

At the door I lift the old-fashioned brass knocker and knock three times.

The door opens, and Victoria blinks at me in surprise.

"What a strange coincidence! I was just about to ring you. Won't you come in, dear?"

"Yes, thank you."

I follow Victoria into her living room. As before, it's lovely, decorated in peaches and creams. The couch, big and comfy with a pretty flower design, is inviting and warm.

The last time I was in this room Helena was holding Nolan prisoner, and she tried to kill me . . . but I try not to think about that.

Today Victoria is just Victoria—long, swishy raven hair that's practically down to her waist, flowing black velvet dress, and lacy black shawl—not platinum-blonde Ms. Warkomski in a hot-pink dress and fishnet tights and Dr. Martens. I *missed* this Victoria—it's nice to see her.

"Please sit, won't you?" she says, gesturing to the flowery couch. "I'll go and get us some refreshments."

She disappears into the kitchen and comes back a few minutes later with a tray. Minty, lemony smells waft through the air.

The tray holds a teapot with a delicate rose design, matching teacups and saucers, and a plate of shortbread cookies. Victoria pours tea into the cups.

"This is a special recipe I make out of peppermint and lemon verbena leaves. Both herbs are very calming for the mind and body."

"Yum. I could use some mind-body calming. Thanks."

I pick up my teacup and blow on it. Victoria sits down on the couch next to me. Close up, I notice the dark circles under her melancholy brown eyes are darker than ever, worse than mine, even with the beige concealer she caked on. She probably hasn't slept much lately. Actually I don't think she's slept much at all since Anna died. Her husband died that day too (the demon that possessed him took his life), so she's been pretty much alone in the world since then. Except for our tiny luiseach tribe of three and a half. Actually four and a half now, with Bastian. And if you count Mom, Ashley, and Nolan, it's seven and a half.

"Is there a specific reason for your visit, dear, or is this just a social call? Either way I'm very happy to see you," Victoria says.

"I'm very happy to see you too! I just wanted to say hi and make sure you're okay. I see you every day in English class, but we haven't had a chance to talk."

"Yes, I'm so sorry about that. Your father instructed me to keep an eye on you at school. But I can only do that as my alter ego, Ms. Warkomski, as Victoria Wilde is no longer. As you know, there's a death certificate for me on file at the Ridgemont county clerk's office. And I wanted to keep a . . . what's that expression? A low profile. I didn't want people to connect us in any way except as teacher and student." She adds, "Perhaps I'm being too overly cautious, though."

"It's okay, I get it. Why 'Ms. Warkomski'?"

"One of my best friends growing up was a girl named Susie Warkomski. In 1987 she became the lead singer for a band called the Hell Girls. I think I may have a couple of their cassette tapes around here somewhere."

Cassette tapes?

I take a sip of my tea and wait for the calm to sink in. "You said before that you were just about to ring me," I prompt her. I love that word, "ring," which sounds so old fashioned and British. "Is there something you wanted to talk to me about?"

"Yes, dear."

Victoria sets her teacup down on a white lace coaster. She gazes across the room at a framed photograph of Anna—not ghost Anna but living, breathing, adorable Anna, laughing and tossing a beach ball in the air while the blue-green ocean shimmers in the background.

"Have you seen her?" Victoria asks me in a voice barely above a whisper.

"Yes! You know, last Saturday. She pulled me out of the demon chasm and saved my life."

"But since then?"

I think for a moment. "N-no. But that's not unusual. She doesn't appear to me regularly."

Victoria twists her hands in her lap. Her eyes swim with tears.

"I haven't seen her in such a long time. I miss her so much . . . more than you can possibly know."

I reach over and squeeze her arm. Victoria seems so fragile. For good reason. I try to imagine what it would be like if something happened to Mom or to me and we were separated forever. Just thinking about it makes me want to start sobbing uncontrollably.

"I'm sure Anna is fine," I say, which sounds so empty. And also really strange, considering that Anna is dead. Also, I'm not entirely sure Anna *is* fine. I've been anxious about the fact that she hasn't crossed over yet. Why has she been lingering on

Earth for so long? How long will it be before she morphs into a dark spirit? By all accounts she's *way* overdue.

Although . . . Victoria told me months ago that Anna hadn't crossed over yet because she had some work to do on this plane.

I remind her about this now.

"Your father said that Anna would come to your rescue at a crucial time," Victoria explains. "But she already did this . . . *twice*. And the thing is, I had a dream about her last night. She was . . . in trouble. Trapped. Someone's prisoner."

"*Whose* prisoner? Where?"

"I don't know."

"Do you remember any details from your dream?"

Victoria shakes her head. "It was all very vague. Mostly just a feeling, like Anna was calling out to me, begging for my help. And I'm not sure if this was something that's already happened or is happening right now or will happen at some point in the future. I feel so confused, so helpless. She's my little girl!"

Tears stream down her cheeks. I reach over and hug her.

"I'll find her," I reassure her.

"Would you please, dear? I would be so grateful."

"Of course. Anything for you."

We stay like this for a while, Victoria silently weeping against my shoulder. She was the first one to tell me—really tell me—what it meant to be a luiseach and to clue me in to the fact that Nolan was my protector. She brought me clarity and comfort at a time when I was struggling, lost in the dark, feeling like a delusional crazy person, probably much like Bastian felt before today.

I owe Victoria so much.

I will find her daughter for her.

And after that I will convince Anna to move on.

Easy-peasy.

CHAPTER 23

The New Luiseach in Town

The whole way home from Victoria's I try to summon Anna, like I did back in Llevar la Luz, but it doesn't work. I've tried to summon her at other times and she didn't appear, though, so maybe there's nothing to worry about?

Or maybe there is? Victoria *did* have that dream.

When I walk through the front door an unexpected surprise awaits me—and not a pleasant surprise either, like pizza or Nolan or a balloon-o-gram.

Helena's standing in the living room.

Not just Helena—there are five others I've never seen before. Three men, one woman, and a teenaged girl.

The woman glares at me with a look of undisguised hatred.

What in the heck is going on?

"What are you doing in my house, Helena? Who are these people? *Where is my mother?*" I demand, suddenly scared.

"I'm right here, sweetie." Mom steps out of the kitchen door-

157

way and into view. Her face is a mash-up of conflicting emotions as she rushes up to me. Worry. Relief. Fear. Bravado.

She throws her arms around me and hugs me tightly. "They showed up a few minutes ago," she whispers into my hair. "They said they needed to speak to you. I pretended to call you, but I called Aidan instead. I wasn't sure it would be . . . *safe* for you to come home."

"Aidan's here too?"

"No, he's out looking for you."

"So this is how she turned out," the woman with Helena says coldly. "She doesn't look very impressive."

I move away from Mom and lock eyes with the woman. "*Excuse* me?"

One of the men—he has curly gray hair and a bushy beard— holds out his hand toward me and murmurs something under his breath. I feel a sharp pain in my solar plexus, as though someone just punched me, and then tiny electric zaps. And just as suddenly the pain and electric zaps vanish.

"What was *that?*" I cry out. I touch my solar plexus, which feels fine now, back to normal.

"She has your physical strength, Helena. And your stamina. Your empathy as well," Mr. Bushy Beard says, ignoring me.

Empathy? *Helena?* I would laugh if this whole scenario weren't so bizarre. And creepy. I want Helena and these freaks to leave right this second. I don't *care* if she gave me a magical mystery necklace. She can't be trusted—not now, not ever.

The front door opens and slams, and Aidan bursts into the living room.

"Sunshine!" he says breathlessly. His gaze moves from me to Helena and the others. "I was trying to . . . your phone kept going straight to . . . but I see you've already met the council."

The council. Of course. The leaders, bosses, whatever, of the luiseach on the other side of the rift. The ones who are going to decide whether or not to eliminate me.

How am I going to get out of this one? Maybe I should tell them about Bastian without mentioning his name? No, bad idea. Knowing them, they'd probably try to torture me for the information. Because that's what we guardian angels do, ha ha.

"We haven't exchanged introductions yet, Aidan. This is Mikhail"—Helena indicates the bearded man who Jedi-zapped me—"and Xerxes and Giovanni." Xerxes is short and bald and brown, and Giovanni has a blue buzz cut and a jagged scar on his face. "And this is Aura and her daughter, Zalea," Helena adds, gesturing to the super-mean woman and the young girl.

Aura. Why does she sound familiar? Has Aidan mentioned her before? And then I remember. Lucio told me about her in Mexico. Aura was Helena's second-in-command years ago when they all lived at Llevar la Luz pre-rift. The one who originally came up with the idea to eliminate the infant me.

That explains the super-mean.

Her presence also stacks the odds against me staying alive.

"Nice to see you again," Aura says to me, her voice dripping with sarcasm.

Zalea, the daughter, studies me with a mixture of suspicion and curiosity. Mostly curiosity. She's tall, reed thin, about my age. Short black hair, intelligent blue eyes. I wonder if her mother has been telling her bedtime stories about me since she was little? *Once upon a time there lived an evil luiseach girl. As long as she roamed this Earth all the other luiseach were doomed to die. And so a brave band of luiseach warriors set out to find her and destroy her in order to save our kind . . .*

I raise my hand. "Okay, so . . . elephant in the room. You're all here to tell me I must be eliminated for the greater good, right?"

"Sunshine, that's not funny. Aidan, *do* something!" Mom cries out.

Helena regards Mom with a cold, detached expression. "There is nothing to be done. It's already been settled."

Settled?

Aidan steps quickly between me and the council members. "What do you mean, Helena? Settled how?" he asks, sounding way less confident and in charge than he usually does.

Helena shrugs. "We've conferred, and it's been decided that such an action wouldn't be prudent at this time."

Aidan's shoulders relax. I start to breathe again. Mom puts her arms around me, although it's not a hug so much as a fierce, protective, if-you-harm-a-single-hair-on-my-daughter-you-will-be-toast hold.

"If Aidan's theory is correct—and we're not saying that it is, not yet—but if it is, then La— . . . the girl's death would be contrary to our purposes," Helena goes on.

Aidan glances sharply at her. "Helena!"

"It's what you wanted, isn't it, *dearest*?" Helena says irritably.

"No, that's not it. You just . . ." Aidan hesitates.

"It was hardly a unanimous vote," Aura speaks up.

Thanks a bunch, Aura.

Next to Aura, Zalea swoons slightly.

"Mother!" Zalea grabs Aura's arm. "I just had another vision."

Wait. Another luiseach with vision superpowers?

"Yes, my pet? What did you see?" Aura gushes. She's practically baby talking, which is the polar opposite of the execution-er's tone she seems to like to use with me.

"The war. It will begin soon!" says Zalea.

"*How* soon?" Aidan asks her.

"Weeks. Maybe days. I saw much fire, many deaths."

"You *saw* that?" I say incredulously.

Zalea nods. "Yes. He calls it the Day of Reckoning."

"Who does?"

"Their master. The one called Dubu."

Silence.

"With all due respect, I don't think we should be making council decisions based on these so-called visions," Xerxes says to Helena.

"Duly noted. But we will be making council decisions based on all the information we have, visions included. In any case, this council needs to do much strategizing and preparing for what may be about to unfold. We also need to continue reaching out to the others, summoning them to Ridgemont. We need to raise an army—and quickly."

An *army?*

I remember Bastian asking me about the number of luiseach left on this planet. "How many luiseach are we talking about? How many of us are there out there?" I ask Helena.

"At last count we had around sixty thousand. Give or take," she replies.

"Wow. Okay, so where are they—"

Helena raises a hand to cut me off. "We don't have time for your superfluous questions. We're not here to indulge your curiosity. We have serious work to do."

With that, she nods briskly at her council and heads for the door. Mikhail, Xerxes, Giovanni, and Aura follow—and Zalea too.

"I'm going with you," Aidan announces.

Helena sighs. "Yes, yes, whatever."

"I'm going with you guys too," I speak up.

"*No!*" Aidan and Helena exclaim in unison.

I startle. "Excuse me?"

"This is a matter for the senior leadership. For the adults. Your job is to stay out of the way and not get yourself killed," Helena informs me.

"She's right, Sunshine," Aidan says. "We have a plan in place for you. The best thing for you would be to concentrate on protecting yourself. Lucio will be back from Mexico soon. And Helena and I will be just down the street."

"Just down the street *where?*" I ask, confused.

"Did I not tell you? I have bought all the houses on your cul-de-sac. For security purposes," Aidan says matter-of-factly.

Bought all the houses on the cul-de-sac?

Before I can ask any more questions, he and Helena walk out the door, conferring in hushed voices. The council and Zalea trail behind them.

I suppose I should be relieved. The council has stayed my execution. I've been ordered to hang out on the sidelines and just keep my head down for a while.

Which is exactly what the old Sunshine, the one who wanted to become un-luiseached, might have wanted.

But no longer.

How can I convince Helena and Aidan to let me help them— and fight with the luiseach army too? After all, it's my job, my duty to help save the world.

CHAPTER 24

The Gemini Moon

Later that night, while Mom and Ashley are asleep, I sneak out of the house in my PJs and fuzzy bunny slippers and head out into the night. Aidan mentioned he and Helena would be "just down the street," so presumably within bodyguarding distance. He also mentioned he now owns every house on the cul-de-sac.

Putting two and two together, they must be in one of these houses. But which one?

I stop at the curb and glance up and down the street. The night air is cold, damp, and thick with the scent of pine needles and fresh spring soil. A silvery-white full moon hangs in the starless sky. Mrs. Hillman's windows are dark, and her red SUV—the one that almost mowed me down—is gone. The two houses that flank hers are also dark; they're occupied—I think—by a couple of young families. *Were* occupied, that is, before Aidan showed up with his never-ending bank account of mystery wealth. How much did he have to pay the neighbors to convince them to pack up and vacate their comfortable, familiar homes—and in less than a week?

On my side of the street there's the house next door that *was* occupied by a middle-aged guy with a truck. His truck is gone now, and his windows are dark too. The house on the other side of us, whose previous owner was a middle-aged woman with three very yippy dogs, is likewise dark.

But in all the darkness there's one house with a lit-up window. The brick house at the very end of the cul-de-sac.

Moving quietly through the shadows, I proceed. As I walk I touch my throat to make sure the necklace is there. It is. For some reason it makes me feel safer, even though I'm not sure if it actually works or if Helena was just messing with me. I still don't trust her, and I probably never will.

Still, there's something comforting about this necklace. Is it just a placebo effect, which, according to Mom, is when you give a patient a fake pill and say it's a real pill and the patient gets better anyway because mind over body?

After a few minutes I reach the brick house. A plaque hangs near the front doorbell; it has a picture of a beaming, dimply angel on it and the words BLESS OUR HOME! Ironic.

I crouch behind an overgrown laurel bush and peer inside the lit-up window. Through the gauzy curtain I can see them sitting around a dining room table: Helena, Aidan, and the council. Helena is at the head of the table with Aidan opposite her. Xerxes and Mikhail sit on one side and super-mean Aura and blue-haired Giovanni on the other. I don't see Aura's daughter, Zalea, though.

Books, maps, notebooks, and coffee mugs cover the table. The six of them seem to be arguing—I can hear the shrill cre-

scendo of their voices, even though I can't make out most of
their words. Just a few here and there:

Pentagram.

The girl.

Adis and Uiri.

Dubu.

Sons.

Prague.

Suddenly Aidan stands up, so abruptly that he knocks over
his chair. Helena stands up too and stares him down with her
cold, eagle gaze. Their postures radiate fury; they appear to be
at some sort of ugly standoff.

Footsteps. A branch snapping.

I whirl around and see a tall, shadowy figure behind me.

It's Zalea. I immediately tense up, wondering if her mother
sent her here to cast some evil luiseach spell on me—or worse.

"Sunshine?"

Her voice is light and friendly, so I relax a little.

"Oh, hey Zalea."

"How serendipitous! I was collecting samples out back and
had this sudden vision you were near me. And here you are!"
Zalea flutters her hands in the air as though sprinkling fairy
dust.

I'm not sure how to respond to this. At least she doesn't seem
hostile or violent. The exact opposite, in fact. In any case, I gesture for her to follow me away from the window so the grown-
ups won't overhear us.

We find a couple of Adirondack chairs in the side yard and
sit down. A black iron grill divides us, crusty with the burnt ves-
tiges of long-ago barbecues, and an old dog leash and a tennis

ball lie in the grass at our feet—remnants of someone's real life before the luiseach patrol showed up and took over the neighborhood.

"So . . . what kind of samples?" is the best I can come up with for small talk. I push up my right coat sleeve and glance briefly at my wrist, which I find myself doing occasionally to make sure the spider-web mark hasn't returned. Yay, it hasn't.

Zalea scoots her Adirondack chair so she's closer to me. She digs into the pockets of her flannel robe, which she's wearing over an old-fashioned-looking white nightgown. Unfurling her hand, she reveals an assortment of small gray rocks.

"These," she says.

"Why are you collecting rocks?" I ask curiously.

"Rocks? They're not just rocks!" Zalea selects one and holds it up. It catches the ambient light from inside the house and the full moon. "See the thin orangey stripe? That's carnelian." She picks up another one. "These white flecks are zeolites. These other samples have copper and chert and agate and jasper and coprolites." She stops and grins. "Do you know what coprolites are?"

"Um, no."

"Fossilized poop!" Zalea breaks into a peal of laughter.

I laugh too. "So where did you find these, um, samples?"

"In these humans' yards." Zalea waves her arm in a wide arc, indicating the now practically deserted cul-de-sac. "These samples will help me understand the soul of your city, its history."

"Really? That's cool. I mean, I have no idea how that works, but it *sounds* cool."

"It is!"

Zalea smiles and regards me with her large blue eyes. "You're not at all like Mother said."

Aura, my number-one fan. "What did your mom say about me?"

"She said you were very frightening and terrible. And very powerful too."

I chuckle drily. "So I'm not frightening or terrible or powerful?"

"No! You're definitely powerful. Extremely so. But you're a kind person. You care about others—maybe too much sometimes."

"Are you basing this on the weird zappy magic trick that guy did to my—" I point to my solar plexus. "This area? And then he said I had a boatload of empathy, just like Helena? Who, by the way, is about as empathic as a killer Komodo dragon?"

"No, I didn't base this on Xerxes's soul assessment of you. I can read your thoughts. Not all of them, but some."

"Excuse me, what?"

Zalea folds her hands on her lap. "Okay. Your cat's name is Lex Luthor because you like the Superman comic books, and your puppy dog's name is Oscar because you like Hollywood movies. You like—no, you *love* a guy named Nolan. Nolan Foster. You spoke to him on the phone earlier tonight and told him about the council's arrival here in Ridgemont. Oh, and you were thinking about him a few minutes ago too, about how much you miss kissing him. You can't wait until your father lifts the spell so you and Nolan can make out all you want."

My cheeks grow hot. Is this girl a witch?

"Now you're wondering if I'm a witch. You used to think your friend was a witch too. The former one, Victoria. I never met her, you know? Why did she give up her luiseach powers anyway? By the way, Mother doesn't like *her* either."

I hug my arms across my chest and shake my head. I need

to stop thinking and empty my brain ASAP so this crazy witch-girl will cut it out with the ESP.

"Now you're telling yourself to stop thinking so I won't read your thoughts anymore. And did you just call me a crazy witch-girl?"

"Okay, please stop doing that!"

"Sorry, sorry!" Zalea slips her rock samples back in her robe pocket. "I've had these abilities since I was little. Mind reading, prophetic visions, dreams. On and off, here and there. Sometimes I can control them, sometimes not."

I blink, confused. "Since you were little? But I thought—"

"I know. Luiseach aren't supposed to come into their powers until they're sixteen. That was true for me too, except for these particular abilities. I'm not sure why. Mother always said it's because I'm special. Of course she says that about everything I do." Zalea grins.

"Huh. I can't read minds, or at least I don't think so. But when I was at Llevar la Luz over the winter I started having visions like you—real-time visions, snippets of stuff happening right that moment in distant places. Sometimes they get mixed up with my dreams."

"Same!" Zalea's face lights up. "Hey, did you know that I was born at Llevar la Luz, just like you?"

"Really?"

When Aidan took me there this past winter it was just him and me and Lucio. Most of the massive compound was full of dust and cobwebs and wistful echoes of its long-ago residents. I like imagining it in its glory days, with hundreds of luiseach living there, working there, raising children there, having babies there.

"I was too young to remember the place, though. Mother and I left when I was only a few months old. But I've seen it in visions. It's very beautiful," Zalea says.

"Yes, it is. In a creepy, *noir* sort of way. Did you ever see that old black-and-white movie *The Letter* with Bette Davis? It's got the same tropical-gothic vibe. What about your dad? Did he leave with you and your mom?"

"Mother never told me who my father was. I've had dreams about him, but I've never been able to figure out his name, not even by trying to probe Mother's memories."

I gasp. "You probe your mom's memories?"

"Yes. She hates it when I do that," Zalea smiles.

"I bet!"

Her smile fades as she tips her head back and stares up at the sky.

"Do you see? Up there?"

I tip my head back too. "See what?"

"The moon."

"Yes, it's big and round and pretty. What about it?"

"Do you remember the last full moon?"

I scrunch up my nose to think. There was a full moon recently . . . wait, was it, like, four or five nights ago? I remember racing downstairs in the wee hours after finding the black tape on Dr. Hoo's beak, speaking with Aidan on the porch, looking up at the full moon in the predawn sky.

That was on Tuesday morning.

Which is not scientifically possible.

"It was Monday night, Tuesday morning. That has to be a mistake, though. Am I misremembering?" I ask Zalea.

"You're not misremembering, and it's not a mistake."

"Um, okay. What are you saying here?"

"You probably already know about blue moons. A blue moon is two full moons in one month, and it happens once every few years," Zalea explains. "Two full moons in one *week* never happens. It's not part of the natural order. It's called the Gemini Moon, and according to legend it only occurs when the world is descending into chaos. The only other time it occurred was right before the First War."

I sit up very straight. Alarm bells are going off in my head. Does this mean a *second* war is imminent, just like Zalea saw in her vision?

"The First War? What's that?"

"That's where this all started. The acrimony between dark and light."

"Because demons and luiseach used to be best friends and hung out and had sleepovers before?" I joke feebly. "Seriously, though, what is it?"

"By the way, did you know that 'acrimony' is another word for the plant agrimony, which has magical powers?" Zalea says dreamily. "Long ago it was mixed with crushed frogs and human blood to treat internal hemorrhaging. It was also a witches' cure for elfshot, which is when invisible elves shoot you with invisible arrows and cause bodily pain."

"That's super-interesting and I'd love to hear more about invisible elf arrows some other time. But right now I need to know about this First War."

"The First War happened several thousands of years ago. It was very . . . awful. Devastating. History altering. The original luiseach king and queen were killed. So were two of the three Markon rulers. When the two Markons died, the demon army

fled and scattered. The luiseach considered themselves victori-
ous, and the eldest daughter of the king and queen immediately
took over."

Whoa. This is *so* much new information. "H-how do you
know all this?"

"It is in our chronicles. Did your father never mention the
chronicles to you?"

"No. My father isn't the sharing type. He dispenses facts and
figures on a strictly need-to-know basis."

Zalea nods sympathetically. "It's not easy being a luiseach
leader, especially with your father's lineage . . . and his burden."

"What lineage? What burden?" Why am I hearing about
all this for the first time? And what's this about him being a
luiseach leader? I thought that since the rift he's basically been
in charge of Victoria, Lucio, and me—and that's it.

Lights flicker on inside the house. A curtain parts and a face
appears in one of the windows.

"Zalea? Are you out there, pet?. Why aren't you in bed?"
Aura calls out.

Zalea rises hastily to her feet. So do I.

"I have to go," she whispers, leaning her head close to mine.
"Mother would not be pleased if she knew I was being so forth-
coming with you."

"But . . . but . . ."

Zalea digs into her pocket, pulls out a stone, and hands it to
me. "A gift. And don't worry. We will speak again. Just remember
this, though: you have the power to end this new war quickly."

"Me?"

"Yes, you. But it means taking your father's burden from
him. Which will not be a simple matter. Good night, Sunshine."

She turns and skips to the back door, humming to herself. I glance at the small gray stone in my hand and then up at the Gemini Moon. The moon that appears only when the world is about to descend into chaos.

The war is coming.

And *I* have the power to end it quickly?

None of this makes any sense, and Zalea seems a little . . . flighty, otherworldly.

Yet. Something deep inside me, some luiseach hive-mind instinct, is telling me she's speaking the absolute truth.

Which is exhilarating.

And also flipping terrifying.

CHAPTER 25
What Happened in Prague

On Sunday Aidan sends me a text to cancel our training.

> I must take care of a time-sensitive matter. Lucio will
> be back from Llevar la Luz in the next day or two. In the
> meantime Helena will be watching out for you..

He's called away on some time-sensitive matter on the very day I need to ask him a zillion questions? About the First War, about the coming war, about his lineage? And most importantly, this "burden" of his that I have to take on?

> We need to talk, Aidan.
>
> > Of course. Soon.
>
> When?

No response. *Argh.*

The day looms before me. Ashley is at a ballet lesson with Madame Gergiev. Mom is working an extra shift at the hospital; the ER has been especially busy lately—more and more random attacks—and as a result, the pediatric wing has been admitting a record number of patients. Nolan has a family event, after which he's planning to go to the library to do more research on pentagrams, wild animals, violent crime rates, and the rest of the subjects on his and Lucio's long, long list.

I could do some homework. Or watch TV. Or clean my—and now Ashley's—room. Or reread *Mansfield Park,* which I've been meaning to do for a while.

Or . . . I could pop down the street and see if I can talk to Zalea some more.

Which is what I decide to do. As I head out I zip up my puffy winter coat and pull on one of my crocheted hats—it's super-cold outside. I don't think I need to worry about killer SUVs or wild animals or the like? I'm wearing my magical mystery necklace under my hoodie, Aidan said Helena is "watching out" for me, and I have my luiseach knife in my back pocket as always . . . so I should be okay, right?

I soon reach the brick house at the end of the cul-de-sac, but it seems like no one is home. The place is quiet, there are no lights on inside, and there are no cars out front. I circle the house and peer inside the windows. I press my ear against the back door and listen.

The door opens suddenly, and I practically fall inside.

Helena stands there, regarding me with an imperious scowl.

"I see you have added trespassing, spying, and breaking and entering to your list of accomplishments."

"No! I was just, um . . ." I haul myself upright and smooth my frizzball back into place—as if that makes a difference. "I wanted to see if, um . . ."

Helena peers over my shoulder. "Are you alone?"

"Um, yes?"

"Since you're here, you might as well come in."

"What? Why?"

She doesn't answer but instead takes me by the wrist and pulls me inside. The next thing I know I'm in somebody's avocado-green kitchen. With Helena. *Alone.*

Argh, I should have just stayed home and read *Mansfield Park.*

I cross my arms over my chest and glance around. This kitchen, the "Bless Our Home" person's kitchen, is so . . . normal. Ordinary. Refrigerator covered with grocery lists and photo magnets. Crocheted oven mitts hanging near the stove. Bottles of dried spices lined up on the counter in alphabetical order.

Helena points to a chrome table with a couple of chairs, and I sit down reluctantly. She remains standing, leaning against the counter, studying me.

"It's time we had a conversation," she announces.

"About what? Politics, the weather, my favorite movies? Ha ha." My awkward sense of humor really kicks into gear when I'm super-nervous.

She raises her eyebrows. "About our current situation."

"By 'our,' do you mean—"

"I'm not your enemy. I know you think that I am, but I'm not. What I did sixteen years ago, what I tried to do again at Victoria's house"—Helena exhales—"it was for the greater good. I trust that you see that. Because some day, sooner than you think, you may have to make difficult choices, *extremely* difficult choices, for the greater good."

I flop back in my seat, confused. Is Helena trying to apologize to me? Or simply rationalizing the two—or more?—times she tried to kill me in cold blood?

"These 'extremely difficult choices,' do they have something to do with my father?" I ask after a moment.

Helena startles. "What are you talking about, child?"

Child?

I make a fist in the air and start ticking off items, finger by finger. "*One*. The First War. *Two*. King Adis and Queen Uiri. *Three*. Dubu's brothers. *Four*. Aidan's lineage . . . and his, um, 'burden'? And what is this about him being a luiseach leader? Thanks to you, he barely has any luiseach to lead!"

Helena stares at me in astonishment.

"Who told you about these things? Surely not Aidan."

I don't mention Zalea's name—I don't want to get her into trouble.

"I know more than you think, Helena. But I don't know everything, so you need to fill me in." I feel less scared and awkward now, more confident.

Helena opens her mouth to speak, then closes it again. She looks very tired all of a sudden.

"Yes, I suppose I do need to fill you in." She sits down in the chair across from me and stares out the window at the view of the side yard with the barbecue grill and the Adirondack chairs where Zalea and I spoke last night. A clock chimes in the living room, just beyond the kitchen. Twelve musical *dings*—it's noon. Would the people who lived here be coming home from church right now? Debating pancakes versus omelets for brunch? I'm often haunted by what *should* be normal in this world and how the darkness has turned all that upside down.

Helena finally turns to face me.

"Adis and Uiri were the first king and queen of the luiseach," she begins. "Several millennia ago they waged war against the darkness to try to eradicate it. Up until then the idea was to maintain a balance between the two sides. But things got . . . *complicated*. And the luiseach leadership decided to eliminate the demons and their minions once and for all. The demons were led by Dubu and his two brothers, Dagon and Drakov. During the war Adis and Uiri managed to kill both brothers, and as a result the army of the darkness fled, abandoned their posts, if you will. Dubu and his remaining soldiers retreated. Unfortunately Adis and Uiri had to sacrifice themselves in order to kill Dagon and Drakov. But their oldest daughter, Laoise, immediately took over the reigns as the new queen of the luiseach, and our side declared victory." She adds, "Laoise is Aidan's grandmother and your great-grandmother."

I gape. "Whoa, *what?* Seriously? So that means—"

"That you are descended from the first luiseach king and queen, yes. And on my side you are descended from Uiri's cousin Fatil, who was also royalty."

"Really?"

"Yes, yes, *really*. Why do you find this so unbelievable? Have you not noticed you possess special powers? Some of your ancestors had some of those same powers. You seem to have inherited *all* of them, in combination, and a few additional powers too, probably as a result of your father and I conducting . . . Anyway, you are unique."

Is Helena actually paying me a compliment? Or just stating a fact?

Royalty. I can't even wrap my brain around the concept. It's like one of those movie moments where the commoner discovers she's actually a princess. Except the commoner-princess is usually super-happy and excited when she finds out. I don't feel happy or excited at all, just overwhelmed.

"Who were *your* parents? And *their* parents?" I ask.

"We can discuss your matrilineal ancestry later. That is another very long story," Helena replies. "Getting back to Queen Laoise, your paternal great-grandmother"—*my paternal great-grandmother*—"she was a magnificent queen. She restored order in the world, which had been torn asunder by the First War. For many, many centuries the demons and dark spirits stayed underground. There were occasional possessions on the earthly plane, but nothing significant. Dubu never resurfaced. Everyone believed him to be dead. Markons, like luiseach, can live very long lives, but they are not immortal."

"But he *wasn't* dead. The other day you told Aidan you knew he was alive. How did you know?"

"Because." Helena looks me square in the eye. She is her usual terrifying self yet appears strangely vulnerable too. "Many decades ago—a century, in fact—I fell in love with another man while I was married to your father. Aidan and I were . . . estranged. We had talked about separating. And then I met this man."

Holy crackers.

"Good golly, who was he?" I ask curiously. I try to imagine Helena in love, the way I love Nolan. Giddy, blushing, butterflies in my stomach, aching to be with him. I totally can't picture it.

"His name was Andreas. He was kind, brilliant, charming, handsome. And he was absolutely devoted to me." Helena squirms uncomfortably. "I thought all along he was human. But he wasn't. One day he revealed himself to be who he really was. A demon, a Markon . . ."

My jaw drops.

What is she saying here?

."*Dubu?*" I practically yell. "You had an affair with *Dubu?!*"

"Yes. Please keep your voice down . . . the others could return any minute. The thing is, Markons have an uncanny ability to shape-shift, to assume alternate identities. They are masters at this. Still, when Andreas—Dubu—told me who he really was, I didn't"—Helena falters—"I found I couldn't turn him in to the luiseach or try to destroy him, as I probably should have done. I was in love with him. He was in love with me. And unlike your father, I had a more . . . *nuanced* attitude toward the darkness. I believed we all possess some dark and some light within us." She pauses. "In some ways I still believe that."

My biological mother had an affair with a super-demon. *The* super-demon.

I thought the royalty thing was a bombshell, but *this* . . .

"Eventually I broke off our affair and reconciled with your father," Helena goes on. "I had no intention of telling Aidan about my relationship with Dubu, but he found out somehow. He went after Dubu—this was in Prague. But before he could get to him, he encountered a demon in a public square. The demon had possessed a university student and was holding a pregnant woman hostage. Aidan came to the rescue and managed to exorcise the demon and destroy it before harm could befall the woman, her unborn child, or the student. Unfortunately that demon turned out to be . . . he was Dubu's firstborn son, Selarion."

Another bombshell.

"Dubu disappeared after that. Vanished completely. Aidan heard from a trusted source that Dubu had perished too . . . that the grief over the death of his son had weakened him, made him sick, and eventually killed him. But I knew he was still alive."

"How?"

"The necklace."

"The necklace?"

"Dubu gave it to me when we were together, to protect me. His existence is what powers it. If he were to . . . *die* . . . it would crumble to dust, disappear."

Oh my gosh.

"This is Dubu's necklace? How *could* you?" Angry and horrified, I reach up to tear it off my neck.

But Helena stops me by grabbing my wrist with supernatural speed. "*No!* You must continue wearing it. It's crucial you stay alive, that you have every means at your disposal to do so. This necklace is a powerful tool."

"I can't, I won't wear something that belongs to him!"

"If you die, you know what will happen. The pentagram spell will be completed. And we believe—the council believes— that the completion of the spell is what will trigger the Second War. We're working frantically to figure out how to stop it, how to reverse it. But until we do, you *must* stay alive."

I sit there, stunned, trying to take all this in.

"Why me, though? Why not one of the other luiseach?"

"You're the most likely candidate. Dubu has made other attempts on your life. You're an extremely powerful and important luiseach. Also . . ." Helena hesitates.

"What?"

"I know him. Aidan took the life of his child. And no doubt he now wants to exact revenge . . ."

My stomach twists.

Helena doesn't finish the sentence. She doesn't need to.

Aidan killed Dubu's son Selarion. So now Dubu is going to kill me.

Even-steven.

And if I die, the pentagram spell will be triggered.

Then . . . apocalypse. No more luiseach. No more humans.

Just darkness.

CHAPTER 26
Visions

That night I sit cross-legged on the pink shag carpet next to my bed and try to conjure a vision. Several visions, actually. As I breathe deeply and try to still my thoughts, I'm aware of the cool, delicate sensation of Dubu's necklace against my skin. I have to fight the temptation to tear it off and throw it into a volcano, Mordor, *anywhere* to make sure it's destroyed once and for all.

But I can't risk it.

So I guess I'll just have to find Dubu himself and throw *him* into a volcano or Mordor or wherever.

The question is how?

Helena said I was unique, a combination of multiple luiseach abilities passed down through the generations. Aidan said once that I'm a luiseach like no other. The two of them also exposed me to who-knows-what while Helena was pregnant with me, which contributed to my luiseach skill set in a bizarre but apparently useful way. Except for the part when my birth released a massive wave that may have caused the spontaneous death of a bunch of unborn luiseach babies and pregnant luiseach women. Helena didn't reference that bit of history during our heart-to-heart.

When Zalea said I could end this war quickly, maybe that's what she meant, that I could do so by using my special, one-of-a-kind menu of superpowers. Aidan thinks it's his burden to find and stop Dubu, but maybe it's destined to be my burden instead?

I just have to figure out how to find and stop Dubu—before he kills me and completes the pentagram and launches the apoca lypse. Dubu, the demonest of demons, who also happens to be the ex-boyfriend of my biological mother . . .

. . . which isn't weird or anything.

I also promised Victoria I would try to find Anna.

So two birds with one stone. It's time for me to go into lui-seach GPS mode.

Dubu, where are you? I ask silently, gazing up at the ceiling. *Make yourself known already. Time to stop playing hide-and-seek. And Anna, where did you go? Your mom's worried. She wants to see you.*

Nothing. Just a faint circle of tiny glow-in-the-dark stars blink-ing down at me. I never noticed them before. The Wildes lived in this house way back when. Did the stars belong to Anna?

From downstairs I can hear the rattling and clinking of plates and glasses, random strands of conversation, laughter. Ashley and Mom are doing the dishes from our Thai takeout dinner: spring rolls, shrimp pad Thai noodles, chicken curry, and jas-mine rice. Mom had a pretty brutal day at the hospital—another violent incident, this one at a little league baseball game, with no fatalities but many injuries. So I'm glad she's able to relax a bit.

"Sunshine State? You want some ice cream, sweetie? Ashley and I are making sundaes!" Mom calls up the stairs.

"In a sec, Mom!"

"Do you want Fudgelicious Frappemocha or boring old vanilla?" Ashley yells.

"Boring old vanilla!"

I uncross my legs and recross them yogi style. I let my eyelids flutter shut to a soft, relaxed half gaze.

Apparently—or according to Aidan anyway—visioning is not a common luiseach ability. He and I both seem to have it, and Zalea too, and also Helena? I'm not sure who else. The thing is that these visions kind of come and go unbidden and are sometimes intermingled with dreams, like the one of Aidan and Helena having a conversation about me and about killing Dubu. I haven't been able to *make* the visions happen yet.

Maybe I can make one happen now.

I just have to go all Jedi in my head somehow.

Lex Luthor purrs and rubs up against my knees. "Not now," I whisper. "I'm trying to have a psychic experience."

I feel him plop down on the carpet beside me and curl up into a warm, furry ball, purring like a motor. Through a crack in the window a cold breeze stirs the curtains and grazes my skin. I hear Ashley exclaim, ". . . *and she ate the entire thing in one bite!*" and she and Mom crack up.

Come on, Dubu. Where are you?

Anna, I miss you! Your mom misses you!

Even though Mom has been a little more cheerful with Ashley around—Ashley *does* have that effect on people—she hasn't let down her guard when it comes to keeping me safe and alive. She continues to text me, like, twelve times a day when we're apart. On Tuesday she had our landlord change all the locks on our doors and install new locks on our windows. I'm not sure locks will keep Dubu and other demons out, but still. She's even talking about getting a fancy, expensive security system with codes and passwords and a Bat phone–style automatic link to the police. Again, not sure how effective the police can be against a Markon and his crew.

My thoughts wander.

Algebra homework. Spring dance committee. Tiffany is mean. I need new socks. Did I eat the last English muffin? Where is Aidan? Helena and Dubu. Nolan. When is Lucio coming back from Mexico? Kirsten. That word she said—ded-something. The spider-web mark. Spiders. Latoya. Hospital food. Anna. I'm descended from luiseach royalty. The guy with the machete. Mrs. Ostricher. Those animals in the state park. Lex Luthor and Oscar. Did I change the cat litter? Zalea. Queen Laoise—did Helena pronounce it like "lee-sha"? Rocks. Fossilized poop. The end of the world.

Random pinpricks of light dance against my eyelids. My muscles start to relax, go heavy. And then an image of Nolan materializes in my head, flittering and floating, and my heart skips a beat. He's sitting in the library, at one of the big oak tables, alone. His tawny hair falls across his forehead as he pores over a big leather-bound book with yellowed pages. The pages are covered with Latin words, charts, and graphs. Also strange illustrations of scientific instruments, celestial bodies, and monstrous beasts. Nolan takes furious notes with one hand while his other hand flies across the pages.

An elderly man, a librarian, approaches him. He's dressed in flannel slacks, a rumpled black shirt, and a black cardigan with one button missing. "We're closing in fifteen minutes, young man," he says, tapping his wristwatch.

Nolan nods without looking up and flips to the next page. And then he straightens in his chair and exclaims, "Queensland, Australia!"

The old librarian stares at him. There's something familiar about the man. Have I seen him before? At that library? But I haven't been there in ages, and in any case I don't remember him—just the red-haired lady who shushes people a lot and the other librarian who's always reading a book of Percy Bysshe Shelley poems.

Then my vision shifts, and I see Anna standing in the middle of a field.

Yes, finally—*Anna!*

I try to call out, but no sounds come out of my mouth. All around her, tall green grass undulates in the wind. The sky above her is a cloudless, Technicolor blue. She's wearing a white cotton nightgown and clutching her stuffed owl.

And then she notices me and waves. She begins to quote Shelley to me in a grown-up voice:

O wild West Wind, thou breath of Autumn's being
Thou from whose unseen presence the leaves dead
Are driven like ghosts from an enchanter fleeing . . .

Anna says something else, but I can't hear the words.

"What, Anna? What was that last part?"

"Be. Careful," she repeats in her normal voice, her ten-year-old voice.

"Be careful of what? And where are you? Your mom had this scary dream, and she's super-worried about you. I'm worried about you too because you've lingered on Earth too long, and you know what will happen if—"

"The enchanter is after you," Anna says.

She giggles and vanishes.

"Anna!" I shout. *"Anna!"*

But she's gone. The wind picks up, and the green grass undulates more violently. Storm clouds pass across the blue sky, gray and boiling.

Wait. That isn't a field of grass. It's a field of rice. Mom and I watched a TV documentary about Japan last summer, and the rice fields there looked just like that.

A light shimmers, and Anna reappears. But no, it's not Anna. It's another girl, taller, older—a teenager, wearing a white kimono. She has long black hair and pale, pale skin. Her brown eyes are wide with terror.

"Ki-yo-tsu-ke-te," she whispers to me.

"What?" I ask loudly, trying to be heard over the rising wind.

"Ki-yo-tsu-ke-te!" she screams.

Trembling, she rolls up the sleeve of her kimono and thrusts the underside of her wrist at me.

I start to tremble too.

No.

She has the spider-web mark, the same one Kirsten, the light-spirit-turned-dark, left on my wrist.

What does this mean?

The kimono-clad girl cries out in pain. On her wrist the mark twitches and pulsates and doubles in size. The ten—no, *fifteen*—short lines that make up the spider-web shape-shift around rapidly.

After a moment they settle into a new shape.

A pentagram.

CHAPTER 27
Urgent News

The next day at school I'm definitely not myself. I am so not myself that when Mr. Okafor calls on me to name three generals from the American Revolutionary War, I blank. Which is not like me, as I'm usually the nerd girl who knows all—my nickname in middle school was the Brainiac.

Of course, as soon as the bell rings and I walk out of the history classroom, a ton of names come to me: Richard Montgomery, Richard Howe, Benedict Arnold, "Mad Anthony" Wayne, and—how did I not remember this one?—George Washington. *Argh.*

I can't stop thinking about my vision from last night—if it *was* a vision, that is. I'm sure the part about Nolan was because I called him right afterward and confirmed he was at the library doing exactly what I saw him doing. I told him about my entire vision, dream, whatever, and he suggested the kimono girl might be linked somehow to the luiseach who died in Japan and that the dead yellow bird I found was indigenous to

Queensland, Australia. As for the part about Anna, was that real too? Or was my subconscious mind just free associating and making up scary, random stuff at that point?

I also can't stop checking my wrist. So far the mark hasn't returned. No spider-web, no pentagram. The mark hasn't returned since a week ago in English class, when it vanished along with Wesley's ghost. If Nolan hadn't seen it, I might have dismissed it as a hallucination.

But I can't help having this sick, bad, worried feeling I haven't seen the last of it yet.

Is the mark related to the demons' pentagram spell?

What do Kirsten and the kimono girl have to do with all of this?

Where on Earth is Anna?

When the last-period dismissal bell rings, I make a beeline for my locker, drop off a bunch of books, and head up to Room 236. In English class I spoke to Bastian briefly and convinced him to meet me at the spring dance committee meeting so we could have a safe place to talk; I want to see how he's doing after his luiseach initiation experience on Saturday. Plus we need to schedule more training sessions if possible—he needs to exercise his powers, learn about them, feel comfortable with them. Later Nolan and I are hanging out at the Dream Bean Coffee Shop so I can tell him about my epic conversation with Helena yesterday along with everything else that's happened.

And speaking of training sessions, Aidan canceled ours again this morning, no explanation.

What's going on with him? I need to talk to him about the new information I learned from Zalea and Helena.

"Sunshine!"

Tiffany stands in the doorway of Room 236 and gives me a big, sparkly smile—bigger and sparklier than usual.

"Thanks so much for coming by again. Hey, you look so pretty today. Love your outfit!"

I stop and stare at her. *Huh?* Tiffany likes my taste in clothes all of a sudden? I'm in one of my usual get-ups: jeans, Chuck Taylors, and a nineties plaid flannel shirt with a cranberry juice stain from lunch. Nothing has changed here. Ashley hasn't been able to corral me into a fashion makeover yet. Is Tiffany being sincere, or is she setting me up for another insult? Likely the latter.

"Your friends are already here. Ashley and Bastian are making decorations. We're up to fifty crepe-paper roses! So only fifty more to go—yay!" Tiffany throws her arms up in the air and does a little shimmy dance.

More bafflement. What happened to Mean Tiffany? Did aliens take over her body?

Except I don't have time to ponder this mystery because *Ashley and Bastian.* It didn't occur to me they might run into each other here, introduce themselves, have a conversation—not today anyway, as Ashley mentioned she had ballet again after school. There's no way she said anything to him, right? Like, "Hey, I hear you're a Loose Peach paranormal superhero! Can you levitate and talk to ghosts and exercise with demons and stuff?" I promised him total confidentiality.

Maybe it was a bad idea to let her read Nolan's notebook.

"Excuse me, I have to . . ." I rush past Tiffany, trip on an extension cord, right myself, and survey the room. I recognize some of the same student volunteers from last week; they're busy with posters, playlists, and updates to the school's Twitter feed, Facebook page, and Instagram.

Ashley and Bastian are by the window making roses. Green pipe cleaners and pink crepe paper cover the table in front of them.

"Ashley, Bastian, hi!" I say breathlessly.

They both glance up.

"Hello, Sunshine. Your friend Ashley is teaching me how to create these very interesting floral decorations," Bastian says by way of a greeting. I notice he ditched his baggy navy blazer and is wearing just the white button-down shirt with the sleeves rolled up.

"Hi, Sun! Did you know Bastian used to live in Washington, DC? And in Europe before that? Switzerland, right, Bas?" Ashley beams at him.

"Geneva, yes. We also lived in London while I was in grades two through six."

"I promised Bas I'd show him around Ridgemont maybe this week. You know, a mini-tour. Here, you want to get started on some roses?"

Ashley hands me a handful of pipe cleaners and crepe paper. On the plus side, it doesn't seem like she mentioned the luiseach business to Bastian. On the minus side—or on the confusing side anyway—why is she offering to show him around Ridgemont? She's been here for, like, all of ten days, ergo she hardly knows the town . . . and Bastian and his family have their vacation home—correction, *mansion*—in the mountains, so he must already be familiar with the area, right?

"I thought you had a ballet class today, Ash."

"I did, but Madame Gergiev had to cancel. She has the flu. Lucky for me!" Ashley beams at Bastian again.

I smile, trying to mask my bewilderment. "Uh huh."

I shift my gaze to Bastian to see how he's taking all this. The Ashley charm offense. But he seems to be okay, or not freaked out by it anyway. He's looping a pipe cleaner around a paper rose slowly, meticulously.

"Is this correct?" he asks Ashley.

"Perfect! So have you got a date for the dance yet, Bas?"

No, no, no. "Ash, could I talk to you? In private?" I say quickly.

"Sure!"

I pull her aside out of Bastian's earshot. I bang my elbow into a metal filing cabinet and stifle a PG-rated swear word.

"Ash, you can't flirt with him."

She shrugs innocently. "Whaaat? I'm just being friendly."

"No, you're not. You're flirting. Or he may think you're flirting. I know it's just your way of talking to guys and it doesn't mean anything, but . . . Bastian is . . . *fragile*. He and I . . ." I hesitate, wondering how to explain this. I want to tell her she can't distract him with flirty, datey stuff. He's my luiseach-in-training. A warrior for the greater good. He has to focus. "You just can't" is the best I can do.

"Sure. Fine. But honestly I'm just being nice. He's new here. And you know, with a little work, he could be super-cute . . ."

"*Ashley!*"

"I'm just saying!"

A motion catches my eye. Someone's waving to me from the doorway.

It's a familiar hot-pink-clad figure. Dyed platinum hair. Dr. Martens boots.

Victoria, a.k.a. Ms. Warkomski.

I wave back. She crooks her finger, gesturing me into the hallway. Maybe she wants to know if I've made any progress on my search for Anna?

Ashley notices Victoria too, and her face lights up. "Hey, is that—"

"*No!* It's *not!* It's Ms. Warkomski, the new sub in my English class. I need to speak to her about . . . um . . . a paper I'm writing. Yes, that's it. On the themes of self-examination and introspection in Jane Austen's books! Just stay here, and don't repeat any of what I said to Bastian!"

"Whoa! Yes, ma'am!" Ashley pretends to salute.

I hurry off. When I reach the door Victoria smiles nervously and directs me into the hallway, presumably so we can have privacy. Well, with as much privacy as we can have with hordes of students hanging out or passing by.

"Hi, Vic— . . . hi, Ms. Warkomski."

"Hello, dear."

I lower my voice. "I'm still working on that . . . *thing* we discussed."

She smiles sadly. "I'm not here about that. I have something for you."

She presses a folded-up note into my palm.

"I think you'll understand," she says and hurries away.

I open the note. It's written on old-fashioned ivory stationery in Victoria's strange, spidery handwriting. The paper smells faintly of peppermint and lemon verbena.

Lucio is back from Mexico.
He has urgent news and is waiting for you.

CHAPTER 28
Four Girls

I read Victoria's note again. I glance around—Lucio's nowhere in sight.

Fading footsteps. I spot Victoria at the far end of the corridor, the one that leads to the gym—the *new* gym, which was completed last fall and is almost the size of the rest of the school combined.

Just before rounding the corner Victoria peers over her shoulder at me. She crooks her finger again.

I feel a little bit like Alice, following the white rabbit down the hole.

She starts down a set of stairs in the back of the building, then ignores the entrance to the gym and instead opens a set of double doors with an ominous red sign: EMERGENCY EXIT ONLY. DO NOT USE.

I cringe and wait for a zillion alarms to go off. But nothing happens.

Whew.

Victoria heads outside, and I trail after her. It's started to rain—a damp, misty, cling-to-your-skin Washington rain. I can feel my hair reacting, puffing out, becoming enormous; the frizzball does not care for humidity. I've never been to this part of the schoolyard. There's a parking lot that's deserted except for a large brown dumpster piled high with cardboard boxes and one lone sneaker. Weeds sprout out of cracks in the asphalt, and the paint delineating the parking spots have faded to ghostly white flecks. In the far distance the cross-country team is doing laps around the track, small as ants from my vantage point.

Some instinct makes me pause and spin around. Behind us the lit-up windows of the school building glow eerily in the mist. In the northwest corner of the second floor a face appears in a window, then vanishes. It looked like a blond girl, but I'm not totally sure. Was it Ashley? Or some random student?

"Sunshine, please! We must be on our way," Victoria calls out.

"I'm coming!"

Beyond the parking lot is a patch of overgrown grass and fuzzy milkweed. Beyond that are dense woods, mostly pine trees but also some maple and birch too as well as a thick undergrowth of motley shrubs and ferns.

Victoria heads straight for the woods, doubling her pace, and I half run so I don't lose her. Here, what little sunlight there was to begin with is immediately snuffed out by the dark canopy of branches overhead. My Chuck Taylors squish and slosh on the muddy path. The air smells like dead leaves.

Something stirs in a shrub. Something *big*. I jump.

"*What was that?*" I shout-whisper to Victoria.

Just then Lucio steps out from behind the shrub. "Good, you're here."

"*Wah!* Lucio, you scared me. Why are you being all cloak-and-daggerish?"

"Because I didn't want anyone to see us. Sorry, didn't mean to scare you." He turns to Victoria. "Thank you for finding her. Where's Nolan?"

"I'll go back and retrieve him, dear. He was just finishing up a makeup algebra test, and I didn't think I should disturb him. I believe teachers—real teachers anyway—get annoyed about that sort of thing."

Victoria takes off her chunky black glasses and blows on the fogged-up lenses. Then she slips them back on and quietly disappears through a stand of trees.

Even as a pretend eighties rocker, she seems mysterious.

The rain intensifies. Lucio frowns up at the invisible sky.

"I think I passed a lean-to around here somewhere."

"A lean *what?*"

"A lean-to. People build them near hiking trails and campsites to keep themselves and their stuff out of bad weather. We're maybe fifty yards away from one of the trailheads for Ridge Mountain."

"And you know this how, Mr. I've-never-been-away-from-Mexico?"

"Nolan gave me a ton of maps. Street maps, hiking maps, geological survey maps. Plus I'm a quick study. Come on!"

He grabs my hand and leads me deeper into the woods. There's something comforting and familiar about Lucio's warm, strong hand grasping mine; he used to lead me around the jungles of Llevar la Luz this way. Of course, that was before things got confusing between us. *I* don't feel confused anymore, though. I wonder if he does?

After a few minutes he takes me off-trail to a small, scraggly wooden hut—or rather, *half* a small, scraggly wooden hut; it's completely open on one side. Twigs, pine needles, and leaves litter the makeshift roof.

"Ta-da! Lean-to," Lucio announces grandly. "After you."

"Allrighty."

I enter awkwardly, head bowed, and manage to trip on a mushroomy log.

"Ow!"

"Easy!"

There's very little room inside, which forces the two of us to stand close together. I comb my fingers through my puffy wet hair. "Sorry I'm such a mess."

"You're not a mess. You look—" Lucio stops and crosses his arms over his chest. "Yeah, so . . . um . . ."

Awkward, awkward, awkward.

"I have a lot to tell you," I say. "But you go first. Victoria said you had something urgent to share? By the way, how did you get down to Llevar la Luz and back so fast?"

"Aidan chartered a private jet. He needed a bunch of files, and besides, he was worried because we left the place in such a rush. He wanted to make sure it was totally locked up, that there hadn't been any attempted break-ins."

"Were there? Any attempted break-ins?"

"No." Lucio reaches inside his jacket pocket and extracts a large manila envelope. "*This* is the urgent thing I wanted to share with you. Nolan too when he gets here. I came across the contents in Aidan's lab. I don't think I was supposed to see them."

He opens the envelope and pulls out several black-and-white photographs.

"Brace yourself," he warns.

"Um, okay." I bite my lip nervously.

He hands me a photograph, then a second and a third and a fourth.

I blink and stare at each one. Then I begin to shake, and not because of the rain or the cold or my soaking-wet clothes and hair.

I clamp my hand over my mouth.

There's a dead girl in each photo—a *different* dead girl. All four girls appear to be lying on morgue tables, partially covered with white sheets.

"Who *are* they?" I whisper, horrified.

"I've been trying to figure that out. What's Aidan doing with these photographs? Obviously, he never shared them with me. And he has no idea I have them now."

"Oh my gosh! This is so—"

"I know, I know." Lucio wraps his arm around my shoulder, and I nestle closer. Dreadful thoughts are swirling around in my head.

What is my father doing with pictures of dead girls?

Outside the lean-to the rain continues to fall. I study the photos again, more carefully, one by one. The images are grainy and somewhat blurry, so it's hard to make out all the details.

When I get to the fourth one I do a double-take . . . and gasp.

"Lucio, I *know* her!"

CHAPTER 29
Nolan's Theory

W hat do you mean, you know her?" Lucio demands.

Speechless with shock, I gape at the girl lying on the morgue table. Dead girl number four. Her long black hair fans out across the steel surface, her pale skin is as translucent and lifeless as marble, and her brown eyes are wide with terror.

"I-I saw her last night," I stammer.

"You *saw* her?"

"Yes. In my vision . . . or maybe it was a dream, I don't know. She was wearing a white kimono. She said something to me . . . I think it was in Japanese? She showed me her wrist, and it had the same mark—the spider-web mark. Except hers got all twitchy and weird and morphed into a . . ."

"Morphed into a what?"

"A pentagram," I whisper.

"*What?*"

My gaze automatically drops to my right wrist. Nothing.

Lucio and I fall silent. I listen to the steady *spit-spit-spit* of the rain on the roof of the lean-to. What's happening? As with the spider-web mark, I *could* have dismissed the kimono girl before—as a hallucination, a nightmare, whatever. But now I absolutely can't. Because my father has a photograph of her.

I pull out my phone and shine the brightly-lit screen on the photo of the Japanese girl. For a second my screensaver is visible, and Lucio catches sight of it. It's a selfie Nolan and I took last fall when we went on a mystery-solving road trip to the university. He's about to start his car, and I'm leaning in with my phone while he's smiling happily at me. A rare beam of Washington sunlight falls across our faces, casting a golden glow.

I quickly slant the screen away. Lucio pretends not to have seen it and busies himself with the clasp of the manila envelope. I'm so lame. I really need to change that image, maybe replace it with that one of Oscar and Lex Luthor fighting over a chew toy. Or the one of me wearing my COME TO THE DORK SIDE T-shirt that Ashley gave me for my birthday last year.

Argh.

But back to the matter at hand. I squint at the photo of the Japanese girl and try to make out a mark on her wrist.

There's something there . . .

"She *might* have a mark. The photo is so grainy, though," I inform Lucio.

He holds up the other three photos. "They *all* are. Looks like they may have been scanned first, or rephotographed and scanned maybe, and then Aidan printed them off the computer? It's hard to tell."

I take the photos and try to illuminate them with my phone. "These other three girls may have marks on their wrists too. *Or* it's just dirt on the camera lens and we're on a wild goose chase or barking up the wrong tree or whatever the correct metaphor is. Do you have a magnifying glass?"

"Yeah, that's the sort of thing I carry with me all the time," Lucio jokes.

"*I've* got one."

Nolan dips his head and enters the lean-to, closing an umbrella behind him.

"Hi, guys. Victoria said I'd find you out here."

I'm so happy to see him and at the same time so not happy to see him. It would have been better if he showed up when Lucio and I weren't squished together inside a closet-sized space.

Lucio and I both step back to try to make more room.

"I assume something has happened?" Nolan asks, his gaze moving between the two of us.

For a second I think he's asking if something's happened between Lucio and me, and I blush furiously. Guilty conscience?

Fortunately Lucio doesn't make the same mistake.

"Yeah, something's happened. Check these out," Lucio says, handing Nolan the four photographs.

He sifts through them. "These are . . . they're very disturbing. Where did you get them?"

Lucio explains. When he's finished, Nolan reaches into his backpack and pulls out a magnifying glass along with a small penlight, poising them over the four photos.

"Look! On the right wrists of each one. Sunshine, hold your phone up a little higher."

I do so, and Lucio and I peer at the photos. Nolan shifts the magnifying glass and penlight from one photo to the next.

All four girls have a small pentagram mark on their wrists.

"So what does this mean? Who *are* they? And why do they all have the same mark?" Lucio says.

"And why does my father have these photos?" I add.

"We should ask him to explain. But I have a theory," Nolan volunteers.

"Really? Great, what's your theory?" I ask.

To my surprise Nolan puts a hand on my shoulder and stares into my eyes. His expression is meant to be reassuring, comforting, but I can tell he's trying to cover up something he feels inside.

Fear.

"Nolan, what is it? Hey, you're worrying me."

"I think these girls are luiseach. The four luiseach who died four years apart in those four places on the pentagram."

The Fifth Girl

The fifth girl is even more powerful than I imagined.

Yes, yes . . . the energy wave, the prophecy. But there's something else.

She can see me and sense me in my current incarnation, unlike anyone else, including her biological parents. Which is most unprecedented. I wanted to remain completely invisible, undetectable, so I can do what must be done with no interference from their faction, not even from my beloved.

But the girl has—how can I describe it?—an extraordinary inner radar. Empathy. She misses nothing and feels, intuits everything.

I must make adjustments so I can obscure my identity from her, at least some of the time.

There's one benefit to her having such a thin psychic membrane, however. I've been able to invade her dreams, manipulate them. Oh, how I enjoy her terror!

Although whenever I enter her psyche, others are there as well—warning her, trying to protect her. The little human-luiseach halfling, the one whose father soul terminated her after my dark servant Bezl possessed him.

The luiseach girl from Hokkaido. The luiseach girl from Queensland who actually sent her a tangible, Earthly warning in the form of a dead bird.

I thought my presence in her bedroom and taping shut the beak of the other bird, that taxidermy specimen, would scare her into silence and submission. Also the red vehicle—that telekinetic display was child's play. Also the spirit of that woman Kirsten: I accelerated her journey to darkness, ordered her to mark the girl, and she obeyed so beautifully. And the four Nemean lions and other dangers I have thrown her way.

But despite all this the girl is still determined. The only thing that gives her pause is her new knowledge that I have the capacity to terminate her. Especially if I am mindful of the clock.

Perhaps I need to rethink the plan.

Perhaps the prophecy can be fulfilled with a slight variation.

Perhaps she can be useful to me in another way.

Fortunately her new charity project continues to distract her. Empathy, indeed! I have also sent another little surprise.

Her pathetic father continues to run around in circles, thinking he can capture me with his absurd pseudoscientific device and his . . . what? Delusions of superior mental and physical acumen? He has no chance. The sooner he realizes this and gives up, the sooner I can lure him into my trap and terminate him.

And claim his mate for my own.

And avenge my firstborn son.

Deditio, *Aidan Adis Cadeyrn.*

Surrender.

CHAPTER 30

Spycraft

I can't reach Aidan. Of course. Again. It's funny (actually, it's not in the least bit funny) that he can be a helicopter parent-mentor when he wants, hovering and micromanaging and being a big, annoying bossypants, but he'll disappear off the face of Earth when he has other plans and priorities—especially with his military-grade, GPS-enabled phone protocol that he forced on all of us.

Fortunately Lucio is able to reach him—or he has access anyway. Aidan prearranged a time and place to meet up tonight (I saw the text: "*Danby Industrial Park, last warehouse on the main service road, 7 p.m., please be punctual*") so he can get the file folders he needed from Llevar la Luz. I asked Lucio what the folders contained—he said there were pages and pages of handwritten notes with lots of abbreviations and numbers. Nolan took a quick look, and not even he could decipher them.

The three of us are on our way to Danby Industrial Park now in Nolan's car. The rain stopped a while ago; now it's just damp and muggy outside—the air isn't warm exactly, but it's thick and oppressive like an unwanted layer of clothes against your skin. As we cruise down Main Street we pass the used bookstore, Spotless Sam's Dry Cleaners, and the Dream Bean Coffee Shop. Through the pleasant, glowy window of the café, I see people I know from school—talking, laughing, drinking tea, studying together. I feel a pang, like I wish I could be doing all that normal stuff right now instead of, say, driving to the middle of nowhere to confront my father—my weird, inscrutable, not-human father—about photos of dead girls.

Earlier I spoke to both guys about everything that's happened: my afternoon with Bastian, the arrival of the council, my conversation with Zalea, my conversation with Helena, and my dream-vision from last night. I left out some details, like about my necklace, because Helena did swear me to secrecy about that, although I really wish I could tell at least Nolan.

They were—are—beyond outraged about Helena's past relationship with Dubu. And Lucio got very stressed out by the mention of the council being in town. After all, one or more of its members may have participated in his parents' execution.

"Turn right at the next light," I instruct Nolan, pointing out the front passenger side window. "According to Granville Perry Swift, the industrial park should be about five miles down that road."

"Five-point-three miles exactly," Nolan says, glancing at the odometer.

"Who's Granville Perry Swift?" Lucio asks me.

"It's my new nickname for the GPS on my phone. He was a nineteenth-century gold miner, plus he was related to Daniel Boone. Like a nephew. Hey, it's awfully spycrafty of Aidan to want to meet up at an industrial park," I remark. Silence. "You know, *spycraft,* as in, stuff spies do. I learned that word from a movie. Mom and I watch a lot of spy thrillers on our pizza-and-movie nights."

"Your mom's really nice. You're lucky," Lucio says. He opens and closes his right hand, staring at the tattoo on the pointer finger that spells out his parents' names. Argi and Jairo. "I don't know a lot about my mom. I was only one when she and Papa were . . . when they died. I know she liked to ride horses and listen to opera and that turquoise was her favorite color. Her favorite gemstone too. She was a botanist who specialized in medicinal herbs. Papa was a scientist too—a microbiologist. He spoke five languages. He looked exactly like me, except taller and with a beard."

This is the most he's ever said about his parents. If we weren't in a moving car, I'd reach back and hug him immediately. Nolan probably would too.

"My grandfather died last year. I was closer to him than anyone in the world. I still miss him every day. I can't imagine how you must feel. I'm sorry," Nolan says.

Lucio nods and swipes at his eyes with the back of his hand. "Thanks, man."

We continue in silence. As we drive away from downtown the road becomes darker and more deserted. We pass an old, dilapidated gas station with a faded FOR SALE OR LEASE sign in front of it as well as a row of boarded-up houses. A rusted-out van lies on its side in the middle of what may have been a cornfield at one time.

As I stare out at the desolate landscape, I think about Lucio's parents. And Helena. I wish I could get her out of my head.

She makes me feel an impossible, inexplicable mixture of anger and confusion and need. But why *need?* That's the part I don't understand. I *have* a mother, the best mother in the world. So why should I need Helena, especially considering who she is and what she's done?

She had Lucio's mom and dad killed.

She tried to kill me multiple times.

She had an affair with a demon overlord who wants to destroy humanity and take over the universe.

Still, something about our conversation last night shifted something inside of me. I'm not sure what it is. But it's bothering me, niggling at my consciousness.

My thoughts drift again to the photographs; the manila envelope containing them sits on my lap. Death and more death. If Nolan is right—and he usually is—then what am I supposed to believe? The subjects of the photographs are four dead girls on morgue tables. Who are probably luiseach. Who look to be about my age. And who have marks on their right wrists, like me. Granted, theirs are pentagrams and mine is—was—a spiderweb pattern. But *still.*

Why does Aidan have these photographs? And why did he keep them a secret from the rest of us?

"There it is. Up ahead," Nolan says suddenly.

He clicks on his turn signal—not that there's anyone around to see it—and swings onto a narrow gravel road called Danby Industrial Park Drive. We've arrived. The park seems to consist of twenty or so flat, windowless warehouses and storage units surrounded by a saggy chain-link fence.

"He said it's the last one on the service road," Lucio pipes up. "Yup, there's his car. See?"

Aidan's silver SUV is parked next to a large warehouse with no sign that stands at the end of the road. His seems to be the only car in this entire place.

As Nolan parks next to the SUV I unstrap my seatbelt and pull out my phone. "I'm going to text him, let him know we're here."

"Why don't you hold off on that, since he's expecting me to be alone?" Lucio suggests. "Let me go in first with the folders he wants, then you guys come when I give the signal. I may be able to get some information out of him about the photos just one on one."

"I guess so. Okay." I put my phone back in my pocket. Even though Aidan is *my* dad, Lucio knows him way better than I do. In many ways Aidan is more Lucio's dad than mine.

Or is Lucio implying that Aidan may be inclined to confide in him about the four dead girls but not in me?

Lucio glances at his watch. "It's not seven yet, but I'm sure he won't mind. I know he really wanted these file folders."

He slides out of the car, tucks the folders under his arm, and strides toward the warehouse door. Nolan and I exit the car too and hover by the side of the building. I'm holding the manila envelope.

Lucio reaches the warehouse door, knocks, and opens it a crack. He pokes his head inside. "Aidan? Are you here? It's Lucio—"

A blood-curdling scream shatters the air.

CHAPTER 31
Smoke

There's another scream. Then another. And another. The screams are coming from inside the warehouse, and they sound like a man's.

My chest tightens. I can barely breathe.

Something horrible is happening to Aidan.

Is it Dubu?

Lucio drops the folders and charges through the door, shouldering it open. Nolan and I run after him—will we get to Aidan in time?

Inside the warehouse it's practically pitch black. No windows, no lights, and the temperature is frigid, like the air conditioning has gone totally haywire. The noxious smells of turpentine and soot mingle incongruously with the sweet fragrance of honeysuckle and butterscotch.

Another scream, except this time it's a girl screaming, not a man.

"Why are you doing this to me?" the girl's voice pleads. "I didn't *do* anything! You've made a mistake. You've got the wrong person. Please let me go!"

"One of you, call 9-1-1," Lucio whispers to Nolan and me.

"I'm on it," I whisper back, trying to stay calm and not freak out. Where's Aidan? Is he even alive?

As I reach for my phone a small circle of light blinks in the darkness. Someone's shining a flashlight on the girl's face.

She looks familiar. Long, dirty blond hair, high cheekbones streaked with soot. Designer clothes. Her eyes are squeezed shut as though in pain.

"*Please!*" she cries out. For a split-second the flashlight illuminates a metallic flash of purple in her mouth.

Purple braces?

Tiffany Ramirez? From school, from my English class, from the spring dance committee?

The flashlight shifts, and I can see that Tiffany is tied to a chair. Her wrists, legs, everything—she's bound not just with rope but also irons and chains.

"*Tiffany!*" I shout.

The flashlight beam wobbles and dips, and suddenly I can make out the identity of Tiffany's captor.

My father.

"Let her go!" I yell.

"Aidan, what are you doing?" Lucio shouts at the same time.

"Sir, this isn't a good idea," Nolan speaks up.

Aidan's head jerks in our direction. "Get out of here! All of you! *Now!*" he roars.

"Is that you, Sunshine?" Tiffany squeaks in a high, terrified voice. "I'm so glad you're here! Please, you have to do something! Call the police! This deranged person kidnapped me on my way home from school and—"

"Don't listen to her. She is not who she says she is," Aidan cuts in sharply.

He turns back to Tiffany and wraps his hands around her throat. She gasps and sputters and coughs.

"I'm asking you one more time. *When is it going to happen?*"

"We have to do something! He's lost his mind!" I whisper frantically to Nolan and Lucio.

"S-Sunshine, help meeeeeee!" Tiffany croaks.

Nolan turns to Lucio. "Is Aidan's behavior here consistent with what you've observed over the years at Llevar la Luz?"

"Nope, not in the least. I have no clue what's going down here. If this weren't Aidan, I'd tackle him and pin him to the ground while the two of you freed the girl . . ."

"But it's *not* Aidan. Or it's not the Aidan we know anyway. Something's really, really wrong," I insist.

Just then Aidan begins speaking to Tiffany in a foreign language. Latin? Greek? He repeats the words over and over, louder and louder, as if reciting a chant.

And then a horrifying thought flits through my brain. Is Aidan possessed? Can demons possess luiseach? I thought that wasn't possible, but lately all sorts of impossible things seem to be happening.

Do I need to perform an exorcism on my father?

Aidan's hands tighten around Tiffany's throat.

She laughs at him.

At first her laugh is a girly giggle, the same one I've heard come out of her mouth lots of times in school. Then the laugh slowly descends, deepens into a low, guttural rumble.

"When the five-pointed star is completed, the world will be washed in fire and be reborn as the kingdom of Dubu," Tiffany growls in a baritone voice—a man's voice. And then the voice switches back again to Tiffany's. "Hey, Sunshine! Do you have a date for the dance yet?" she trills.

Oh.

Now I get it. *Tiffany* has been possessed by a demon. Not Aidan. Why didn't I realize it sooner? That's why we thought a man was screaming before.

And why isn't Aidan exorcising the demon, like, immediately? It could kill Tiffany in a heartbeat. Not just *kill* her, but erase all traces of her permanently. Not even her parents will remember she ever existed . . .

Quickly and carefully I weave through the darkness to the middle of the room where Aidan holds Tiffany and her demon prisoner. I can hear Lucio and Nolan right behind me.

"Sunshine, I said, get *out!* You too, Lucio and Nolan!" Aidan yells.

"*No!* Why aren't you exorcising the demon? It'll destroy her!" I scream.

"This is not your business. Now, *go!*"

Lucio and Nolan step forward and flank me on the right and left.

"What's the plan here?" Lucio whispers nervously. Aidan continues to chant at the Tiffany demon.

"She's obviously in a state of possession. If Aidan won't perform an exorcism, I will."

"Are you sure that's what you want to do? We don't know what kind of demon it is," Nolan points out quickly.

"I know, but there's no other option. Lucio, help me. Like we did in Mexico."

"Anything you need."

Lucio weaves his fingers through mine and squeezes my hand, giving me strength. He's never exorcised a demon on his own. But he held my hand like this when I destroyed the fire demon in the village near Llevar la Luz and it worked—it was like he was passing double, triple, quadruple luiseach energy to me through his touch.

Feeling stronger, braver, I close my eyes and focus on the creature inside of Tiffany. At first I can't see it or even sense it. My vision sweeps through her organs—heart, liver, kidneys. Where *is* it?

And then I find it. It's a smoke demon. *Ugh.* No wonder I couldn't discern it right away. Aidan told me once during a training session that smoke demons are notoriously elusive, difficult to detect.

Aidan stops chanting. Clearly he's realized what I'm up to.

"Sunshine, I am ordering you to stop! I am not finished with it yet!"

"Don't listen to him, Sunshine! We're friends, aren't we? Practically *best* friends? You have to help me!" Tiffany pleads in her girly Tiffany voice.

I tune them both out and concentrate, really concentrate so I don't lose track of the demon. *There.* I latch on to it with my mind and follow its black, amorphous form seeping through Tiffany's body like a poisonous fog.

It reaches her trachea and begins filling it up. Then it travels to her right lung and begins filling that up too . . . and then her left lung . . .

The reddish pink lung tissue sags and dilates and starts to turn black.

Oh no. It plans to suffocate her from inside.

I've never dealt with a smoke demon before. *What should I do?* But I can't exactly take a break midexorcism and ask Nolan to look it up on the Internet: *How to Defeat Smoke Demons.*

Maybe it'll respond to a taunt?

Let her go. It's me you want to fight, not her. Or are you afraid of me?

In response Tiffany—or rather, the demon—begins to laugh its guttural laugh again. Is it my imagination, or do I feel short of breath? I gasp, trying to suck in oxygen, but it's like I've suddenly been transported to an impossibly high altitude.

Lucio squeezes my hand again. "You're okay. Breathe. You've got this."

I try to breathe. A little better, but still not enough. My connection to the demon is suffocating me somehow. I have to hurry and exorcise it. Otherwise . . .

I feel Dubu's necklace growing hot against my skin. Is it going to help me? But at the same moment a wave of energy hits me and makes me stumble backward. The demon? No, it's not the demon. Aidan is reaching out to me, murmuring an incantation—a *different* incantation.

But he's not trying to help me—he's trying to *block* the exorcism.

So now I'm battling the demon *and* Aidan.

Why is he so determined to keep the demon inside Tiffany?

Obviously he's lost his sanity. Or maybe a demon—another demon—possessed him after all?

I close my eyes again and concentrate harder, visualize the toxic smoke creature inside of Tiffany. I lock my mind on to it.

There. I have it. I focus harder, secure my hold on it. It groans and shrieks, trying to escape my mental hold. I search blindly for my luiseach knife—there it is, in my jeans pocket. I pull it out and will it to manifest.

I can feel Aidan trying desperately to stop me with the force of his mind, to pry the knife out of my grip. But he can't. The knife trembles in my hand and glows silver-blue for a split second, then flies up into the air and blinks into nothingness . . . and rematerializes as a hurricane-like gale of wind, whistling and screaming and slamming against the walls of the warehouse. It gusts at Tiffany and knocks her over along with the chair she's bound to. Its force is so powerful that Tiffany's hair stands on end while her skin ripples as though it might fly right off of her bones.

"*Sunshine!*"

I can't tell who's shouting my name. The wind continues to pummel Tiffany's body.

Let. Her. Go, I command the demon.

Just then a long plume of black smoke blows out of Tiffany's mouth and immediately dissipates in the wind. Gone. Vanished.

Seconds later the wind stops and everything's still. My knife blinks back into existence and clatters to the concrete floor.

I flop down next to it, exhausted, gasping for breath. Lucio's still holding my hand. Nolan kneels beside me and takes my other hand. I can feel the necklace growing cooler against my throat.

Footsteps. Aidan is standing over me, staring down. I brace myself and wait for the shouting, the rebukes, the rage at my disobedience.

But . . . *nothing*.

Instead, my father looks . . . defeated. Not just defeated. Stunned.

Was he not expecting me to best him?

CHAPTER 32

The Interrogation

Aidan drives me home in his silver SUV while Nolan and Lucio take Tiffany back to her house in Nolan's car.

"She will have no memory of this when she wakes up. I also made sure to use her mobile phone to text her mother earlier, saying she was at a friend's house and would not be home until late," Aidan informs me as he turns onto my street.

"*Why?*" I repeat for the millionth time. He has yet to explain why he wouldn't exorcise Tiffany—and not just that, but why he tried to block my efforts to do so.

Aidan parks the car in front of my house and cuts the engine. In the darkness I can make out a glimmer of light through the thick stand of pine trees. I picture Mom, Ashley, Oscar, and Lex Luthor inside, and I can hardly wait to be with them, put this horrible day behind me, nestle into my cozy life. As cozy as it can be, anyway, given the rest of it—the pentagram spell, Dubu, photographs of dead girls, smoke demons . . . *everything.*

Aidan drums his fingers against the wheel. He still won't answer my question—my questions.

"She could have died. Or worse. That demon could have destroyed her soul and erased any trace of her from people's memories. *For-e-ver*," I emphasize.

"Point taken. But she is fine. She will probably have an unpleasant headache for a few days, but that is it."

That's it?

"Okay, so I'll ask you again. Why?"

"Because." Aidan sighs and turns to me. "There is every sign that the darkness is not just growing but escalating—rapidly, exponentially. You know about the mall arson and the other violent occurrences in Ridgemont. The same thing is happening all around the world. There have been disturbing climatological and celestial changes as well. Temperature averages are dropping everywhere, quite dramatically . . . and the other night there was a rare lunar phenomenon—"

"The Gemini Moon," I cut in.

"How did you know about that?" he asks, surprised.

"I know a lot of things." *Your lineage . . . my lineage . . . Helena's affair with Dubu . . . Dubu's son Selarion . . . Dubu's personal vendetta against you . . . the First War . . . the Second War,* I say silently to myself. "But the stuff you're saying, it still doesn't explain why you did what you did—and didn't do—back there."

"Since arriving in Ridgemont, Helena, the council members, and I have been busy exorcising multiple demons. Yesterday I was about to exorcise a demon that had possessed an elderly man when he—the man, the demon—let slip a piece of information about Dubu. This gave me the idea to interrogate him. Unfortunately the man . . ."

Aidan stops.

"He *died?* The demon killed him before you could get your precious intelligence?"

"He did not die. He was about to go into cardiac arrest. I exorcised the demon immediately and rushed the man to the emergency room. He is recovering now."

"That's sick!"

"It was necessary, Sunshine. For the greater good."

"Now you sound like Helena!" I say angrily.

"Nevertheless. The information I got from the man led me to another demon. The one who had possessed your friend Tiffany. I was in the process of interrogating her when the three of you interrupted."

"We didn't . . ." I stop and hold up my hands. "Back up. I just thought of something. I saw Tiffany in school just hours ago, at the spring dance committee meeting and in English this morning. I saw her in school a bunch of times last week too. Why didn't I pick up that she was possessed?"

"I believe she was possessed very recently. Perhaps as recently as this morning. Did she act any differently when you saw her at school today?"

I scrunch up my nose trying to remember. "Yes, actually. Not in English, but at the spring dance committee meeting . . . she was nice to me, and she's usually kind of mean. But 'nice' isn't very demonic is it?"

"Actually it can be. Any change in behavior can be an indicator."

"Huh. *Really?*"

I try to take this all in. Demon possessions are on the rise here in Ridgemont and around the world. Tiffany was possessed by a demon.

If *she* was possessed, and I totally missed the signs, then who else might be possessed? Other kids at my school . . . teachers . . . neighbors . . . random people I pass on the street? Is anyone I know acting differently, not themselves? When Mom was possessed, it took me a while to figure out she wasn't just stressed or sick or having a nervous breakdown. Of course that was back when I was just beginning to learn about the paranormal world.

I'm supposed to be good at this stuff now after all my training in Mexico.

Am I losing my touch? Or are the demons becoming more clever and cunning? They're dangerous, deadly creatures, especially when they're in the guise of humans and can move freely through the community, wreaking havoc and destruction.

"Back to your question of *why*," Aidan goes on. "I had no intention of keeping Tiffany captive any longer than I had to. I planned to exorcise the demon as soon as I extracted some useful information out of it. But it turned out the demon knew much more than I had anticipated. In fact, it was about to tell me when the pentagram spell was going to be completed. An actual *date*."

I gulp. "T-there's an actual date when the spell's going to be completed?"

"It seems so."

"Does that mean . . ." Suddenly I feel cold. Not dark-spirits-cold but I-want-to-crawl-under-the-covers-and-never-get-up cold. I slink down in the passenger seat, trembling, and wrap my arms around myself. "Does that mean Dubu knows when I . . . when he's going to try again to kill me?"

If Aidan were any other dad, this would be the time for him to reassure me, tell me everything was going to be all right: *No, honeybunch, don't you worry. I promise to keep you safe!* I have no idea where I got the "honeybunch"—I think heard a TV dad calling his TV daughter that particular term of endearment. But it's Aidan, so no "honeybunch." He just sits there for a long, tense moment gazing out the window, then he steeples his hands under his chin.

"We don't know what Dubu intends. That is what I am trying to find out so I can stop him. This is why I had to conduct the interrogation on your friend."

"She's not my friend" is all I can manage to say.

And then I remember the photographs. The reason Nolan, Lucio, and I wanted to speak to Aidan to begin with. The manila envelope is on the floor of the car next to my backpack. I pick it up and pull them out.

"These," I say coldly.

He takes the photographs from me, and as soon as he sees the first one he sets them all down without looking at them.

"Where on Earth did you get these?"

"Lucio found them by accident when he went to Llevar la Luz to pick up your folders."

"Lucio had no right to—"

"This isn't about Lucio. Aidan, tell me the truth. Are these the other four luiseach who died four years apart? In Japan and Australia and those other places?"

He hesitates only for a second. "Yes."

So Nolan was right.

"Why do you have these?" I press on.

"I wanted to learn more about the girls' deaths. There were no autopsy records, no records whatsoever. So I have been doing some investigating, running tests."

Tests?

Alarm bells go off in my head. Tests are why I was born the way I was, why I triggered a massive energy wave that may or may not have doomed our race. "What *kind* of tests?"

"Chemical analyses of the exhumed remains of the victims. My notes were in the folders I asked Lucio to retrieve. I need to determine the cause of death in each case."

"Why?"

"So I can prevent it from happening to you."

When he says this I feel something give way inside. Aidan wants to protect me. He cares about me.

Or does he? Maybe he just wants to keep Dubu from killing me so the spell won't be unleashed. The greater good.

"Why didn't you tell me all this before?"

"I'm telling you now. There's a reason all four victims are as young as they are. They are—were—sixteen years of age at the time of death. Markons can kill luiseach, as I mentioned, but it's very difficult for them to do so. I believe these particular girls were targeted because luiseach are most vulnerable during the first year after they come into their powers."

"Luiseach are most vulnerable . . . *what?*" I practically shout.

"It's more than that," Aidan continues, ignoring my outburst. "I believe Dubu is working off an ancient demonic text called the *Book of Prophecy*. I've never come across it, although your mother—your *birth* mother, Helena—saw it briefly on one occasion. So we are certain of its existence, even though we don't know its exact contents, or at least not *all* its contents in their entirety. There have been stories and speculations."

I shake my head, trying to sort through this flood of new and awful information, trying not to have a complete psychotic, freak-out meltdown. I'm still trying to process the part about luiseach being most vulnerable between their sixteenth and seventeenth birthdays.

I do the math. Today is April 10. My birthday is August 14.

Which means I won't be turning seventeen for another four months and four days.

Which means there is a four-month, four-day window during which I'm a sitting duck, a bull's-eye target. Markon fodder.

"My current working theory is that your birth may have been foretold in the *Book of Prophecy*—and with your birth, an instruction for the forces of darkness to unleash a spell. The pentagram spell." Aidan sounds like he's describing an academic article he's writing versus, say, my life. My life that is now on a clock—actually, ticking time bomb may be a better metaphor. "According to my hypothesis, the pentagram spell calls for the death of five luiseach girls four years apart, starting in the year of your birth and during their most vulnerable year—their sixteenth year. Furthermore, these deaths are to fall on very specific coordinates around the world that make up a kind of pentagram. You see, the pentagram is very significant in demonic lore . . . very powerful . . ."

"Yes, demon lore. Yes, very powerful. But again, *why*?"

"Why what?"

"Why didn't you tell me all this before?"

"Because I didn't want to frighten you, make you lose your focus."

"Seriously? Maybe you haven't noticed, but my focus is pretty darned sharp these days. Better than yours," I add pointedly. "Or have you already forgotten? About a certain luiseach who exorcised a smoke demon even though you tried like heck to stop her?"

Aidan raises his eyebrows in surprise, and then he does something completely un-Aidan-like.

He laughs. I laugh too, although I start crying at the same time.

And then he does something even *more* un-Aidan-like.

He hugs me.

The Day of Reckoning

He almost learned of our plans from Diadrl.

Fortunately the girl gave in to her empathy and chose to destroy him in order to save the human named Tiffany.

Diadrl will be missed—he was one of my most devoted servants—but his loss is for the best, considering.

I have been doing exactly as the Book instructed: growing the darkness, ordering more and more servants to take over human bodies. Especially now that the Day of Reckoning is near.

But the Book did not anticipate the consequence: our servants, in the wrong hands, can be detrimental to our cause. They can be captured and interrogated, forced to give away valuable secrets.

And so I must be more careful—especially when it comes to the girl. My intention was to surround her with my servants, keep her close, keep her distracted. Perhaps also learn their *valuable secrets.*

However, I see now this approach comes with risk. Even if Aidan hadn't detected Diadrl's presence in the human named Tiffany, the girl would have figured it out soon enough. Her powers are growing daily, dramatically, whether she knows it or not.

Fortunately her powers are not enough—will never be enough—to detect the presence of my most valuable servant.

Also, there is one more human in her circle I intend to claim. I will simply have to take care not to disseminate crucial details to the servant I choose to do the deed.

Just for a short while longer now.

The Day of Reckoning is almost at hand.

The 119th Blood Moon of the Tertiary Cycle of the Second Millennium of the Reign of Dubu.

Or, as they say in the language of the lesser beings: April 15.

CHAPTER 33
Plan B

Another bad night of sleep. This is going to have to stop or pretty soon I'll turn nocturnal. Mom used to tease me about that when I was little: "Sunshine, you're going to turn nocturnal!" She told me that when I was a toddler I would wake up at 2 A.M. full of energy, pulling toys off the shelf, ready and revving to start my day. Between my nocturnalness and her insane hospital hours, the two of us were usually out of sync with the rest of the world and sometimes even with each other. She once joked she should have named me Starshine, not Sunshine.

I glance at my alarm clock: It's 5:10 A.M. Aidan has canceled our training for the third day in a row—he had another interrogation to perform—so I could snooze a bit if I wanted . . . if I could. But there's zero chance I'll be able to go back to sleep at this point. Ashley is conked out on her air mattress, snoring and sleep-talking, and I know Mom is at the hospital covering a colleague's shift. I pull on my robe over my Powerpuff Girls nightgown, grab my phone, and tiptoe out of the room, stepping over small, rumply piles of Ashley's outfits. Oscar and Lex Luthor follow, no doubt hoping for an extra-extra-early breakfast.

Downstairs it's eerily quiet. I snap on the kitchen light, feed the animals, and make myself an English muffin and a pot of strong coffee. I place my phone on the counter and set it to silent so it doesn't wake up Ashley.

After Oscar's done eating I open the back door and let him out to do his business. I pour myself some coffee into an *I Heart My Heart Health* mug (our house is full of free stuff Mom brings home from the hospital) and follow him into the backyard. The predawn sky is still inky black, although streaks of light are starting to appear on the horizon. The grass is dewy beneath my feet. The first birds of morning chirp invisibly in the trees.

I take a sip of coffee and breathe in the cool green morning air. Being out here like this, time feels infinite somehow. Suspended. Which is just fine with me because I'm not ready to face whatever the day holds. Aidan dumped a lot of heavy stuff on me last night. Like demon possessions are escalating all over the world. Like I'm definitely Dubu's target because I'm a luiseach girl, I'm sixteen, and I live in Ridgemont, the fifth point of the pentagram. Like there's an actual date when I'm supposed to die and unleash the spell. Like, like, like . . .

And there's all the stuff I learned from Helena and Zalea too.

Maybe I should run away to Llevar la Luz, lock myself in, and not come out until after my seventeenth birthday? Or ever? Maybe the world will be a safer place that way?

I shake my head and stare out at the sky. There's one last leftover star from the night, twinkling in the east, oblivious to the fact that its shift is done, that it's time for the sun to take over. Last year I *would* have tried to run away from all this. From Dubu.

From the spell. From demons and dark spirits. From Aidan. From Helena and her council. From my obligations as a luiseach.

But I guess that's not me anymore. At some point between then and now—closer to now—I stopped wanting to hide from my problems, from the world's problems. I need to confront this. I need to be all in.

I need to be the luiseach I was meant to be.

The question is: *How?*

Crunch. The dew beneath my feet has morphed into ice.

Puzzled, I take a step. *Crunch, crunch.* Come to think of it, the air has grown colder too.

I set my cup down on the ground and glance around warily—could it be demons?

No, not demons.

There are twelve light spirits wafting toward me through the pine trees, white and shimmering. A passenger train derailed on its way from Portland to Seattle. A couple on their honeymoon, four college students going to a sold-out rock concert at Safeco Field, a family of six visiting the grandparents.

I wonder why they didn't go to Aidan or Helena or Lucio—or the members of the council? Or Bastian, for that matter?

But no matter. They're here, they came to me, and it's my job to help them.

And yet . . . I hesitate for a second, waiting to see if they're just pretending to be light spirits. Will they turn dark as soon as I touch them, like the Kirsten spirit?

Don't be afraid.

The words bubble up inside me—not for them, but for me.

Don't be afraid. You're a luiseach. You have the strength and wisdom to handle whatever this is.

I nod to myself and extend my hand to the spirits.

Don't be afraid. Let me help you cross over to the other side, I tell them.

The spirits drift slowly, uncertainly toward me. And then I remember: I'm not just a luiseach. I'm a unique, special luiseach with unique, special skills. In Llevar la Luz I directed spirits to cross over on their own without my help. According to Aidan, I'm the only one who's ever been able to accomplish this.

If the world comes to an end soon because Dubu is triumphant, if there are no luiseach left on this planet, then at least I can leave this gift to the humans who remain. The ability to cross over on their own independently, without luiseach, and thus avoid an eternity of darkness trapped on the earthly plane.

Focus on the light. Do you see the light?

Aidan's Plan B for humanity. Another small, shining ray of hope.

Walk over to the light, not to me.

The spirits obey.

Yes, yes, keep going! You're so close to the light now.

And then it happens. One by one they pass into the radiance. So much peace. So much beauty. As they disappear they glance over their shoulders one last time and smile serenely at me.

A slight movement. I spot Anna sitting on a tree branch, hugging her stuffed toy owl, watching the spirits curiously.

"Anna!"

She turns slowly to gaze at me and gives a little wave.

"Where have you been? I've been looking all over for you! Your mom misses you, she's worried about you."

Anna kicks her heels against the tree.

"You know that you need to cross over. Soon. Maybe even immediately. Let me help you."

She shakes her head.

"Why not? It's been so long since . . . you know what can happen!"

Anna points to something behind me.

There are two dozen, three dozen spirits, even more. They're not just from the Northwest but from farther away, from all over—California, New Mexico, Texas, the Midwest, the East Coast, Florida.

I turn my attention to them.

No, not to me. To there. You can make the journey on your own. You can find peace.

The spirits obey and drift away, becoming one with the light.

New spirits keep showing up. They're coming from all around the world, drawn to the energy, the quiet miracle of whatever is happening here. For the next minute, the next hour, the next *six* hours—I can't tell—dozens, hundreds of spirits shimmer and billow and cross over on their own.

I laugh and begin to dance. It's working!

Joy. Everything is joy. I spin around on my bare toes, my nightgown flapping and fluttering like butterfly wings. Spirits flock toward me and I send them on their way—no, they send *themselves* on their way, drawing just the slightest breath of inspiration from my presence, but no more. I am becoming unnecessary to them, which is exactly as it should be. Soon light spirits everywhere will be able to move on by themselves.

If I survive—if the luiseach race survives—then we'll be able to do other good. Exorcise demons, destroy them, keep the balance in check. But *this* work, the work of moving on light spirits, will happen whether we're here or not.

Plan B. I can't wait to report this to Aidan.

"Sunshine?"

Anna rarely speaks to me, uses words, says my name.

"*Sunshine!* Look out!"

I was so lost in joy, love, and miracles that I didn't notice the other thing. A new spirit rips a jagged path through the shimmering veil of light souls and knocks me to the cold, icy ground.

What the—

In the distance I can hear Oscar barking. Where did he go, where is he? I try to stand up, but the *thing,* the strange new spirit, knocks me to the ground again, so hard I feel as though my spine has been paralyzed.

And then it dawns on me—*oh my gosh,* this is a wind demon. Aidan told me about them in Mexico. How ironic—or actually not—that my luiseach knife manifested into a fierce wind last night in order to defeat the smoke demon inside Tiffany. Now the same weapon has been turned against me by the dark forces . . .

My luiseach knife. I reach for it, but it's not there. *Argh,* it's under my pillow, which is where I always keep it while I'm sleeping. How can I defeat this thing without it? I realize too that I left Helena's necklace on my nightstand. I know she told me never to take it off, but it was bothering me in the middle of the night.

"*Anna!*" I shout. But the tree branch is vacant. I don't see her anywhere. Where did she go?

The wind demon swirls around me, gathering momentum, and begins to lift me into the air. What is it doing? And then I know. It's going to catapult me against the tree, over and over again, until every bone in my body is shattered to smithereens . . .

No.

I clench my fists and focus my mental energy on resisting the wind. I make myself strong, heavy. Heavy as lead. I am cemented to the ground. I am immoveable.

It works. The wind demon comes back, battering, shrieking, screaming. All around me the trees, grass, the chain-link fence, everything is flattened, bent practically in half by the maelstrom.

But not me. My body has become something else—a boulder, a monolith—and the wind can't touch me.

Seconds pass. Minutes. Eventually I hear the wind die down and all is quiet again.

I've defeated it.

I sit up slowly, making sure it's truly gone. I spot Oscar cowering under the back porch, whimpering.

"It's okay, boy! I'm sorry you had to experience that. *Bad demons!* Come on, let's go inside and get you some treats . . ."

That's when I notice the face in the kitchen window, staring out at me.

The man in black.

Dubu.

CHAPTER 34

The Return of the Man in Black

No, no, no.

Dubu is in my house.

He watches me from the kitchen window, his lips curled up in a half-smile. But his eyes aren't smiling at all—they're black, hard, full of rage.

And then I remember Ashley's upstairs asleep.

I scramble to my feet and make a mad dash toward the kitchen door. "Stay away from her!"

But there's no one in the window.

Where did he go?

I reach the door and open it slowly. My heart is knocking against my chest so hard that it feels like it'll jump right out. I survey the kitchen. Everything's the same as before. The half-filled coffee pot making little gurgly noises. The dirty dishes in the sink. My half-eaten English muffin on the counter. But there *is* something different—a faint, buzzy energy in the room. Is that the Markon energy signature Aidan's always talking about? The thing that his weird silver Renaissance device detects? How is it possible I can detect it *without* the device?

Footsteps creak on the stairs.

It must be him. He's heading up to the second floor. I look around wildly and grab a kitchen knife out of the wooden knife block. It's not my luiseach knife, not even close, but it's the only weapon that's readily available.

On the counter next to the knife block is my phone. Yes! I pick it up and text Aidan quickly:

Dubu in house.

He texts back immediately:

On my way get out of there NOW.

But I can't. I'm not about to leave Ashley alone with Dubu. I'll just have to keep my fingers crossed that Aidan will be here soon.

I silence my phone and tuck it into my robe pocket, then I clutch the kitchen knife and tiptoe cautiously toward the stairs. Once I reach the landing I glance up. No Dubu. What should I do? Should I yell up to Ashley and warn her? But even if she were awake, there's no way she could defend herself against a Markon.

Not that I'm in a much better position to do so, especially with a lame kitchen knife. But I have to try, at least until the cavalry arrives.

A door opens and closes.

My heart practically stops.

Is he in my room? With Ashley?

The heck with caution . . . I hurry up the steps, taking them two at a time.

My bedroom door is closed. Lex Luthor sits there, blinking up at me.

"Lex, get out of the way," I whisper.

In response Lex Luthor begins to levitate in the air. His green eyes gleam as he extends his claws at me, hissing and growling.

"Lex, *no!* It's *me!*"

He flies through the air at my face. I duck just in time.

And then I gather some momentum, leap to the door, and throw my body against it.

No Dubu. My room is the same as I left it. Ashley's fast asleep on her air mattress, her face turned toward the wall.

The buzzy energy I felt earlier is gone.

Something touches my ankles.

Startled, I glance down. Lex Luthor is rubbing up against me and purring.

"Lex?"

He meows and paws the carpet, which is his way of saying he wants more food. Is he back to normal? What did Dubu *do* to him? I'm afraid to reach down and pet him.

Just then I hear a strange moaning sound. It's coming from the air mattress. *Ashley!*

I hurry to her side. She's struggling to sit up.

"Ash?"

She stares at me with terrified eyes and points to her mouth. It's covered with black tape.

Her Power Is Beyond
What I Imagined

I tested the girl with one of the strongest weapons in my arsenal.

She handily fended off Serepan, the wind demon, and without the use of her own weapon.

Her power is beyond what I imagined. Soon her abilities will surpass those of her biological father and mother—perhaps even her ancestors, the Original Ones.

I must rethink everything.

At least the halfling is out of the picture. She is in my possession now, scooped up as easily as a tadpole out of a pond, and she is awaiting her fate in one of my underground prisons.

What an annoyance she has been. An enigma too, and I do not care for enigmas. By all accounts, she should be one of us already. Her spirit has been lingering on this Earth for more than a year. Why hasn't she turned dark by now?

Does it have something to do with the fact that she is half luiseach? Are half-luiseach spirits able to linger here on Earth in their light states indefinitely or at least for longer than their human counterparts?

For that matter, what happens to luiseach spirits when they leave the earthly plane? The Japanese girl and the Australian girl are still here. The ones from Russia and Rapa Nui seem to have vanished entirely—but to where? And the other luiseach who have passed on, the memorable ones, anyway . . . where did they go? I have not seen them or heard them or even sensed their altered existence in this or any other realm, not for many centuries. Like the Original Ones. Like Laoise, their eldest daughter, who ruled the luiseach until the beginning of the Renaissance. Like Laisren, Laoise's eldest son and Aidan's father.

Like I said, I do not care for enigmas.

Halflings of all kinds do seem to have unique abilities. My two children, for example—or rather, my child, my sole remaining child, as the other was lost to the Great Darkness. His own rather spectacular halfling abilities could not help him when Aidan terminated him during a so-called exorcism. I know Aidan justified his action, claiming he simply wanted to save the life of an innocent woman and her unborn child, that he'd had no knowledge of the identity of the demon inside her. But I have never believed that. Clearly he had vengeance on his mind, given what he'd learned about his mate the day before.

The Book of Prophecy did not prophesize this. If it had, I might have saved my son from this terrible fate.

It did, however, prophesize the coming of Aidan's child. A luiseach like no other whose birth would pave the way for our own renaissance.

But the little halfling called Anna, she has interfered one too many times. And I do not want her interfering on the day the spell shall finally be completed. The Day of Reckoning.

Perhaps I can hasten her journey to darkness somehow as I did with the Kirsten spirit?

CHAPTER 35
Carpe Diem

"Is everything okay with your friend Ashley?" Bastian asks me.

It's Wednesday after school, and we're in Room 236 for one of the last spring dance committee meetings. The dance is in three days. Bastian and I are at a corner table finishing up the rose decorations. I was getting pretty sick of making them—the same crepe-paper flowers *over* and *over* and *over* again—but today I'm grateful to have something boring and repetitive to do with my hands so I can concentrate on my zillion and one problems and how to solve them.

"Ashley?" I say to Bastian, casually, like I don't know what he's talking about. "What do you mean?"

Bastian blushes and drops his gaze to the floor. His hair falls across his eyes, and it occurs to me he must have gotten a haircut—it's less bowl cut and more preppy, collegiate.

"She hasn't been in school all week. I, um, took the liberty of telephoning her yesterday to see if she was all right. She said it wasn't a good time and hung up. I believe she may have been crying?"

Ashley gave Bastian her telephone number? I'll have to remind her about the no-dating-Bastian rule. When she's better and not in nonstop panic-attack mode 24/7.

"Oh, that. Yeah, um . . . she got some bad news from home," I improvise quickly. "From her family in Austin. She's been pretty upset."

"I hope everything is all right?"

"She'll be okay. She just needs a little time."

"Right. Of course."

I busy myself unraveling a pipe cleaner knot. The thing is, I have no idea if Ashley will be okay. She pretty much hasn't stopped crying since what happened Monday morning. She doesn't remember much—just that she had a nightmare about a "scary killer monster" and woke up gasping for air and totally freaked out because her mouth was covered with black duct tape.

By then Aidan had arrived—practically knocked the front door down as he charged into the house, ready to defend me against Dubu. But Dubu was long gone. All that remained was a scared-out-of-her-mind Ashley. Plus Lex Luthor, who *seemed* to have recovered from his levitation ordeal. (Which, as far as I can tell, I didn't hallucinate, although I haven't let him sleep in my room since then. Trust issues.) Aidan swept the house with his silver device and told me he'd changed his mind: he wanted me to leave for Llevar la Luz immediately and lay low for a while. I refused. We had a big argument, typical father-daughter stuff, but he could see that I'd made up my mind to stay in Ridgemont and not run away from Dubu, from any of this.

I came really close to telling him about Bastian.

But not yet. First I have to make sure he and Helena aren't going to go all Dr. Frankenstein on the poor guy.

I came really close to asking Aidan about his "burden" too. And repeating what Zalea had said about me being able to end the war quickly. *Me.*

But I didn't because it's possible—probable even—that whatever Zalea is talking about is highly dangerous, which means there's a good chance Aidan won't let me get involved. Because, overprotective.

Of course there's a chance *I* won't let me get involved either. Or Nolan, my protector. Because, also overprotective, in his own way.

"So, Bastian, how are you doing?" I ask him. I lower my voice and add, "Have you had any more, you know, *experiences?*"

Tiffany is yelling across the room at some volunteers—who decided to use this ugly font on the new posters and why hasn't anyone called the rental place about the disco ball and does she have to do everything herself? Whew, she's back to her old self. It's so weird she's so *not* nice in real life and super-nice when possessed by a demon. I always thought possessed humans were nasty and dangerous or, at the very least, super-creepy.

Bastian is beaming and whispers, "Yes, I had another experience. Last night. I was in my room studying when everything grew very cold and an elderly woman appeared. She had just died in the hospital of a brain disorder. An aneurism perhaps. I was frightened at first, but I tried to remember what you said. I tried to remember what I did with that other ghost too . . . the drowning victim, Tomas . . . how I helped him disappear."

"Cross over."

"Yes, cross over. I closed my eyes and sent the old woman kind feelings. Compassion. She touched my shoulder, and when I opened my eyes she was gone."

"Bastian, that's *great!*"

"Is it?" He blushes again.

"It's fantastic!"

"My father almost walked in on me during the crossing-over procedure. But it was fine!" Bastian says quickly when he sees my reaction. "I explained that I was rehearsing for a drama audition, a school play."

"Oh whew. Good one! Way to think on your feet!"

"Yes, it was fortunate. If he and Mother found out . . ." Bastian stops and shakes his head grimly.

"So you haven't said anything to anyone? About being a lui-seach, I mean?"

"No, absolutely not! This is absolutely our secret: I cannot risk the possibility of—"

"*You guys!*"

I glance up, startled, to see Ashley coming across the room toward us. She looks gorgeous and super put-together in a pale-pink dress, matching wedge shoes, and just enough makeup to make it look like she's not wearing makeup, that she's just naturally and effortlessly beautiful. Which she is. Her long hair is swept up neatly in a high ponytail and adorned with a single sparkly barrette.

Before I left for school this morning she was curled up in a fetal position on her air mattress, in her PJs, weeping softly while Mom tried to convince her to eat something, anything.

So, big contrast. I'm really relieved she's better.

When she gets to our table she gives me a long hug and then

she gives Bastian a long hug too. His face turns several shades redder.

"I am *soooo* glad to see you both!" Ashley gushes.

"Hey Ash. I thought you were staying home with Mom today? Are you sure you're okay to be here?"

"I'm better than okay! In fact, I had an epi-phony. Is that how you pronounce it? I realized I can't just hide in my room—well, *your* room—crying my eyes out because the world is a scary place. So here I am! In fact, I had *the* best idea. Sunny-G, why don't the four of us go to the dance together this Saturday? The three of us and your cute genius boyfriend. You and I can go shopping for dresses at the mall, the guys can wear matching tuxes . . ."

"I-I had not planned on going," Bastian says, squirming uncomfortably. "I do not dance."

"Well, now you're going! I'll teach you! It's going to be a blast! Sun, what's that Spanish phrase about seizing the day? It sounds like a kind of fish. Carp something?"

"Latin. *Carpe diem.*"

"Yes, that! We all need to *carpe diem*. Sunshine and I aren't taking 'no' for an answer!"

What has gotten into Ashley?

Bastian gazes at me helplessly. Maybe this is where I should jump in and rescue him. He seriously looks as though he'd rather jump off a cliff than go to a high school dance. Besides, I'm the one who didn't want him getting all datey with Ashley and losing his luiseach focus.

However, Ashley seems pretty excited about this—actually, ten cups of espresso in her system excited—so maybe I should back her up? It's better than watching her sobbing nonstop because her life just turned into an R-rated horror movie. Besides, it doesn't sound like a romantic double date as much as four friends hanging out at a dance together.

Nolan and I are going as just friends technically speaking, so why not two more just friends?

"You could just go and not dance?" I say feebly to Bastian.

"What is the point of going to a dance if you're not going to dance?" he counters.

"Stretch limo!" Ashley bursts out. "Is there a place to rent stretch limousines in Ridgemont? I'm thinking one of the ones with the sparkly neon lights and high-tech sound system. And a moon roof! Or a sun roof—is there a difference? Oh, and those free bottles of water and packs of M&M's—"

Just then Tiffany marches up to our table. She has a large piece of yellow poster board tucked under one arm.

"I need your opinions, people. Well, I need *your* opinion, Ashley, as you're the only one in this little group with any style or taste."

Yup. Back to her old self.

"This is the new poster design. Is this too plain? Should we add some artwork? And if so, what kind? Photos? Illustrations? The font's going, by the way, obvi, because it looks like little pieces of cat throw-up."

Tiffany holds up the poster for us to see.

SPRING FLING!
Ridgemont High School Gym
This Saturday, April 15 at 7 P.M.
Live Music by Angry Jell-O
Refreshments, prizes, fun!
Updates at Ridgemontspringfling.com and
@ridgemontspringfling

Ashley leans back and taps her finger against her chin as she scrutinizes the poster.

"Hmm. Maybe a photo from the band's website here? And a few pink and green roses to match our decorations here and here?" she suggests, pointing. "Oh, and this isn't poster related, but we should get an audio clip from the band and put it on our website! Plus do a Twitter blast!"

Tiffany claps. "Brilliant!"

Bastian is staring at the poster.

"So what do you think?" I ask him. He takes off his glasses, rubs the bridge of his nose, and blinks. "Bastian? No one's going to make you go, if you really don't want to."

"Yes." He puts his glasses back on. "I just remembered, I actually have a family obligation that night. But I hate to deny Ashley her request. So I believe I can do both. As long as I don't have to dance."

"No worries. I'm a horrible dancer too. We can stand on the sidelines together and watch all the beautiful people gyrating and head bobbing," I joke.

"All right then."

Bastian nods to himself and turns away.

But before he does I swear I catch a glimmer of a smile.

What's *that* about?

CHAPTER 36

Guera Spirito

Later that night Nolan and I meet at Ridgemont Pizza. It's not a date, exactly, obviously, although of course there's always an overlay of datey whenever I'm around him. Mostly he just wanted to get together so we could catch up on everything that's been happening. I love this restaurant, which mysteriously—because Ridgemont is a tiny, middle-of-nowhere town—has better pizza than back in sophisticated, big-city Austin.

Also the air always smells yummy here, like garlic, oregano, and tomato sauce. And they have a sweet old tabby cat, Mr. Mike, who wanders around and greets the customers.

"How are you?" Nolan asks. His brown eyes are sweet and tender as they take in my no doubt exhausted-looking face, my Goodwill outfit (ruffly blouse with extra-long sleeves and peasant skirt), and my frizzball that is semitamed-but-not-really under my crocheted hat.

"Mostly okay. Sometimes confused. Sometimes freaked out. But mostly okay."

Nolan slides his hand across the table and squeezes mine briefly. I smile at him, and he smiles back. Then he pulls away and busies himself with his extra-cheese slice, neatly cutting off the crust with a plastic fork.

"How's Ashley doing?" he asks.

"Strangely better," I reply.

"Why strangely?"

I glance around the crowded restaurant to make sure no one's listening. We're sitting in a semisecluded corner next to a big window that overlooks the parking lot and Ridge Mountain beyond. At the only table within apparent hearing distance six burly guys wearing Washington State College letter jackets are competing to see who can cram the most fried mozzarella sticks into their mouths. With all the yelling and laughing and snorting, we probably don't need to worry about eavesdroppers there.

Still, I lower my voice and lean across the table toward Nolan. We bend our heads together. His hair falls across his eyes, and I want to reach over and push it back, but I don't.

Nolan's just-friends-until-I'm-out-of-danger policy. Sometimes it's easier for me to follow than others. Sometimes it's darned near impossible.

"Ash was a complete wreck after what happened the other morning. She wouldn't even get out of bed, she was so terrified. Then a couple of hours ago she showed up to the spring dance committee meeting at school all . . ." I take a bite of my pepperoni slice and chew thoughtfully. "Dressed up and super-cheerful and carpe diem about everything."

"'*Carpe diem*,' as in the Latin phrase? Seize the day?"

"Yup. And one of her carpe diem ideas was for you, me, her, and Bastian to all go to the spring dance together on Saturday."

"Seriously?" Nolan grins in amusement. "Ashley and Bastian? I thought she liked Lucio. That's the impression I got anyway. Not that I can always tell about those things. Actually I can *never* tell about those things so don't listen to me."

"She *does* like Lucio. Did. I don't know. In any case she's kind of taken Bastian under her wing. Or something. I told her before I didn't want him to be distracted by a relationship, so hands off and stick to friendship, and she seemed to understand. I'm not sure, though."

Nolan chuckles. "Wow, Sunshine. You're sounding like your dad."

"Excuse me?"

"Aidan doesn't want you distracted by a relationship either. Ergo the spell."

"Huh. You're right. Hmm, maybe I should cast the same spell on Bastian?"

"I'm sure he'd love that. Speaking for myself, I'm counting the days until Aidan banishes the spell he put on you," he adds softly.

I blush. "Me too. Days, hours, minutes, seconds, milliseconds . . . and whatever is tinier than milliseconds."

"That would be a microsecond, which is a millionth of a second, and then a nanosecond, which is a billionth of a second."

"Yup. Those."

We lapse into silence. Of course I don't remind Nolan *he's* the one who insisted the spell stay in place until Dubu is out of the picture. But I understand—or I'm trying to understand—that Nolan just wants me to be safe. He's my protector; that's his job. I know he wants to hold me and kiss me as bad as I want to hold him and kiss him. To be a real couple.

"Soon," Nolan says, reading my thoughts as always. "Speaking of . . . what's the current plan? What if the war happens even if the pentagram *isn't* completed? What are Aidan, Helena, and the council doing to prepare?"

I think this is Nolan's way of refusing to acknowledge to himself or to me that the pentagram *could* be completed.

Because that would mean . . .

"I know they're trying to raise some sort of army, trying to mobilize all the luiseach on the planet," I explain.

"How many is that?"

"Helena said around sixty thousand?"

"That's impressive. I had no idea there were so many luiseach out there. So are Helena and the council trying to get all these luiseach here before . . ." Nolan hesitates.

"Yes. Fingers crossed that by . . . *whenever,* there will be a big, scary luiseach army right here in Ridgemont, Washington, ready to defend."

"Good." Nolan nods.

Then he pulls his notebook out of his backpack, splays it open, and hands it to me. "Lucio and I have made some progress. And I've also written down all the stuff you told me. Take a look."

I sip my ginger ale, take the notebook from him, and start reading:

It's possible that the luiseach girl who died in Hokkaido, Japan, came to Sunshine in a dream or vision in order to warn her. (In the dream/vision the girl, who was wearing a kimono, had a spider-web mark on her wrist that mysteriously morphed into a pentagram mark.) The girl who died in Queensland, Australia, also came to Sunshine—not in a dream or vision but in real life, in the form of a bird that is indigenous to that area. Of course, this is all speculation; we don't know for sure.

*Lucio and I have not managed to find any references to pentagram spells or, more importantly, how to reverse or stop them. This is a very high-priority item, however, so we will continue researching it.

*Violent crimes are increasing not only in Ridgemont but nationally and internationally as well. Earlier Helena mentioned that such a spike in violent crimes also happened before the deaths of those four luiseach girls.

*A mysterious climatological change has been occurring as well. In the past few months a sort of "global un-warming" has been taking place, with temperatures falling to below-record levels across the world.

*Also, the Gemini Moon.

*Also, the sun has been setting earlier and earlier each day rather than the other way around. (It is now April, and this should not start happening until the summer solstice on June 15.)

*Lucio and I finally came across some references to Markons during our research. Markons have been called other things in other cultures throughout history: Balor, Fan Wujiu, Popobawa, and the Generals, for example. Apparently they are extremely *difficult to kill; the only way may be a highly dangerous ritual called "guera spirito."*

I glance up from the notebook and stare in amazement at Nolan. "*Guera spirito?* Good golly, what's that?"

"The phrase 'guera spirito' was mentioned briefly in an essay written by a thirteenth-century monk and historian living in Venice, which back then was not a city in the country of Italy but a city in the Republic of Venice. The subject of his essay was a painting that at the time was hanging in his monastery. Lucio and I had to translate the text from Venetian, which we thought at first was a dialect of Italian. But Venetian is actually its own language, so it took a while.

"Unfortunately the monk-historian didn't go into the details about the ritual," Nolan continues. "The essay was mostly about the painting, which was by an unknown painter. Some have theorized he was an ancestor of Michelangelo. Anyway, the monk wrote that the painting depicts two celestial figures, maybe angels, maybe some other entities, using guera spirito to destroy the indestructible super-demons, which he referred to as 'il demoni potente.'" He adds, "Lucio and I did manage to translate the phrase from Venetian to English, though. It means 'spirit war.'"

"Spirit war," I repeat. "Can you and Lucio try to find out more about it?"

"Yes, of course. Lucio is at the library right now. I'm meeting him over there after I drive you home."

Our server comes by and hovers over our table. "Can I get you guys a refill on your drinks?" she says cheerfully.

"Yes, please . . . *Rebecca*," Nolan says, peering at her nametag. "Coke for me. Sunshine?"

"Yes, more ginger ale, please."

While Rebecca is busy with our drinks, I turn my attention back to Nolan's notebook.

"Is that a new necklace?" Nolan asks suddenly.

"Hmm?" I glance up from the notebook.

Nolan points to my neck. "It's unusual. What's that symbol on it? Is it a hieroglyph?"

Oops.

Somehow I absent-mindedly pulled Helena's—*Dubu's*—necklace out from beneath my blouse and started twirling it around my fingers.

"No! I mean, yes! I mean, um, I found it in my jewelry box the other day."

Nolan cocks his head and frowns. He can always tell when I'm lying.

"You don't have to make up some story. Did Lucio give it to you? Because if he did, it's fine. I mean not fine exactly, but . . . what I mean is, I know you two are close. Platonically speaking, that is. I mean . . ." Nolan stops and looks away. I've never seen him like this, so awkward and agitated and fumbling around for words—that's *my* thing.

"No! I mean yes we *are* close, platonically speaking. But no, Lucio absolutely didn't give it to me," I assure him.

"Look, Sunshine, I don't want to act like the jealous boyfriend about this. I'm not the jealous type. Well, I wasn't before I met you because I didn't have anyone I . . . anyway, I trust you, and I know things have been a little weird and not normal between us because of Aidan's spell and Dubu and this whole end-of-the-world thing, and—"

"Helena gave it to me," I blurt out.

"Wait, what? Helena, your biological mother who tried to kill you? Or a different Helena?"

"The former. She said it would give me an extra level of protection against demons—and Dubu."

"Oh. *Oh!*" Nolan knits his brows. "So . . . Helena is actually trying to keep you safe? Above and beyond being one of your luiseach bodyguards? I want to say 'that's so nice of her,' but that doesn't seem like the right sentiment somehow. I mean Helena—"

"I know, I know," I agree. "So far the necklace kind of seems to be working. I think? I can feel it grow hot against my skin when it's about to amp up my demon-fighting powers and then cool down after it's over."

"Wow." Nolan looks impressed. "So what does that symbol on it mean? 'Hero' or 'strength' or 'bravery' or something similar? Is it proto-Celtic?"

"I'm not sure actually." Which is the truth.

I hope and pray that it doesn't mean "Dubu."

I hate hate hate having to lie to Nolan. Not that I lied exactly. I just omitted the part about how the necklace actually belongs—belonged—to Dubu. Also the interesting factoid that if Dubu perishes, his necklace will perish too.

Our server, Rebecca, returns with more drinks. Mr. Mike wanders over to our table and rubs up against our legs, purring. Nolan and I continue eating our pizza and shift the topic from demons and darkness to the spring dance: who's picking up whom and when, what we're all wearing, what the dance will be like. Neither of us has ever been to a school dance, so it's kind of a big deal for both of us.

As we talk, though, I can't seem to be in the here-and-now

and enjoy our not-datey date. My thoughts keep returning to this guera spirito thing.

Is *that* what Aidan plans to use in order to try to eliminate Dubu?

What exactly is it?

Just then I feel a familiar warmth against my neck. Helena's necklace is kicking into gear. My senses on alert, I glance around the restaurant, trying to detect the presence of a demon or dark spirit.

Nothing. No one.

The necklace subsides to cool. It must have been a false alarm.

CHAPTER 37
May Day

Nolan drops me off before heading off to the library to meet Lucio. He waits at the curb to make sure I get inside, then he honks and takes off.

"Mom? Ashley? I'm *hoooome!*" I call out. Lex Luthor prances up to me and sniffs at my ankles curiously, no doubt detecting Mr. Mike's scent. Oscar jumps up to be petted, and I oblige, mentally reminding myself to give him a bath and doggie shampoo soon—he's about a year overdue.

All of a sudden Aidan appears in the hallway.

"Aidan, you scared me!"

"My apologies."

The expression on his face is somber—more somber than usual, that is.

My heart plummets.

"Aidan, what *is* it? Did something happen to Mom? Where is she? Where's Ashley?" I cry out.

"Your mother and Ashley are fine. Ashley is upstairs. She complained of a headache and went to bed early. Your mother got called to the hospital a few minutes ago. She just left, in fact. There was another . . . violent incident. This time at a restaurant. Someone with a baseball bat."

"Oh, no! Were there any . . ."

"About a dozen injuries, including six college students."

"Who were they?"

"The police have not released their names yet, but they were apparently from Washington State College."

Washington State College.

Six burly guys in letter jackets scarfing down fried mozzarella sticks.

"Aidan? Which restaurant was it?" I ask slowly.

"It was Ridgemont Pizza. Xerxes is at the scene now, taking care of the . . . exorcism."

My stomach twists, and a cold, clammy sensation sweeps over me.

"Sunshine, what is wrong?"

"Nolan and I just left Ridgemont Pizza, like, fifteen, twenty minutes ago. We had dinner there."

"*What?*" Aidan's face turns deathly pale. "You must have just missed the . . . dear God, Sunshine, are you all right?"

"Yes, I'm fine. Who was the attacker?"

"One of the servers. A young college student named Rebecca Packer."

Rebecca, our server.

With a trembling hand I reach up and touch Helena's necklace, which is hidden under my blouse. No wonder it grew warm at the restaurant. Did it protect me against the demon inside Rebecca?

Voices. All of a sudden I realize there are people in the living room, talking quietly.

"Who's here?"

"The council. Or the council minus Xerxes anyway. We have news."

"*More* news?"

"Yes. But this news is more . . . well, shall we say, constructive."

Aidan takes my arm and leads me into the living room.

Helena, Giovanni, Mikhail, Aura, and Zalea are seated on the couch and in various chairs. When Aidan and I enter the room they stop talking abruptly and look up at us with serious expressions. Except Zalea, who smiles and gives me a small wave.

"We have uncovered a date," one of the men speaks up . . . Mikhail, the one who zapped me before—Zalea called it a "soul assessment."

"A date . . . for what?" I ask.

"A date when Dubu expects to complete the pentagram spell," Aidan explains. "Earlier today Mikhail and I captured a possessed human and interrogated it. It turned out to be one of Dubu's highest-level servants."

I set my backpack on the floor, trying to wrap my brain around this. "But . . . how did you know it was one of his highest-level servants?"

"Because it knew things about Dubu that only someone very close to him could possibly know," Mikhail replies. "In any case, it revealed the date to us under . . . extreme duress."

"'Extreme duress.' Is that a euphemism for torture?" I ask, not really wanting to know the answer.

"Aidan and Mikhail did what had to be done," Giovanni pipes up, running a hand through his short blue hair. "Anyway we now have a date. *The* date. It's the first day in the month of May, in accordance with the Gregorian calendar. And logic tells us this information is correct."

I run through the dates in my mind. Today is Wednesday, April 12. May first is . . . eighteen, no, nineteen days away. "Why does your logic tell you this, Mr. Spock?"

Giovanni doesn't smile at my super-dork *Star Trek* joke.

"The first of May is May Day, which is a holiday in many countries under different incarnations," he states matter-of-factly. "In most cases it's celebrated approximately halfway between the spring equinox and the summer solstice. The Gaelic version is called Beltane, and an important part of the celebration of that holiday is fire."

Fire. I try to remember what the demon that possessed Tiffany Ramirez said when Aidan interrogated it. "'When the five-pointed star is completed, the world will be washed in fire and be reborn as the kingdom of Dubu,'" I recite out loud.

"Precisely." Aidan nods. "Several demons we have interrogated have repeated the same phrase to us."

"There's a so-called May Day Festival at the state park on the first of May," Mikhail pipes up. "According to various advertisements and articles it appears to be some sort of outdoor party involving a maypole, music, dancing, food sold for consumption, a craft fair—whatever that is—and so forth. Apparently it takes place annually."

"The articles suggested that historically this particular May Day celebration draws a sizeable crowd, nearly a thousand people, not just from Ridgemont but from surrounding areas," Aidan adds. "We are theorizing that the . . . *event* may take place there."

The event.

"There's something else," Aura speaks up, weaving her fingers through Zalea's. "The first of May is when Dubu's child Selarion . . . *died*. So this would be the anniversary of his death. A symbolic date." She slants a sideways glance at Aidan.

Oh.

I flash back to my conversation with Helena. If she's right, Dubu intends to kill me not just to activate the pentagram spell, which is awful and calamitous enough, but to also exact revenge on Aidan.

If this is the case, I'm doomed.

So doomed.

But, more importantly, the world will end on May 1 if we can't stop Dubu.

I feel the cool metal of the necklace against my skin. Helena said it would provide me with "enhanced protection," not "absolute protection."

Aidan notices my reaction. "Obviously, Sunshine, you cannot be in Ridgemont on that day. I will arrange to have you flown to an undisclosed luiseach compound, perhaps the day before. If I move you any earlier, Dubu might find out and try to search for you to bring you back to Ridgemont."

"But . . . couldn't he just move the date back again? I mean, May first isn't carved in stone, is it? It's not a date decreed by their little prophecy book, is it? If I leave town, he'll just do this thing on, say, May fifth or June sixth. Or even *August thirteenth*," I point out, mentioning the day before my seventeenth birthday.

"It will be the first of May. Helena and I have formulated a plan to make sure of it," Aidan says.

I turn to Helena, who hasn't said a word this entire time.

She's sitting by herself, looking unusually distracted, smoothing an invisible wrinkle in her dress.

"What kind of plan?" I ask.

Helena glances up, and our eyes lock.

"You don't need to know the details," she says tersely. "Your father and I will take care of it."

"Take care of it *how?*" I persist.

Zalea reaches into her pocket and pulls out one of her stones. She holds it up to the overhead light. "My stone tells me this plan is not likely to work."

Mikhail throws up his hands in exasperation. "Really, Helena? Must we indulge these pseudo-mystical pronouncements?"

"Why isn't the plan going to work, Zalea?" I ask her nervously.

Aura glares at Mikhail, then me, and tugs on Zalea's hand. "Come on, pet, we must be going."

"Yes, of course, Mother."

"We *all* need to be going. We have much to do," Mikhail states. And with that, he gets up, sweeps past me, and heads for the front door. The others follow.

As Zalea passes me, she leans close. "Do you still have *your* stone? The one I gave you?"

"What? Yes, of course."

"That's wonderful. Hold onto it. It will bring you luck."

"Um, okay. Thanks. Why isn't their plan going to work?"

"I'm not sure. It was a fleeting vision, no more. Something about a shiny, spinning celestial body . . ."

Aidan's the last to go. I put a hand on his arm. "Can you stay for a minute? We have to talk."

"I only have a few minutes."

After the others are gone I sit down on the couch and motion for him to join me.

"You need to tell me," I state firmly. "Whatever you and Helena are planning. I have to be in on it. Especially given what Zalea said."

"I would not take stock in Zalea's fancies. She has a vivid . . . imagination."

"Still."

"I am not going to tell you the details of the plan, Sunshine. Leave it be, please."

"No. It's time you started treating me like a . . . well, like not a child. I'm sixteen. You say I'm a luiseach like no other. That I may be the key to the survival of humanity because I can teach light spirits to move on by themselves. I need you to include me in whatever is happening here because I want to help. I *need* to help. I can't just stand on the sidelines and watch Dubu and his evil minions take over the world!"

Aidan stares at me. His lips curve into a smile, but his eyes are heavy and sad.

"You are very much like your mother—like Helena, I mean. Stubborn and determined. Also very brave."

Normally I'd complain bitterly—throw a major tizzy fit even—about being compared to Helena. But for some reason I don't take offense this time. Part of me is actually a tiny bit pleased.

"I *am* stubborn. And I am *de-ter-mined* to keep you here until you tell me everything."

Aidan steeps his hands under his chin. His face is sallow and drawn, and there are fatigue lines around his eyes. It's like he aged ten years—or in his case a hundred, two hundred, three hundred years or more—practically overnight.

"Helena told me this morning that she explained our history to you, about Adis and Uiri, about your lineage," he begins. "What she didn't reveal is the fact that she and I are . . . that is to say . . . we are the king and queen of the luiseach. We have been for many centuries."

"I'm sorry, what? You're a *king?*"

"Yes. Although when the rift occurred sixteen years ago almost every single luiseach followed your . . . followed Helena. So my title as 'king' became somewhat moot, meaningless. As far as most of the luiseach community was concerned, Helena was their sole ruler."

Holy moly. My parents are a luiseach king and queen. Does that make me a princess? Not just "of royal blood" but an actual princess? The thought would make me laugh if it weren't so surreal and unbelievable.

Except it appears to be true.

Princess Sunshine?

"Helena and I have discussed it at length. There is only one way to kill Dubu, and as the king of the luiseach, it is up to me to carry it through."

"Your burden," I say, the pieces suddenly coming together. "Killing Dubu is your burden as king. And it will end the war swiftly, minimizing the loss of life."

Aidan frowns at me in confusion.

"And you're going to use something, some ritual, called guera spirito, aren't you?"

"How in heaven's name did you—"

"What is it, Aidan? What is this 'spirit war' ritual you intend to use?"

He stands up abruptly, walks over to the window, and pushes

the curtain aside to gaze out into the dark night, at the wind blowing through the pine trees. The fog is rolling in, blanketing everything in a wet, ghostly gray.

"Guera spirito is how my great-grandparents and your great-great-grandparents, Adis and Uiri, killed Dubu's two brothers, Drakov and Dagon. It is a ritual that was likely described in the demons' *Book of Prophecy*. I am not sure how Adis and Uiri learned of it—everything in the *Book of Prophecy* is closely guarded by the darkness—but they did. And before they perished, they passed on the knowledge of this ritual to their daughter Laoise, who then passed it on to her son Laisren, my father, who then passed it on to me."

A chill runs down my spine. I want to know what guera spirito is, and yet I don't. Some instinct tells me that it's not going to be easy to hear.

Aidan sits back down, takes my hand, and looks into my eyes. "It has already been decided, so you must accept what I am about to tell you," he says gravely.

I nod slightly and clasp my hands together, trying to still their trembling. "O-okay."

"Helena and I have planned that she will communicate with Dubu on May first and ask him to . . . ask him to . . ." He hesitates, and for a second his eyes darken with torment. "She will ask him to reconcile with her and pretend to join his side, which will cause him to be sufficiently distracted, at least for a few minutes, to allow me to initiate the ritual. And if the ritual is successful, he will never get the opportunity to activate the pentagram spell. The world will be safe."

"And how do you initiate the ritual?"

"I must die and then battle Dubu on the spiritual plane."

My breath catches in my throat, and I choke back tears.

"You have to *die?* No, no, you can't!"

"The term 'die' is not simple in this context. The ritual is . . . complex. I must physically die, my body must die, in order for me to enter the spiritual plane and battle Dubu there. But as long as I can destroy him permanently before my brain and heart have completely shut down, I will return to the earthly realm. Worse for the wear, to paraphrase an expression. But I will return."

"But you might not? There's no guarantee?"

Sighing, Aidan wraps his arm around my shoulder and hugs me for the second time in our brief lives together as father and daughter. I can't hold back my tears anymore, and for a second it seems like he's on the verge of crying too.

"No, there is no guarantee. I must do this regardless. For the greater good. Only then can I hope to eliminate him from this universe once and for all. And no matter what happens, you will go on. You *must* go on. You are the king and queen's daughter. After me, after Helena, you will be the leader of the luiseach."

A creak on the stairs. Aidan and I both stand up.

Ashley stands at the landing, dressed in her PJs.

She rubs her eyes and blinks. "Sun? Sorry, I fell asleep. Monster headache. Is everything okay?"

"Everything's fine!" I plaster on a smile. Did she overhear any part of our conversation? Probably not, or she'd likely be freaking out right now. "Dance Saturday, remember? You have to take me shopping," I add with forced lightness.

"I haven't forgotten. Aidan, you'd better give her all your credit cards, because we're going to be spending some serious money!"

Nope, she definitely didn't overhear.

As she turns and heads back up the stairs, I wonder how I'll be able to do these normal things—shop for dresses, go to a school dance . . . go to school, period—when I know that my father, whom I'm just getting to know and love, may be dead in nineteen days?

At Last

The pesky mosquitoes are so easy to fool. Really, I should do this more often.

They now think the Great Reckoning will occur on the first of May—the humans' absurd holiday with their maypoles and flower garlands and pagan flute music and annoying little dancing children.

They even have a plan to draw me out and defeat me.

How sweet.

I am practically beside myself with excitement, anticipating the expression on Aidan's face when the fifth girl is terminated and the pentagram spell is complete. Ah, the glorious drama when the five points across the globe erupt in a rapture of death and darkness. My servants will arise, war will commence, and the whole world will be washed with fire.

First I will terminate her, and then him.

And take what is mine.

My queen.

My kingdom.

Finally, at last.

CHAPTER 38
Dress Shopping

On Thursday after school Ashley takes me to the Ridgemont Mall to dress shop for the dance. The mall was closed for a while after the incident with Mrs. Ostricher (who's receiving tons of psychiatric tests and other evaluations in prison; no one can figure out what mental illness, exactly, caused a sweet little old lady to just snap and commit arson). It's open now except for the Food Court, which is still roped off with yellow police tape, and also Candles 'N' Wicks because its owner, Marylee Mumford, had taken an unfortunately timed break to get a smoothie at Jolly Juice and was one of the victims.

Ashley stands in front of the fountain, which marks the center of the mall. The water inside glitters with pennies and nickels and dimes from all the wish makers.

I dig into my pocket, pull out a penny, and throw it in.

Please, please, please keep my father safe.

I throw in the rest of my change too for good measure.

Ashley puts her hands on her hips and slowly turns, carefully scanning the three wings of the mall that are distinguished by the wall colors—red, yellow, and blue. "This place is sad. Don't you even have an H&M? Or a Forever 21?"

"Sorry, we're not the big city. I think there's a department store down this way, though." I point to the red corridor. "We really don't need to find me a dress here. If we just stop by Goodwill on our way home, I know they'll have something for me. Like a prom dress from the seventies. Really, we should concentrate on you."

"Nope, nope, nope. It's time you got a full makeover. I'm talking dress, shoes, hair, makeup—you need the works."

"Wow, you sound just like Tiffany Ramirez," I joke.

"Well, Tiffany's not wrong, is she?"

"Ouch! When did you get to be so judgey?"

"It's just a little tough love, dude. You should thank me. I'm going to make you so hot that Nolan won't be able to keep his hands off of you!"

Ashley hooks her arm through mine and pulls me toward the red wing. "Soooo . . . what's the latest on your demon drama? I'm dying to know!"

"Um, there's a lot going on. Lots of possessions and so forth. And we're preparing for a possible, um, attack. In May." I want to keep Ashley in the loop, but I don't want to freak her out either—especially after what happened to her on Monday.

"An attack? That doesn't sound good. Should we get out of here and road-trip it to Mexico, after all?"

"I'm not sure. I'll keep you posted."

"You'd better. *Ohmigosh*, look who's here!"

I follow Ashley's glance. Bastian is walking out of Tux Depot.

"Bas!" Ashley waves and runs over to him. She throws her arms around his neck and gives him a long, squeezy hug.

This time he doesn't blush. Is he getting accustomed to her PDAs? Instead, he smiles happily and says, "Hello, Ashley. What a pleasant surprise. What are you and Sunshine doing here?"

"Shopping for drop-dead gorgeous dresses for our date on Saturday night, of course!" Ashley gushes.

"Hey," I say, walking up to him. I haven't had a chance to fill Bastian in on my conversation with Aidan about May first. As it is, I've told him very little about the pentagram spell and the rest of it—I didn't want to scare him and make him resign from the luiseach club just when he's getting started. I want to keep him focused on our next training session, which we've planned for the day after the dance. "Renting a tux?" I ask breezily.

Bastian reaches into his jacket pocket and pulls out a crumpled Tux Depot receipt. "Yes. I've never rented a tuxedo before. It's quite complicated, really. Choosing colors, styles, ties, a cummerbund versus no cummerbund, shoes . . ."

"So what did you decide?" Ashley asks.

"I wasn't sure, so my mother suggested I go with a classic black tuxedo. She and Father are at the frame store now, picking up some prints. Perhaps I can introduce you to them."

Bastian's parents? I've heard so much about them from him—mostly bad—that I become immediately nervous at the thought of actually meeting them face to face. I think about how they had him institutionalized and majorly medicated in January because he thought he was seeing ghosts—or, actually, light spirits.

A cold breeze blows through the corridor as though someone just turned up the air conditioning in the mall. Goosebumps prickle my skin.

Speaking of spirits . . .

Bastian drops his Tux Depot receipt and picks it up again. He stares at me with wide eyes.

"Ghosts?" he whispers.

"What did you say?" Ashley asks him.

I turn to her. "Ash, could you, um . . . head over to the department store and do some reconnaissance? You know, pre-select some dresses for me to try on? Bastian and I have to discuss a, um, surprise for you. For the dance. I'll be there in, like, ten minutes."

"Oooh, a surprise! Sounds juicy. I'll go pick out some dresses for you, Sunny-G. I'm thinking maybe bright red or purple or yellow—you know, to make you look less blah and boring."

Ashley flutters her fingers and takes off down the corridor.

Less blah and boring?

But I don't have time to feel insulted by my best friend. There are light spirits nearby.

I think this is Lucio's shift to bodyguard me or whatever, which means he must be nearby somewhere. Even though we now know May first is *the* date, Aidan wants to continue the around-the-clock protection. In any case, the light spirits seem to be seeking out Bastian and me, not Lucio, so it's our job to help them move on.

I stand next to Bastian, close my eyes, and concentrate. There are two spirits—I can visualize them now. A couple, Jason and Jonathan, who were attacked while hiking in the state park by a pack of strange wild animals.

Oh my gosh. A pack of strange wild animals? Could they be . . .

"Do you see them?" Bastian whispers to me.

"Yes. Do you?"

"Yes. Those poor men, they must have suffered greatly."

"Send them your love and compassion, Bastian. Your kindness. Try to connect with them."

"I will do that."

We reach out our hands at the same time. The spirits of Jason and Jonathan billow toward us. They were in their thirties, both of them biologists and assistant professors at the university. Jason specialized in butterflies. Jonathan was a rain forest expert.

Come to us. Just a little closer now. We will help you reach the light, I say silently.

"Sebastian? What on Earth is going on here?" a woman's voice interrupts.

My eyes fly open. Jason and Jonathan's spirits shiver, retreat, and recede. I try to summon them back, but they pass through a wall next to Tux Depot and disappear.

A man and a woman stand in front of Bastian and me. The man is tall and broad shouldered with short blond hair and icy blue eyes; he's wearing a casual shirt, slacks, and tweed jacket that quietly exude expensive designer labels, plus a tweed wool cap and leather driving gloves. The woman is likewise dressed in a simple but perfectly tailored black dress that matches the shade of her closely cropped hair. Behind her glasses her blue eyes are as chilly as his.

"Sebastian? Please explain," she repeats.

Bastian flushes bright red. "Um . . . hello, Mother, Father. This is my friend Sunshine. Sunshine Griffith. We were just, um . . ."

His parents. The super-scary law professor and psychiatrist.

"Sorry, my fault!" I jump in with a bright smile. "I was just showing Bastian, I mean Sebastian, a move I learned in my tai chi class. I know we must have looked so dorky, doing tai chi in the middle of the mall! It's like that scene in *Pride and Prejudice* where . . . except, what am I saying? Of course they didn't have tai chi in Victorian England! You must be Mr. and Mrs. Jansen. It's really nice to meet you both!"

Mrs. Jansen narrows her eyes at me, then turns to Bastian. "This is your friend? From your English class?" Bastian is crumpling and uncrumpling his Tux Depot receipt. Now he rips it in half and stuffs it back into his pocket agitatedly. "Sebastian? I am speaking to you," she says.

"Y-yes, Mother, that's her. She has been very helpful to me, especially since I joined the class so late in the y-year."

Mr. Jansen is staring at me as though I were a particularly fascinating insect that was pinned under a magnifying glass. "Tai chi, did you say? Do you go to a local studio?" he asks in a deep voice with a trace of an accent. German? Scandinavian?

"What? No! I used to go to a studio in Austin—that's where I'm originally from—but now I just study, um, privately," I improvise. "So you guys are from DC, right? How are you enjoying Ridgemont?"

I realize that I'm babbling and blathering and in general making a fool of myself, but for some reason Bastian's parents make me nervous. *Really* nervous. Part of it is what I know about them and the fact that they basically walked in on us trying to move light spirits to the other side—which, based on recent history, could get Bastian in terrible trouble and land him back in a mental hospital.

But it's something else too. There's an aura about them . . . of what? Coldness? Cruelty? Like if they were driving along and saw a deer in the road they'd steer *toward* it rather than *away* from it? But that's a harsh thing to think about two people I just met, based on nothing but a creepy feeling plus the super-mean way Mrs. Jansen spoke to Bastian just now.

"Sebastian, we must go. Cook is preparing dinner for seven o'clock," she says, tapping on her slim diamond wristwatch.

Cook? Now *she's* talking like a character in a Victorian novel.

"It was a pleasure to meet you, young lady," Mr. Jansen says, tipping his tweed cap.

As they walk away, Bastian throws me a desperate look over his shoulder. I know he's worried about what his parents may or may not be thinking. I know he's worried about Jason and Jonathan's spirits too.

Who are no longer there.

I close my eyes and try to sense them, wherever they are.

Nothing. Hopefully they moved on by themselves or found Lucio or another available luiseach.

Sighing and shaking my head, I hurry down the corridor to the department store where Ashley's waiting with some dresses to un-blah me.

CHAPTER 39

Just for Tonight

"You look so beautiful, sweetie!" Mom gushes as she zips the back of my dress.

I peer at the long, flimsy mirror that hangs on the back of my closet door and inspect my outfit. My vintage black party frock with the lace top and sleeves is only *faux* vintage—it was the best I could do at the department store, and the most "me" out of the dozen outfits Ashley had preselected—but it's really pretty anyway. Definitely prettier and more me than the maroon velvet mini-dress she tried to push. Besides, it *feels* authentically vintage when I think of it as a "frock."

Mom finishes zipping and closes the fisheye hook at the top. She pats my shoulder. "There. Done!"

"Thanks, Mom."

"I can't believe you're going to your first school dance. Oh, Sunshine, you're going to look back on this night when you're older and cherish the memories. Speaking of memories . . . you need to let me take lots of pictures before you go. And a video. And maybe—"

I turn around laughing and kiss her on the cheek. "The guys are picking us up in about five minutes, so I'm not sure if we have time for the full celebrity photo shoot treatment."

"Maybe just a few pictures then. Like twenty or thirty or forty." Mom's gray eyes shimmer with tears, which she swipes with the back of her hands. "My baby is all grown up!"

"Hardly! I'm only sixteen. I have a long way to go before I'm all grown up."

She leans back and smooths my frizzball with a tender smile. "You and I both know that's not true. Still, deep in my heart you'll always be my baby, Sunshine State."

"Aw, thanks, Mom. I love you to the moon and back."

"I love *you* to the moon and back."

"*Ta-da!*"

Ashley prances into the bedroom and twirls around. She's been in the bathroom for practically an hour doing her hair and makeup.

"Ladies, check . . . this . . . out!"

She starts strutting across the floor as though she were a model catwalking on a runway. Her dress is way shorter than what she usually wears and also tighter, with a super-low neckline. I tried to talk her out of it at the mall and steer her toward one of the other less Las Vegas-y dresses, but she absolutely insisted on this one and reminded me a little tersely that *she* was the fashion expert, not me.

Of course she looks gorgeous as always. It's just that, speaking of sixteen, she appears *way* older, like she's an adult, especially with her heavy makeup, corkscrew curls, and body glitter.

"Oh my!" Mom's eyes move from Ashley's neckline to her hemline and then back up again. I can practically hear her trying to formulate a diplomatic response. "That's quite the, um, outfit, Ashley. Should we take a quick photo and text it to your mom and dad?"

"Good one, Kat, ha ha. Sun, you need more makeup. Come on, I've got tons of stuff in the bathroom!"

"Thanks, Ash, but I'm fine," I say quickly. The pink lip gloss and shimmery green eye shadow she insisted on earlier are about all I can handle; I've never been comfortable putting creams and powders on my face.

"Suit yourself." Ashley slips her feet into a pair of pointy stiletto heels that are the same red as her dress. "The boys should be here any sec. Let's wait for them downstairs!"

"Okay."

"I'll get my camera," Mom says, heading for the door. "I think this occasion calls for a real thirty-five-millimeter versus my cell phone, don't you? It's not as fancy as your Nikon, Sunshine, but it should do the trick, and I don't have to futz with all those complicated settings."

"Sounds good."

Before I leave my room I do a full sweep to make sure I have everything. Helena's necklace hidden under my vintage Chinese silk scarf. *Check.* Mom's vintage beaded purse with my Luiseach knife and cell phone inside. *Check.*

"Come on, come on," Ashley says impatiently, holding the door open.

"All right already."

"After you, Sunny-G."

I walk past her and start down the stairs, holding my taffeta skirt up with my hands and squeezing the beaded purse under my left armpit. Not exactly graceful.

Suddenly I feel a shove from behind, and I scramble to stay on my feet. I let go of my skirt and the purse and grab the railing.

Was it my imagination, or did Helena's necklace just grow hot and then cool? It must have been my imagination because the necklace feels normal now, like it's barely there.

Behind me Ashley's on her knees, clutching the railing too. "Ow! I'm so sorry. These stupid shoes . . . one of the heels caught in the carpet and I fell. Are you okay?"

"I'm fine," I reassure her.

"Is my makeup still okay?"

I laugh. "Yes, your makeup's still okay."

We rise to our feet and straighten our dresses and hair.

"Are you girls ready for pictures?" Mom calls up from the living room.

The doorbell rings. Ashley and I hurry downstairs.

Mom runs to the door and opens it. The guys walk in carrying corsage boxes. Nolan looks *so handsome* in a 1980s powder-blue tux, white ruffled shirt, and bow tie. And sneakers. Bastian is uncharacteristically dapper in his elegant black tux get-up. He seems to have replaced his crooked tortoiseshell glasses with contacts, his skin is smooth with a hint of a new tan, and his hair is styled neatly.

Nolan's eyes light up when he sees me. "You look . . . exquisite."

I beam. "Why, thank you, sir!"

"Seriously, you two are *such dorks*," Ashley whispers in my ear.

Bastian stares at Ashley, looking a little star-struck. Or like a sixteen-year-old guy swooning in front of his crush. I really need to get him to rein that in. "You too, Ashley. That is a lovely dress."

"Thanks, Bas! I love your tux. Yours too, Nolan."

I introduce Mom and Bastian to each other as Ashley and I pin on our corsages—mine is white gardenias, hers is a big, exotic yellow orchid. (At the department store I lied to Ashley and said that the "surprise" Bastian and I had to discuss privately was a choice of her corsage.) Then Mom takes a ton of pictures in different combinations: me alone, me and Ashley, me and Nolan, Ashley and Bastian, all four of us together.

At one point while Mom is posing Nolan and me on the couch, Ashley grows impatient.

"Come on, let's start this party!" she says loudly.

Mom frowns a little. "This is the last one. Um, Nolan, honey, what time did you say you're bringing the girls home?"

"Eleven o'clock, Mrs. Griffith . . . *Kat*," he replies. "The dance is supposed to be over by ten, ten-thirty at the latest."

Bastian glances at his watch. "Yes, we should go. I believe the festivities are beginning at seven?"

Ashley winks. "Yes, Bas. The festivities are beginning at seven!"

They both laugh.

Nolan glances at me and raises an eyebrow.

"I think Bastian's in love," I tell him in a low voice. "I'm definitely going to have to put an Aidan spell on him."

"Good luck with that."

Now *I* laugh.

The four of us head out into the night. It's cold, and I shiver in the thin velvet stole I borrowed from Mom. Nolan wraps his arm around me and keeps it there—and I don't feel queasy in the least, just tingly-happy from his touch. I'm not sure why Aidan's spell isn't kicking in, but I'm not complaining. In front of us Bastian holds Ashley's elbow as she teeters on her impossibly high heels.

Nolan leans his head toward mine. "Hey, just for tonight, let's forget about spells and pentagrams and demons and all that," he whispers. "Promise?"

I reach up to adjust my green silk scarf, and my fingers graze Helena's necklace. Aidan said both he *and* Helena would be bodyguarding me tonight—and that Lucio, Aura, Zalea, Giovanni, Xerxes, and Mikhail would also be standing by near the high school because the dance, with its anticipated high attendance, might be a potential magnet for demonic activity.

With all this protection I can afford to breathe a little, right?

I just need to turn my busy, anxious brain off for a few hours.

"I promise," I whisper back.

CHAPTER 40
The Spring Dance

The shiny new Ridgemont High gymnasium is jam-packed with students and the dance is in full swing by the time the four of us arrive.

Earlier in the day Ashley and I had come by to help Tiffany and the other volunteers decorate. I pause and admire our hand-iwork in the gym. White tablecloths, heart-shaped glitter, and vases of pink crepe-paper roses cover the tables. Pastel-colored streamers and balloons hang from the rafters. Tiny flecks of light from the disco ball spin and shimmer across the floor.

On the stage the members of Angry Jell-O—two guitarists, a bass player, a drummer, a singer, and a girl on electric piano—play a cover of a popular song I think I may have heard on Ash-ley's car radio but can't name for the life of me because that's how knowledgeable I am about popular songs. *Ha.* Hundreds of students are on the gym floor bopping and wiggling and gyrat-ing. I also have zero knowledge about how to dance like this—the best I can do is awkwardly imitate dances from Jane Austen movies, like the English country dance or the cotillion or the Boulanger or the minuet.

"Come on! What are we waiting for?" Ashley tugs on Bastian's hand and pulls him toward the middle of the floor.

"B-but I told you. I don't dance," he stammers.

"It's time you learned. I'll teach you!"

Bastian hesitates.

"*Baaaas!*"

"All right, Ashley, whatever you say. You are very persuasive."

The two of them disappear into the crowd as I turn to Nolan. "Hey."

"Hey."

"Alone at last."

"Well, not exactly"—he grins and nods at the swarm of dancing bodies—"but alone enough."

"I'm trying really hard not to think about . . . you know." I plaster on a big, goofy pretend-smile. "I *will* relax! I *will* have fun!"

Nolan cocks his head and grazes my cheek with the back of his hand. I lose the pretend smile and lean into his touch. He doesn't know everything. I've told him about May first and the plan to whisk me out of town to some secret luiseach compound right before then, but I haven't told him about Aidan's plan to go through with the guera spirito ritual or even what the ritual is. I've been percolating some ideas about it, and I don't think Nolan will be thrilled about them.

"Earth to Sunshine." He pushes back a loose strand of my frizzball hair. "I completely understand if this"—he sweeps his hand in a wide arc—"isn't helping to take your mind off the ongoing, um . . . situation. If you want, we can just bail and grab some coffee at Dream Bean and talk. I guarantee we'll be the best-dressed people there."

"That's really sweet, but you know what? I promised you I'd try to forget about that stuff and enjoy myself tonight. So if you're game, I'm game. How about some punch and cupcakes?"

"Sounds good. But if you change your mind, the offer stands."

Nolan takes my hand and we wander over to the refreshment table where Tiffany is barking orders at several student volunteers. It's weird, but I find her meanness comforting now. Victoria, dressed as Ms. Warkomski, is one of the adult volunteers along with about a dozen other teachers from the school—also Principal Henderson, Vice Principal D'Angelo, and Coach Martinez.

Victoria is manning the punch bowl. She catches sight of us and waves eagerly.

"Hello, dears," she says when we walk up to her. "How are you enjoying the dance?"

"Hi, Ms. Warkomski." I've gotten very good at that, calling her by her alias. "We just got here. It seems like a big success. The place is packed."

"Punch?" She hands Nolan and me two paper cups.

As I take the cup she lowers her voice and says, "About the matter we discussed. Are there any updates?"

I had told Victoria about Anna appearing in my yard on Monday morning and warning me about that nasty wind demon's presence. Victoria had been really glad to hear I'd seen her daughter, but she was still worried about her dream, which she felt might be prophetic, and wanted to make sure Anna continued to "check in."

"No updates, Ms. Warkomski. But I'm keeping my eyes and ears open."

"Of course, dear. I have complete faith in you."

Victoria turns to help Vice Principal D'Angelo unpack a box of compostable cups. Nolan and I grab a couple of cupcakes from a platter and wander away from the table.

Just as we're finishing up our punch and cupcakes, the band switches to a slow number. Nolan reaches his hand out to me and bows. "May I have the pleasure of this dance, Miss Griffith?"

Aww. My courtly, old-fashioned suitor.

I curtsy. "Yes, you may, Mr. Foster. I believe yours is the first name on my dance card. Actually yours is the *only* name on my dance card."

Nolan grins and wraps his arm around my waist as I lean my head against his shoulder. We sway, not exactly in time to the music because we're both rhythm challenged, but I don't think either of us cares. I wait for the nausea to kick in. It doesn't. I wait for Nolan to pull away and hold me at a just-friends distance. He doesn't. I close my eyes and breathe in the warm, familiar scent of his skin, and in that moment I'm truly able to forget the bad stuff and pretend I'm just a regular, happy, love-struck sixteen-year-old girl dancing with her amazing, wonderful boyfriend at the high school dance.

Either that or I'm Elizabeth Bennett dancing with Mr. Darcy at the Netherfield Ball.

Ashley and Bastian are dancing nearby, holding each other very close as she caresses his back and shoulders in a slow, seductive way. He kisses the top of her head, and she tips her face so their lips meet. They kiss for a long moment—a passionate, making-out kiss.

Whoa. When did they go from just friends to *that?*

I really, *really* have to nip this in the bud. Bastian needs to keep a clear head for his luiseach training.

"*Sunshine!* There you are!"

Someone grabs me from behind and yanks me out of Nolan's arms.

"What the . . ." Nolan exclaims.

I turn around—it's Lucio. His face is bright red, and he's panting for breath. He looks out of place in his jeans and hoodie in the sea of tuxes and suits.

"Lucio? What are you . . . what's wrong? Is my mom all right? And Aidan?" I'm suddenly panicked.

"No, it's not that. Sorry, I . . . I sprinted from the parking lot and . . . why aren't you two picking up your phones?"

"What are you talking about?" I pull my phone out of Mom's beaded purse and push the ON button. It doesn't light up. "That's bizarre. I just charged it this afternoon."

Nolan checks out his phone. "Mine seems to be dead too, which doesn't make sense because—"

"Guys, guys!" Lucio holds up his hands. "It doesn't matter. There's no time. Sunshine, we have to get you out of here. Your dad will be here in a sec and Helena and the rest of the council too. They're putting the evacuation plan in place. Your dad has a private jet waiting."

A chill runs down my spine, and my heart begins to hammer in my chest. "An evacuation plan? Private jet . . . what's going on?"

"We had the wrong date," Lucio replies grimly.

Nolan frowns. "What?"

"We thought Dubu planned to complete the pentagram spell

on May first. But it's *not* May first. Helena found out somehow. Dubu faked us out by having one of his demons give us false information. He's not waiting until then. He plans to complete the pentagram spell *tonight*."

CHAPTER 41

Escape

"onight?" I repeat numbly. "You mean, like, here in
Ridgemont?"

"Yes, here in Ridgemont. At this dance likely, since you're
here and so are about a thousand other people. As in, maximum
potential casualties." Lucio grasps my arm and points to the
exit. "Come on."

But I can't move.

This isn't happening.

Nolan puts his hands on my shoulders, squeezes, and stares
deeply into my eyes. "I know you're scared. I promise it's going
to be all right. But Lucio's right—we need to move."

"But . . . what about Ashley and Bastian?"

"I'll go and grab them. And Victoria too," Nolan offers. "Lucio, please get Sunshine out of here. Keep her safe. I'll be right
behind you with the others."

"Shouldn't we evacuate this whole gym, in case the pentagram spell . . ." I can't finish the sentence.

"The first priority is to keep the spell from being completed. That means extracting you, stat," Lucio tugs on my arm. "Now come on!"

I take a deep, shuddering breath. This isn't just about me. It's about the safety of everyone at the dance . . . everyone in Ridgemont . . . maybe everyone in the entire world. "Yes, okay. I'm ready."

Nolan kisses me quickly. "I love you, Sunshine. For always. Now *go!*"

He turns and disappears into the crowd.

"I love you too!" I call after him, but the music drowns out my words.

Lucio and I make a beeline for the exit, or we try to, but it's not easy with the crush of bodies now dancing to some loud, screechy song about a revolution. As I run I touch Helena's necklace under my scarf, and I can feel the weight of my luise-ach knife inside my purse.

Courage, I tell myself. *I know how to do this. I know how to protect myself.*

But what about Aidan? This means he has to move up the timeline on his guera spirito ritual, that he has to die, physically die, and engage with Dubu on the spiritual plane—*tonight.*

I remember noticing on Wednesday how tired and old Aidan looked, as though he'd aged overnight. I remember too last weekend how he tried to keep me from exorcising the ghost in-side Tiffany Ramirez, and I managed to resist him completely.

My father trained me well.

Will I have to say good-bye to him tonight? Am I ready?

Lucio and I are about thirty feet from the exit when, lo and behold, there's Aidan himself. He rushes into the gym and pauses in the doorway, looking this way and that. Behind him are Helena, Aura, Xerxes, Mikhail, and Giovanni. Zalea's here too, peering around in wonder, her curious gaze landing on something on the ceiling.

Aidan spots us and waves agitatedly. "*Hurry!*" he shouts.

Lucio and I head toward them. I trip on someone's feet, and Lucio clutches my arm to right me. I glance around quickly to see if Nolan has Ashley, Bastian, and Victoria, but I can't locate them—there are too many people.

"Hurry, Nolan," I whisper.

Lucio and I are almost at the exit now. Just then I notice that Zalea's wandered away from her mother and is walking into the crowd, her eyes fixed on . . . the disco ball? What's she *doing?* She's acting like she's hypnotized or maybe just having one of her visions? Aura's conferring with Helena and doesn't seem to notice. None of them seem to notice.

"Zalea!" I yell, although there's no way she can hear me— she's moving in the opposite direction and the band is playing at full volume.

But she *does* hear me somehow. With her keen ears or with her telepathic mind. Zalea stops and turns slightly; her gaze falls on me.

She points to the disco ball, and her lips move.

At that exact same moment a tall figure seizes her from behind and lifts her in the air . . . and runs.

"*Zalea!*" I scream.

The tall figure and Zalea melt into the crowd. I change course and start to pursue them.

But Lucio catches hold of my arm. "What are you doing? Wrong direction!"

"Someone took Zalea. We have to help her!"

"*What?* But there's no time!"

"Let me go!"

I twist out of his grip and take off. He tries to follow but gets immediately blocked by a group of girls who surround him, trying to make him dance with them.

I trip and wind my way through the crowd, barely making out the top of Zalea's captor's head, much less Zalea's. The captor seems to be carrying her toward the center of the gym. What does this person want with Zalea, and why isn't anyone helping her? Of course it's incredibly loud and chaotic in the gym . . . maybe everyone is just oblivious.

I peer over my shoulder. Is Lucio somewhere behind me? I feel bad about ditching him back there, but I know he'd try to keep me from rescuing Zalea so I can make my escape, which I'll do as soon as I can do what my gut's telling me: *save Zalea.* I assume that Aura and Aidan and the other luiseach have figured out she's missing. They must all be frantically combing the gym—for her, for me. But the room is wall to wall with bodies.

Just then I spot Bastian and Ashley squeezing their way through two dancing couples.

"Guys! Where's Nolan?" I call out.

"He went to find Victoria. He told us we have to leave the dance immediately. What's wrong?" Bastian asks anxiously.

"Come with me and I'll explain!"

Bastian hurries to my side. Ashley removes her stiletto heels and trails after us.

"This is *the* lamest high school dance I've ever been to," she complains loudly.

"Bastian, it's happening," I say breathlessly. "The pentagram spell, the thing I told you about. It's tonight!"

His jaw drops. He pulls a white handkerchief out of his tux pocket and mops his face with it. "That is very bad. All right, please tell me what you need me to do."

"Someone kidnapped Zalea . . . she's one of us, she's a luiseach. I have to help her. Can you get Ashley out of here?"

"Yes, of course. But what about you?"

"As soon as I have Zalea I'll get out of here too. Aidan has a plane standing by."

"A plane? Why?"

"I'll explain later. Just—"

I halt in my tracks, as do Bastian and Ashley. We've reached the center of the gym. Something's wrong. The crowd there has parted and formed a circle.

I shoulder my way through a swath of bodies.

Coach Martinez stands in the middle of the circle holding Zalea in his arms.

Black tape covers her mouth.

The coach's eyes gleam red as he gazes up at the disco ball.

"When the five-pointed star is completed, the world will be washed in fire and be reborn as the kingdom of Dubu!" he shouts.

Someone screams, and the band stops playing. The lead singer taps on the microphone, "Hey, is everyone still having fun out there? Or—"

The students begin yelling randomly, incoherently.

Call 9-1-1!

My phone's dead.

Mine too!

Let's get out of here!

There's a mass exodus—at least half the students anyway. The other half stays behind, gawking at Coach Martinez and Zalea and trying to take photos and videos with their phones, which aren't working.

"What's the coach doing?" Bastian whispers.

"I don't know. He's obviously possessed. We have to stop him before he hurts her!"

"But why does he want to hurt *her?*"

"Because . . ."

Zalea suddenly spots me in the crowd and stares wildly, her eyes wide with terror. Above her the disco ball spins around and around, peppering her body with flecks of light.

A fleck of light catches her wrist.

Oh my gosh.

Of course.

There's a pentagram mark on it.

Zalea is a luiseach.

Who's also a girl.

Who said she was a few months old when she and Aura left Llevar la Luz . . . so she must be sixteen?

Just like me.

If she dies here tonight, the pentagram spell will be activated.

CHAPTER 42

The Penumbra of Darkness

I turn to Bastian, trying to keep my panic at bay as I improvise a hasty rescue plan. "I have to perform an exorcism on Coach Martinez! You have to make sure no one tries to stop me!"

Bastian nods, although his expression is strangely calm. Has fear shut him down? He seems frozen in place, like I was a few minutes ago.

"Bastian, *focus!* I need you!"

"Yes, yes, of course."

Ashley clutches his arm and whispers something in his ear. He nods again.

Fingers crossed Bastian will do his job. Regardless, I need to act quickly and carefully. First and foremost I inch to the right so I'm out of Coach Martinez's sight line. Then I close my eyes, trying to tune out the confusion and commotion, and extend my hand toward him. I have to try to find the demon inside him, lock on to it, and destroy it.

I see nothing.

Keep trying!

My inner vision sweeps through his entire body. Still nothing. I bite back my frustration—at this rate the demon will kill Zalea and then kill Coach Martinez . . .

But . . . *wait.* This doesn't make sense. A demon can't permanently destroy a luiseach. The creature inside Coach Martinez might hurt Zalea, but he can't kill her.

Unless . . .

Is Dubu here? Is he going to finish what the Coach Martinez demon started with Zalea and activate the pentagram spell after all?

My eyes fly open and I spin around, scanning the entire gym. Bastian is next to me. I search for him—the man in black, the penumbra of darkness, the king of all demons and dark creatures—but I don't see or sense him anywhere. Students are running en masse toward the one exit that seems to be open—why are the other exits closed? There's a huge logjam of bodies, people pushing and shoving, total chaos. Did Nolan get out safely? And Victoria too? Where are Aidan and Helena and the others?

Then I get an idea.

Its magic could annihilate Coach Martinez's demon, seek out Dubu, end this now. Keep everyone I love safe.

I extract my luiseach knife from my purse and balance it on my palm. Coach Martinez's back is still turned to me so he—or rather, his demon—isn't aware of my actions . . . at least for the moment.

"Manifest!" I order.

My knife doesn't move.

"Sunshine, you have a weapon!" Bastian says, sounding relieved. "Are you going to use it?"

"Not now, Bastian. *Manifest,* darn it!"

It still doesn't move.

"We are running out of time!" Bastian points out.

And then, before I can react, he takes the knife from me and grasps it by the blade, which grazes his skin. Wincing, he turns it upside down so that he's holding it correctly. The blood that trickles from his wound is dark red, almost black.

"Bastian!"

I try to take the knife back, but he twists away, keeping it out of my reach.

"You must let me help you, Sunshine. You are my friend, my mentor."

"No! You can't exorcise a demon with that . . . you don't know how! You'll only hurt Coach Martinez!"

Ashley materializes at my side just then and grabs hold of my hand. I can feel her long manicured fingernails digging into my flesh. "Let him be the hero, Sunny-G. He's ready," she murmurs into my ear.

"You don't know what you're talking about . . ."

But Ashley won't let go, and her grip is surprisingly strong. Bastian holds the knife against his side and sneaks up behind Coach Martinez as though he were "it" in a ghoulish game of hide-and-seek.

Bastian lifts the knife in the air and prepares to strike . . .

"No!" I shout.

Coach Martinez whirls around, Zalea captive in his arms.

Bastian stabs her in the chest.

I scream soundlessly as Zalea slumps to the ground, her eyes wide open, her mouth taped shut as her blood seeps onto the gym floor. Tiny flecks of light from the disco ball dance across her lifeless body.

The floor beneath my feet begins to rumble. Then the ceiling above begins to shake, and the disco ball swings back and forth precariously.

Bastian glances at me, still holding the bloody knife.

And smiles.

Why is he smiling?

"No, young lady. He is not possessed," someone says.

Mr. Jansen—Bastian's father—is standing there.

Except he's not Mr. Jansen. He *is*, but he's someone else too.

The man in black.

The penumbra of darkness.

Bastian strides up to me. The awkwardness and shyness are gone, and in their place is an air of supreme confidence.

"B-Bastian?" I stammer incoherently. What's happening? He's supposed to be my friend, my apprentice, my hope for the future of the luiseach race.

To my horror Ashley prances up to him and twines her arm through his, her eyes glowing red.

Oh my gosh, Ashley too?

"I'm sorry, Sunshine. I don't believe I have properly introduced you to my father," Bastian says smoothly. "This is the man whom you know as Dubu. Father, this is Sunshine."

Bastian is Dubu's son?

Dubu smiles, and his smile is identical to Bastian's. "Finally, at last. The daughter of Aidan Adis Cadeyrn."

CHAPTER 43

The Sacrifice

Dubu holds out his hand as if to shake mine, and I see he has six fingers on each hand. Just like in my dream, my vision, my nightmare. I stumble backward, trying desperately to get away from him . . . and from Bastian . . . and from Ashley, who isn't Ashley anymore.

Bastian is Dubu's son.

I want to fade away, disappear, right here and now for messing everything up so badly. I brought the enemy into our camp. And now Zalea, poor Zalea, lies on the floor staring up at the ceiling with dead eyes. I want to run to her, try to save her, but it's too late. *I'm* too late.

Everyone was so fixated on protecting *me* . . .

The floor rumbles some more, and a thin crack ripples from wall to wall.

It's beginning. The fifth point in the pentagram, the doomsday spell.

I need to stop it.

I can do this.

First, I need backup. "*Aidan!*" I shout at the top of my lungs. "*Lucio!*"

"They will be here shortly along with the rest of your lui-seach . . . *posse*. I ordered my dark servants to detain them. But of course I very much want them here for the finale. Your father especially," Dubu smirks.

"The finale?"

A terrible creaking sound . . . I glance up and realize the disco ball is about to come crashing down. People continue running for the exit, except that more cracks are forming along the floor. Several students fall in, screaming.

A giant flame plumes out of one of the cracks, and another, and another. Smoke seeps into the gym, and fire ignites.

"*Look out!*" someone yells.

A whooshing sound. I glance up and see the disco ball falling, coming straight toward us. My necklace burns hot against my skin as I dive out of the way just as the disco ball hits the floor and shatters into a million pieces.

A dozen students and also Coach Martinez lie there bleeding, covered with glass shards. Dubu smiles and moves his arms as though he were conducting a symphony. Bastian and Ashley nod and clap.

Oh my gosh, Ashley.

More cracks tear across the floor. The gym starts to cave in, and then demons and dark spirits begin flying out of the earth. Not just a few, but dozens, then hundreds, then more. The humans in the gym can't see them, and the creatures take advantage by attacking them and entering their defenseless, unsuspecting bodies, possessing them en masse.

The apocalypse is here.

I turn and trip and right myself, making a mad dash away from Dubu and Bastian and Ashley and toward the black hole of demon activity. As I run I try to exorcise demons one by one, but there are just too many. Dubu said his servants were "detaining" Aidan and the others. Does that mean I'm on my own here, fighting against an entire demon army? My necklace continues to scorch and sizzle. My necklace, Helena's necklace, Dubu's necklace—which is awful and ironic, as it may be the only thing that's keeping me safe and in one piece right now.

But to what end? Because if the pentagram spell worked, this very same thing is happening in those four other places across the world. Soon the darkness will no doubt spread beyond the five points of the unholy star and take over the entire planet.

Smoke, fire, whirling demons. Humans are falling right and left, turning dark, eradicating any semblance of balance. I don't know how much longer I can stay here, stay alive. If an on-slaught of light spirits can kill me, what will an onslaught of dark spirits do?

I pray that Nolan escaped and Victoria too.

The thick gray smoke parts slightly, and I make out the faint outlines of Aidan and Helena and the other council members. And Lucio too. They have formed a tight circle, their backs against each other, their hands reaching out to perform exor-cisms at an impossible rate. The elder luiseach especially are immensely powerful that way.

But not powerful enough. There are only seven luiseach here—eight, including me. Hundreds of demons swirl through the air, attacking, possessing. More continue pouring out of the ground. We are horribly, horribly outnumbered. At this rate Dubu and his evil minions will take over the school, Ridgemont, the country, the world in a matter of hours.

Is this the end?

But it can't be the end.

Sucking in a deep breath, summoning every last ounce of strength and courage, I step over flames, bodies, and hurry toward the luiseach circle.

Just before I reach it, Aidan sees me.

"*Sunshine!*" he shouts, his face white with shock. "I thought you were . . . how did the pentagram spell . . ."

"Where is Zalea? Where is my daughter?" Aura cries out.

They don't know.

Before I can reply, something grabs my neck from behind and lifts me swiftly up in the air.

My necklace grows almost unbearably hot against my throat, like it's burning through my flesh. Dubu is so strong that he holds me by my neck as though I were weightless, a feather. I twist and struggle in his inhuman grip, but it's no use.

Aidan breaks away from the circle and rushes toward us. "*Let . . . her . . . go!*"

"Dubu, no!" Helena screams. "*Please.* She is my daughter too!"

"Hello, my beloved," Dubu says, squeezing my neck a little tighter. "I know this is what you want too, deep inside."

"No! Not anymore!"

Lucio also starts to break away from the circle, but a new onslaught of demons comes after him and the other luiseach. He throws me a desperate look as he tries to fend them off.

Aidan's eyes, full of fire, lock onto Dubu's. "It's me you want. Let her go. This is about you and me."

"Oh, Aidan." Dubu laughs. "You do continue to amuse. You are as ignorant as you are arrogant. This isn't just about you and me. I mean, yes, terminating your daughter is—what do they call it?—icing on the cake. A delightful sideshow for the entertainment of all. And a suitable judgment for your own terrible crime a century ago. But first and foremost this is about the Great Reckoning. The pentagram spell has been completed in accordance with the prophecy. Right now in Hokkaido, Rapa Nui, the Cape York Peninsula, and the Chukchi Peninsula, the earth is bursting open and releasing my dark servants into the air, the same as here. It is the apocalypse. The end of the world. When this day is done, millions will be dead . . . and the luiseach will be no more."

"Not if I can help it."

Aidan closes his eyes and lifts his hand. But Dubu does something—I don't know what, but I feel a terrible burst of energy emanating from his body—and Aidan flies backward.

Helena's face twitches angrily, and then she too lifts a hand in Dubu's direction.

"Don't, beloved. Do not test me," Dubu says to her.

Helena disregards Dubu's warning and continues to attack. The two of them lock horns in a fevered exchange of energy. Aidan struggles to his feet and joins Helena.

As the three of them fight, I gasp and struggle to breathe. I have to do something, anything, now to free myself. But what?

A flash of hot pink emerges from the smoke.

Victoria is carrying something. *Oh my gosh*, it's my luiseach knife. Victoria was the one who gave it to me in the beginning when she told me about my luiseach heritage; there are only five in existence.

Did she find it near Zalea's body?

She moves quietly toward Dubu, who's still battling Helena and Aidan. Xerxes, Giovanni, Mikhail, Aura, and Lucio continue to fight off the ever-increasing demons around them. No one seems to notice Victoria's presence but me.

Is she attempting to sneak up on Dubu and stab him, distract him, weaken him temporarily?

She catches my eye and puts her fingers to her lips, signaling me not to give her away.

I shake my head and mouth: *Don't.*

Victoria smiles sadly and mouths back: *This is for Anna.*

I shake my head again, but she isn't looking at me anymore. She tiptoes up to Dubu from behind and lifts the knife in the air.

Without even turning around, Dubu lets go of me and raises his free hand behind him. The knife clatters to the floor a few feet from where I land as Victoria screams and goes flying through the air.

"*No!*" I cry out.

She slams against a wall so hard that I can hear her spine shatter.

Her broken body slumps to the floor.

"*Victoria!*" I shout.

Tears pouring down my face, I rise to my knees and reach for my knife. Aidan glances at me and then at Victoria. His expression is furious and also tormented as he white-knuckles his hand into a tight fist and lets go, trying to increase the force of his attack against Dubu.

I know my father is trying to figure out how to save the world and me at the same time.

But he can't.

I won't let him.

The time has come for me to step up, to assume the burden.

I close my eyes, and as I do, I mourn Victoria and Zalea and pray for everyone I love—Nolan, Lucio, Aidan, even Helena. And Mom . . . where is she? Is she safe at home, or has the demon onslaught already spread throughout Ridgemont?

I compose a special message for Nolan and hope his mind-reading abilities are still operational. *Nolan, I love you. For always. No matter what happens.*

I pray for Aura and send her a wave of compassion for the loss of her daughter.

And Ashley . . . where is she? Is it too late for her? I pray Lucio or Aidan or one of the other luiseach will be able to exorcise the demon in time when this is all over.

Because I won't be there to do it myself.

The cold steel of my knife twitches in my hand. I hold it up and see Zalea's blood shining against the blade. More tears fill my eyes—and then rage.

My father was right. I am stubborn and determined, like my birth mother.

Aidan knows what I'm going to do. "Sunshine, *no!*"

Just before I lift the knife in the air, something explodes outside the gym. A wall comes crashing down, and soldiers leap over the broken cement blocks and swarm into the gym.

Hundreds of soldiers.

Luiseach soldiers.

They've come from around the world to join us in the fight, to exorcise the demons, to save humanity.

A familiar figure in ladybug and sunflower scrubs rushes through the collapsed wall just behind the luiseach soldiers.

Somehow, through the smoke and fire, her gaze zeroes in on me. She begins running toward me, leaping over rubble and fallen bodies like an Olympic hurdler.

Which makes this so much easier and also so much harder.

I say another prayer and send Mom love, infinite love.

And point my luiseach knife at my chest.

And end my life.

The world explodes in a tidal wave of energy.

This Is Not How It Was Supposed to Happen

This is not how it was supposed to happen.

It was supposed to be Aidan and me here in the invisible realm, in our long-awaited duel to the death. His death.

There was a very precise order.

First he was supposed to watch me terminate his daughter while he stood by helplessly, revealing himself in front of my beloved Helena to be the pathetic weakling that he truly is.

And then he was supposed to suffer as I did, weep as I did, boil in torment as I did when he took my first son from me a century ago.

Yes, that was the order of things.

How did it go awry?

How did the girl know about the ritual? Surely he would not have told her?

But it does not matter. I will easily terminate her in this realm. She is young, so young, and lacks experience. And wisdom. And strength.

She may be special, but she is no match for a Markon.

When I am done with her I will turn my attention back to the earthly realm and finish what I started with him.

And undo the damage she caused just now with that unexpected energy wave.

And bring my dark servants back to life.

Battlefield conditions. One must be flexible when it comes to an apocalypse.

CHAPTER 44

The End of the End

id I die?

My physical self is gone. The Sunshine Griffith with her frizzball and milky green cat eyes and super-dork style is no more, probably lying on the floor of the Ridgemont High gym with a gaping chest wound and no heartbeat.

Are they all mourning for me? Or are they too busy trying to destroy Dubu and his demon army?

Except . . .

My mind, my consciousness, whatever I am now, spins around like a disco ball, casting flecks of light that scatter and flutter around and reintegrate in a new pattern.

I remember.

Something I hadn't foreseen, something *no* one had foreseen.

At the very moment I died my body released a massive wave of energy. The same wave of energy that I supposedly released when I was born.

I understand it now. Aidan and Helena were wrong—the

entire luiseach community was wrong. When I came into the world at 7:12 P.M. Central Standard Time on August 14, my body took *in* that existing universal energy, the energy that sustained all luiseach, into itself. Which is a big part of the reason why I became a kind of super-luiseach, a luiseach like no other, with unprecedented luiseach superpowers.

That energy was what had sustained the luiseach race for many millennia—and at that moment I sucked it all in like a paranormal vacuum cleaner. Unwittingly and accidentally borrowed it, hoarded it. For sixteen long years.

Now it's back in the universe where it belongs.

At the moment I died and the energy was released, the demons everywhere began to vanish slowly, gradually, one by one.

Including Dubu.

Which means he may be in the spiritual plane with me, right now, waiting to duel to the end. Guera spirito. Aidan's burden. Now mine.

But how does this work? How do I fight Dubu when I have no body?

I should have asked my father for more details before I committed to this path.

Maybe this was all for naught.

Or maybe . . .

A cold wind or something that *feels* like cold swirls around this entity that I've become. The cold sensation then morphs into colors—gray, blue, then black. Then the colors morph into waves of emotion. Terror, anger.

Dubu is here.

I don't know how to do this.

Of course I know how to do this.

I concentrate, concentrate. A buzzy sort of electricity, a life force, courses through this new me.

There he is.

I can't see him, but I can see him. And then, without warning, he comes at me full force, unrelenting, trying to crush me out of existence. No mercy.

I'm in a dark room, and the walls are closing in, pushing against me.

I don't know how I'm pushing back or what is unfolding here . . . I'm driven by pure instinct. Whenever that was—time feels irrelevant now. Dubu crushes back, and for I'm not sure how long, perhaps an eternity, we're caught in an impasse: steel against steel, immovable mountain against immovable mountain.

The image of his face and then his body appears, suspended in pure white ether.

Is this an illusion? Or a trick?

No, it's neither. I'm growing more powerful, able to combine past sensory memories with the ethereal, nonlinear, nonspatial present.

"You are brave but foolish, just like your father."

Ah, I can hear him too.

"It is time for you to let go. Deditio, Laoise."

"Laoise?" I repeat.

"That is your birth name, after our enemy, your great-grandmother, the daughter of my brothers' murderers. Now . . . surrender."

"I don't think so."

At my defiance, Dubu becomes pure hatred, pure rage. He

comes at me again, the blackness of his soul a weapon that threatens to obliterate whatever light remains in me.

I don't know how to do this.

Of course I know how to do this.

"Sunshine, gather the light!" Anna's sweet voice.

Yes, yes, that's it. I'll gather the light.

I summon all the light spirits of the world to come. And they do. There are so many more than ever before—not just because my power has reached its apex but because tragically, so many new spirits were created by Dubu's minions in Ridgemont, Russia, Rapa Nui, Australia, Japan—everywhere.

Their deaths will not have been in vain.

"Stupid child," Dubu laughs cruelly. "You think you can stop me with your band of friendly ghosts?"

The light spirits swirl and swarm around Dubu. He continues laughing, mocking, even as they pin him down and immobilize him.

"Most amusing. But your parlor tricks will not work here, Laoise."

Then I summon the light of my great-grandmother and of Adis and Uiri, of Aidan and Helena, of their parents and their other blood ancestors, of all the luiseach that came before me and will come after me. I concentrate all this light, this glorious light, into a single, perfect, unforgiving blade of radiance and direct it at Dubu, willing it to forever destroy the king of darkness.

No mercy.

Somehow, though, Dubu breaks away from the spirits, and the blade misses him. I feel cold, freezing cold, as he rushes at me—furious, unstoppable.

Is this the end?

A vision comes to me. I can see the earthly plane below. There's Ridgemont High, the gym. Hundreds of luiseach soldiers are exterminating the last of the demons and saving the humans.

And there I am—or rather, there's the body of Sunshine Griffith. Blood gushes out of my chest where I stabbed myself with my luiseach knife. Mom presses down on the wound with her wadded-up scrubs, desperately trying to save me.

My blood pressure is dropping, dropping.

Is this the end?

Aidan touches Mom's shoulder gently. "Not yet. She must finish what she has started."

Helena leans down next to Mom and whispers something in her ear.

Mom begins to cry. So does Helena. My two mothers bend their heads together, weeping.

This is the end, and this is the beginning.

Sunshine Griffith is no more, in body or spirit.

I am Laoise, the past and future queen of my kind.

The light spirits fly at Dubu again and overcome him. His face and body begin to disintegrate. The air fills with his screams.

His screams grow fainter and fainter as the light—*my* light, the light of all luiseach—grows bigger and bigger.

And then I see a small, ordinary gray rock suspended in the air.

Thank you, Zalea.

You're welcome, my friend.

Crying and laughing—or perhaps neither—I reach out and touch Zalea's lucky rock. It morphs into a massive boulder. I send all the light spirits, my beautiful light spirits, to the other side. Or perhaps they do that themselves—my last gift to the universe.

Actually my second-to-last gift.

I order the boulder to crush what remains of Dubu.

It does.

"You can save her now," Aidan says to Mom.

CHAPTER 45

Good-byes

White walls, beeping machines, the smells of iodine and disinfectant.

My eyes flicker open, and blurry faces swim in my vision.

"Sunshine! Oh thank *God!*"

I feel a soft, warm, vanilla-scented hand touching my face . . . and drops of rain. No, teardrops. Who's crying?

"We thought you were . . . the doctors had all but given up, but . . . oh, we are so incredibly happy to see you!"

I take a deep breath with great effort and open my eyes completely.

Mom's weeping and laughing at the same time.

"I love you," I mumble groggily.

"I love you too. To the moon and back and then a million times around the whole entire universe. How are you feeling, sweetie?"

I do a mental scan of my body. My chest hurts. My head

hurts. Actually everything hurts—a *lot*. A zillion wires and leads are connected to my body and IV tubes too.

I touch the area near my heart. My fingers sift through layers of gauze and bandages, and below that, a bumpy scar that is criss-crossed with surgical thread.

"W-what happened?" I ask.

More faces swim into my field of vision. Lucio. Aidan. Helena. *Nolan.*

They're all alive.

Lucio steps forward and grins. His right arm is in a sling, and there are cuts and scrapes all over his body.

Aidan and Helena look pretty battered too.

"Sunshine. You had us pretty worried," Lucio says.

"I did? Why?"

Nolan comes to my side and kneels down on the floor. His beautiful brown eyes swim with tears as he takes my hands between his own. "Because you went through with the guera spirito ritual. You sacrificed yourself and fought with Dubu on the spiritual plane."

"You mean . . . I died?"

Nolan nods, and now the tears pour down his cheeks. "Yes. You won and came back."

Helena walks over. Her mouth, identical to my own, curves up in an enigmatic smile as she leans down so our faces are almost touching. "The necklace is gone," she whispers.

"What?"

"The necklace is gone. It crumbled into dust. Which means he's gone too. For good."

"Oh!"

Helena stands up and moves to Aidan's side. He smiles at her, then turns to me and strokes my hair.

"You saved us. You saved the world. But I assume you know that?"

"I did?"

"Your . . . death, your successful execution of the guera spirito ritual . . . Helena and I were wrong about the energy wave."

I squeeze my eyes shut and try to remember. The spiritual plane. Dubu's death. The image of thousands, millions of demons perishing as the energy wave lit up the universe.

"Is everyone okay? The luiseach, the humans?" I ask weakly.

"There were . . . fatalities. But because of you, the war ended very quickly," Aidan says.

"Ashley?"

"She's fine. I exorcised her demon," Lucio speaks up.

Then I see the image of Dubu flinging a helpless woman against the wall.

"Victoria?"

Mom chokes back a sob. "I'm so sorry, sweetheart. She didn't make it."

"But when she died before, at New Year's, she—"

"Not this time," Aidan says sadly.

Grief washes over me. *Victoria*. My dear friend, my wise teacher. She died trying to save me, save us all, from Dubu.

And of course there's Zalea.

"What happened to that traitor? That monster? Bastian?"

Even now, saying his name makes me want to scream and shout and throw things. I was his luiseach mentor. Except he wasn't a luiseach. He pretended to be so he could get close to me, spy on me, toy with me, confuse me . . . whatever demented assignment his father had given him. How did I not see through that?

"We don't know," Aidan replies gravely. "It seems he disappeared in all the confusion. Or he might have been exterminated along with the other demons. He is—was—half Markon, half human. As such, we're not exactly sure *what* his powers are." He hesitates. "There's one more thing."

"What?"

"The release of the energy wave back into the universe was an extraordinary thing. Not only did you essentially stop the war and vanquish all the demons, including Dubu, but you also restored the future of the luiseach race. We predict that new luiseach babies will be joining our community—our new community, our *reunited* community—for centuries, millennia to come."

I smile uncertainly. "So that's a good thing, right?"

"Yes. It's a miraculous, wonderful thing. But"—Aidan falters, searching for words—"that, combined with the fact that your heart and brain activity stopped during the time you and Dubu were fighting on the spiritual plane, means you have lost your luiseach powers. You are now a human. I'm sorry, Sunshine."

I am now a human.

I sit up in my bed—or I try to anyway, before the pain in my chest and head and everywhere else makes me stagger back against the pillows. I'm no longer luiseach.

I am now a human.

The ramifications are so staggering, I can't even think straight, form a reaction. Does this mean Aidan won't want to have anything to do with me anymore? What about Helena and Lucio and all the other luiseach?

A tall, handsome doctor walks into the room. "Sunshine, it's very nice to see you awake. We're going to need to do an examination and run some tests. Could we have some privacy? Kat, you can stay of course."

"I appreciate that, Dr. Kothari."

"We'll be right outside," Nolan says, pointing to the hall.

Aidan leans over and kisses my forehead. Wait, has he ever done that before?

"You get some rest. We can talk later. But I just want you to know: nothing changes between us. I am your father, and you are my daughter. In fact, I feel quite privileged."

"Really?" I say, touched.

But before we can continue with the poignant father-daughter moment, he rises to his feet and walks briskly out the door.

Yup, *some* things are still the same.

Now I feel exhausted, spent, full of confusion and relief and sadness and about a million other emotions.

A couple of nurses come into the room carrying collection tubes and syringes and all kinds of other equipment. Dr. Kothari and Mom confer in quiet voices as they scroll through a laptop computer together, discussing my vitals and stats.

The temperature in the room dips.

Obviously it can't be a light spirit, as I'm not a luiseach anymore. Maybe the air conditioning is wonky?

The temperature dips some more.

I blink.

Oh my gosh.

Victoria and Anna are hovering across the room. They look so . . . happy. Joyous. Victoria holds Anna's hand tightly—Anna's other hand is clutching her white owl—and they're smiling at each other, mother and daughter finally reunited.

I know what I have to do.

I close my eyes and try to help them both cross over.

I don't know how to say good-bye to you both. But I have to. I want to. You belong together in the light, forever and ever.

Am I crazy? What am I thinking? I'm not a luiseach any-more. I'm being delusional—there's no way I can pull this off . . . but how am I able to experience them now if I'm no longer luiseach?

A peaceful calm settles over the room as I open my eyes in surprise.

Anna drifts over and hands me her stuffed white owl. "Take care of him for me. Good-bye, Sunshine!" she whispers.

She goes back to her mother, and the two of them bloom into a beautiful ball of light.

And disappear.

CHAPTER 46

Eighteen Candles

"Happy birthday to you, happy birthday to you, happy birthday, dear Sunshine! Happy birthday to you!"

I lean over the cake laughing and blow out the seventeen—no, eighteen—candles as my friends and family finish singing. They're all here, sitting around our dining room table: Mom, Aidan, Nolan, Ashley, Lucio . . .

But not Helena. Because Lucio has brought along two extra guests.

Mom starts cutting the cake, which is my favorite—carrot with extra walnuts and raisins. HAPPY 17TH BIRTHDAY, SUNSHINE! is spelled out in yellow across a thick layer of cream cheese frosting. A bright sun with dark sunglasses grins in the upper-left-hand corner, and pink and orange flowers form a cheerful border across the bottom.

"Of course you get the S," Mom says, putting a big slice of cake on my plate. "You've always insisted on the S ever since you were old enough to point."

"Knowing Sun, that must've been when she was, like, one day old?" Ashley jokes. "J-K, Sunny-G. But let's face it, you *are* a brainiac."

"Guilty," I say with a grin.

She hugs me, and I hug her back. I'm so glad my best friend is here to celebrate the big one-seven with me. After school ended in late June she went back to Austin but talked her parents into letting her drive up here for my birthday and beyond. Senior year doesn't start for a few weeks, so we both have some time to chill and hang out.

Yesterday Ashley insisted on taking me on a back-to-school shopping trip. I said it had to be at the Salvation Army or Goodwill or a thrift shop, and she not only agreed but bought herself a cute vintage sweater at the new used-clothing store downtown. I let her buy me some new lipstick at the drug store. So, détente. And progress.

I don't think Jane Austen's spirit will be *too* offended if she sees Wild 'n Sizzling Scarlet on my lips.

It's a rare sunshiney day in Ridgemont, and faint beams of light pour in through the windows. We play a Hell Girls cassette on Mom's ancient cassette player in honor of Victoria. Oscar and Lex Luthor are parked under the table, patiently waiting for scraps of cake to fall—or for Ashley to sneak them crumbs from her slice, which she totally does.

Lucio sits between his parents, Argi and Jairo, his arms draped around both their shoulders. His dad looks like a taller, older version of him. His mom is small and pretty, with long dark hair and serious eyes. She brought me a pair of turquoise earrings for a birthday present and thanked me for my being such a good friend to their son.

Unbeknownst to Aidan or anyone else, Helena lost her nerve sixteen years ago. She wanted to have Argi and Jairo executed for what she considered to be their betrayal in not giving up my location. She couldn't go through with it, but she also couldn't have the rest of the luiseach community perceive her as weak.

So she pretended to go through with the execution. At the same time she lied to Argi and Jairo, telling them their young son Lucio had died of some rare illness, and sent them away, exiling them to a remote island off the coast of Argentina.

After the almost-apocalypse in April Helena confessed to Aidan what she'd done. Aidan was beyond furious with her but also relieved and overjoyed that Argi and Jairo were alive.

When they broke the news to Lucio, he cried for a long time. Helena apologized to him repeatedly, but he didn't offer forgiveness—just demanded to see his parents immediately.

Aidan arranged for Argi and Jairo to be flown to Ridgemont to be with their son.

And now they're together, and I've never seen Lucio so happy.

So much tragedy.

So much joy.

"More cake, sweetie?" Mom asks me.

"No, thanks. Listen, can I be excused? I need to go upstairs for a second."

Her face immediately clouds with worry. "Are you all right?"

"Yes, I'm fine! I'm good! This is an amazing party. I just need to, um, take a mental health moment."

"Got you. Take all the time you need, Sunshine State."

Nolan catches my eye as I head toward the stairs. He starts to rise from his chair, then nods and sits back down. Still a mind-reader, which is one of the reasons I love him.

Upstairs I throw off my shoes and flop down on my bed. There's no AC in this house, so my room is actually warm, even a little stuffy. I open the window and lie back down. A breeze blows in, smelling like pine needles and fresh grass as well as roses from the bushes Mom planted in the backyard last summer.

I'm now seventeen, which would have made me a less vulnerable luiseach. But I'm not a luiseach anymore. It's been four months since I stopped being a super-guardian angel with superpowers . . . since I've seen any spirits, light or dark.

Now I'm a mere mortal like everyone else.

However, I no longer have difficult, sometimes impossible luiseach duties that fill up my days and nights and tear at my emotions and yank me in two different directions 24/7. I actually have time—normal time, like normal people. Since April I've finished junior year with straight A's. I've reread all my Jane Austen books. I've dusted off my Nikon F5 and taken a bunch of photos downtown and in the state park. I've texted, spoken to, or Skyped with Ashley almost every day. I've had weekly pizza and movie nights with Mom.

And last but not least, I've gotten to spend time with my boyfriend. For real. Aidan finally lifted the spell, although he said I had basically outgrown it anyway—rendered it moot. Which explains why Nolan and I were able to touch so much without me getting queasy.

Since the official spell-lifting Nolan and I have—how to put it in Jane Austen terms?—exchanged much affection. (Translation: kissed, hugged, held hands nonstop.)

Still, I kind of miss being a luiseach.

But I guess I'm stuck with normal for the next how many ever years I have left in my human life span.

"Sunshine? It's time to open more presents!" Mom calls up the stairs.

"Coming, Mom!"

I rise out of bed and smooth my frizzball, which has grown out to a respectable frizzball length. Things aren't so bad, though, all things considered. In fact, my life is one big, huge birthday present. I have Mom. And Aidan. And Nolan. And Ashley. And Lucio.

And even Helena, who's gone back to Peru with the rest of the council. Aidan joins them from time to time to help reorganize the new, united luiseach community.

The last time he was there, he reported back that Aura has finally started participating in council activities again. Just barely, but it's something.

I reach into my pocket and finger Zalea's small gray rock. I always carry it with me now for luck. My luiseach knife is locked away in a safe in my bedroom closet. These days it's more of a museum artifact than a weapon. Maybe I should consider giving it to Aidan to give to one of the other luiseach.

As I start to leave the room I glance back at Dr. Hoo, who's resumed his usual place on the shelf next to my glass unicorn collection. Next to him is Anna's white stuffed owl.

Anna did ask me to take care of him, after all.

Just then I think I see Dr. Hoo wink at me.

I must be seeing things. I stare at him for a moment.

He winks again.

I smile. Maybe Aidan wasn't telling me the whole truth after all. Typical.

I wink back at Dr. Hoo and head back to my party.